JC

Heartache
and Christmas
Cakes

D1341634

Amy Miller

Heartaches
and Christmas
Cakes

bookouture

Published by Bookouture
An imprint of StoryFire Ltd.
23 Sussex Road, Ickenham, UB10 8PN
United Kingdom
www.bookouture.com

ISBN: 978-1-78681-236-0
eBook ISBN: 978-1-78681-235-3

'If you aren't in over your head, how do you know how tall you are?' T.S. Eliot

Prologue – Autumn 1939

With a threepenny bit in her clenched hand, Audrey Barton pushed her way through the jostling crowds on the platform. Bournemouth Central railway station was crammed with people waiting to board the train bound for Southampton docks and Audrey's eyes skittered from face to face as she tried to locate her brother. Trembling in her blue swing coat, her dark blonde hair resting on the collar, she tried not to stare at the drama all around her. With sunlight slipping through the station ceiling and casting beams of light like spotlights onto the platform, the concourse felt to Audrey like a giant stage. Except that this was real life, she thought solemnly, and nobody was acting. There were fathers wordlessly shaking their sons' hands, misty-eyed mothers and grandmothers handing food parcels to their beloved boys and dear, sweet infants and toddlers in their fathers' arms, not understanding the gravity of what this farewell kiss, planted heavily on their young cheeks, might mean. Already on board the train were young, fresh-faced recruits leaning out of the windows, one writing on the train door in chalk, '*Look out Mr Hitler we're coming to get you!*'

And what of the sweethearts? The fragrance of Evening In Paris scented the air and Audrey could almost hear lovers' hearts breaking above the hiss and whistle of the steam engine. One girl was balancing on the shoulders of her friend so that she could kiss a young soldier leaning out of the train window. When he gripped her around the waist as if he would never let go, a ripple of applause broke out. Another girl clutched a bunch of lavender handed to her by a strapping uniformed man over six feet tall with shoulders almost as wide. He kissed her softly on the forehead while she tried to hold in her tears. Since Chamberlain's declaration of war less than a month earlier, there had been a rush of weddings in the town. Barton's, the bakery Audrey ran with her husband Charlie, had had more orders for wedding cakes than she'd known what to do with. Now some of those young newlyweds would begin their married life wrenched apart, unsure of when, or if, they would meet again. Audrey's throat ached with the emotion of it all.

She swallowed hard and, glancing at her pocket watch, began to panic. She had arranged to meet her brother William before he left, but he was nowhere in sight. Though she was privately terrified by him joining the British Expeditionary Force, she could not let her fears be known. What good would that do to anyone? Besides, William could think for himself and had never been swayed by anyone else's view.

'Sis!' said William, appearing beside her. 'I couldn't see you in all the faces. Is Elsie with you?'

William was tall, slim and had long limbs that had earned him the 'gangly' name tag at school but that he'd grown into as a twenty-one-year-old, giving him the easy elegance of Jimmy Stewart. He had a heart-shaped face, pronounced by his wavy hair combed back from his forehead and the fine vertical line that ran between his eyes, almost as if drawn on with a pencil. He had been courting Elsie for a year, and they made the most handsome, head-turning couple.

'I thought she'd be with you,' Audrey answered, standing on tiptoes to look for Elsie in the throng. 'Gosh, where is she? Maybe Beales wouldn't let her out. Her boss in the Needlework Department rules with an iron fist.'

'You don't think she's had doubts about me?' he said. 'Maybe I'm not as good at the mouth harp as I'd like to think.'

William's harmonica was as much a part of him as his arm or leg. Where most men could be seen cradling a cigarette to their mouths, William's habit was playing the harmonica. During his breaks at the bakery, where he'd worked as an apprentice baker until now, he'd perch on one of the huge sacks of flour and play tunes that rivalled the songbirds.

'Don't be daft,' she said. 'That's one of the reasons she fell for you. She says your heart beats to a Larry Adler tune. I'm going to miss listening to you play and…'

Words failed her, as she battled not to tell him how desperately worried she was about him going. She hugged him tight instead. William grinned, dipped into his pocket and handed Audrey the battered red case of his M Hohner harmonica.

'Can you give her this?' he asked. 'Inside there's… well, it's not the most original thing… and it's not exactly a rock. I wanted to give it her myself and do things properly and take care of her like a husband should, but there's not enough time and the war won't wait…'

For a moment, despite his stature and dashing good looks, William seemed lost, like a five-year-old boy on his first day at school. Audrey felt suddenly fiercely protective of him, and held his face in her hands.

'William,' Audrey said. 'I'll make sure she gets the ring. There's something I want to give you too.'

She placed the threepenny bit in his palm. 'Can you remember when Mother used to put this in the plum pudding at Christmas? You bit into it one year and broke your tooth! It was supposed to bring us luck. Not that our mother has brought us much luck over the years, quite the opposite, but I've always kept this coin…'

The thought of their mother, and the fact she wasn't there to wave William off like the dozens of other mothers on the platform, infuriated Audrey. She smiled ruefully and William laughed gently, tucking the coin into his breast pocket. He put his arm around her and she resisted the temptation to cling onto his coat and not let him go.

The trainmaster blew his whistle and there was a sudden push towards the train doors, puffs of steam billowing into the rafters and scattering pigeons.

'It'll be over by Christmas,' William said, jumping onto the train and pulling shut the door. 'And I'll join you for plum pudding!' he called out above the din. 'And tell my Elsie I'll marry her when I come home, if she'll have me.'

'I will,' said Audrey. 'Farewell William!'

'Farewell Sis!' he called, raising his palm.

As the train moved off in a cloud of steam, a rousing chorus of male voices singing '*Homeland, Homeland when shall I see you again…*' burst through the windows. Audrey waved until her body swayed with the force of it, not just at William but at all the young men leaving their lives in Bournemouth for an uncertain future. Tears escaped her eyes and she swiped angrily at them. She mustn't let William see her cry.

Now, with the train gone, the station was eerily quiet and Audrey walked slowly to the front of the building, lined with sandbags, with a heavy heart.

'AUUUDREY!' she heard Elsie yell. Audrey turned to see Elsie running towards her, overcoat hanging off her shoulders, stockings ripped at the knee and with one of her smart work shoes in her hand. Her cheek and forehead were oil-streaked and her breathing, as she stopped running and bent over to rest against her knees, was ragged.

'Goodness, Elsie,' Audrey said, gently pulling a green leaf from Elsie's shiny dark curls. 'What on earth has happened?'

'My bicycle!' she said. 'The wretched chain fell off. I came flying off, bent a wheel and then lost my shoe in the road under a wheel of a bus. I tried to get the chain back on, but my fingers were shaking so badly I couldn't do it! I ran all the way here and now… now I've missed him, haven't I? The train's gone, hasn't it! That wretched bike, it's as useless as a chocolate teapot!'

Elsie looked at the sky and growled in exasperation. A moment later, hand shielding her eyes, her small frame shook with angry sobs.

'Oh Elsie, you poor girl,' Audrey said, hugging Elsie and glancing at the harmonica box. 'Come on. Wipe your eyes and let's go home. I've got something to tell you that might help heal your heart.'

Elsie's lovely face – hazelnut eyes, peachy cheeks, lips painted in 'Theatrical Red', with deep dimples like full stops either side of her mouth – turned towards Audrey. She managed a watery smile and breathed in, visibly pulling herself together. Audrey handed her a cotton hanky and she blew her nose noisily. Together they walked away from the station as William's train rumbled towards Southampton docks.

While the girls linked arms, William stood in the corridor of the packed train watching the town that he so loved blur and eventually disappear, the threepenny bit in his breast pocket, close to his pounding heart. And so it all began.

June 1940

Chapter One

Audrey opened the bakery shop window blind to a sky so blue and spit-shine spotless, for a fleeting moment she could almost believe there was no wretched war to worry about. Living with the blackout these last months made daylight all the more sweet. Unlocking the door of Barton's Bakery, the brass bell merrily jingling, and releasing delicious wafts of sweet-smelling fresh bread into the neighbourhood's nostrils, she suppressed a deep yawn. Up since before dawn, scaling and moulding the dough for loaves and buns, and preparing the counter orders; another busy day lay ahead.

'Morning,' she called to two scrawny evacuee boys from Portsmouth – no more than six years old – who were leaning their backs against the bakery wall, the bricks warm after the night's baking, waiting for a spare crust, like sparrows searching for crumbs.

'Mornin' miss,' one boy said, his gaze fixed on the young delivery boy, Albert, who was wobbling on the delivery bicycle down the street with the neighbourhood's orders of warm, fresh and perfectly golden tin, Coburg and bloomer loaves stacked in the basket, a hungry seagull above tracking his route. Albert would be gone for hours – some of the spinsters he delivered to looked forward to their cup of tea with Albert more than the bread itself! 'I spend more time doing odd jobs and drinking tea than I do delivering bread,' he'd told an amused Audrey last week. Knowing how lonely some folk were, Audrey was glad of Albert's patient nature and friendly open face.

'Keep up the good work, Albert,' she'd told him. 'You make some people's day.'

Audrey stood for a moment blinking in the early sunlight, like one of the sand lizards in the dunes, trying not to feel disappointed that the cramps of her monthlies had arrived last night, regular as clockwork. Another door to motherhood slammed. After five years of trying to fall pregnant, she should know better than to expect any different. *It's not meant to be*, she thought, busying herself watching Fisherman's Road, the street in Southbourne in east Bournemouth she lived in, coming to life.

Barton's Bakery was on the south side of Fisherman's Road, part of a bustling parade of shops including the chemist, dairy, shoemaker, stationer, draper, café, grocer and the Post & Telegraph Office. The grocer, Old Reg, opposite Barton's, was opening up and wiping down the enamel Red Seal Toffees sign outside his shop, whistling a Gracie Fields song. Since rationing had started, Old Reg said he had aged twenty years. He had many a story to tell about disgruntled customers forgetting to bring in their ration books, or who expected Reg to have precious oranges saved 'behind the counter' for them, at which point he'd gesture to his shelves filled with jars of loose biscuits, tins of Fray Bentos soup and gooseberry pie filling, OXO cubes and the slab of cheese and cheese wire on the counter and say 'This is your lot! Like it or lump it!' It wasn't easy being a shopkeeper these days. With Hitler's U-boats attacking shipping bound for Britain, limited imported goods and raw materials were getting into the country.

'How are you, Reg?' she called to him as he knelt down to polish his front step, as he did every morning, until it shone like a new penny.

'I'm all right, Audrey,' he said. 'It's just the rest of 'em that ain't!'

Audrey smiled but the smile quickly vanished from her face when she caught sight of Mabel, the postwoman. Giving a small wave, Mabel shook her head regretfully and cycled on by without stopping. Audrey's stomach twisted into painful knots. They hadn't heard from her brother William since February when he was posted overseas after he'd completed his military training. With all that was now going on in the war – there was news of the German forces invading Belgium, Holland and Luxembourg by air and land, and, according to the new Prime Minister Winston Churchill, a German invasion in Britain was now a real possibility – the war felt very close to home. Just to hear a word from William, even if only 'Okay!', would be a blessed relief. For a letter to arrive for next week, when it was Elsie's birthday, would be perfect timing.

'No news is good news,' Audrey told herself, taking a lungful of fresh air. You could taste the sea salt on the breeze today blowing in from the Channel, she thought, tucking an escaped strand of hair behind her ear. Audrey was forever thankful for where she lived – one-hundred yards from the cliff top where sweet-smelling yellow gorse and sea pinks were flowering, and down steep stone steps, or a zigzag path, to the water's edge. On hot summer days when the shop had closed, she would sometimes wade into the water up to her ankles and cool off, scrunching the wet sand between her toes. But that was before the war. Now, with the pillbox lookout posts, concrete 'dragon's teeth' anti-tank obstacles and rolls of barbed wire to deter the German army from landing on the coast, even the beautiful beaches seemed threatening. Many of the hotels across the town, formerly enjoyed by holidaymakers, had been requisitioned for military accommodation or were closing down too, and there had recently been talk of all the entertainment on Bournemouth pier being cancelled – a sad thought.

'Audrey?' she heard Charlie's voice from behind her. 'Morning goods ready for the shop! The boy's taken the delivery order. I'll take the van out for the final deliveries. Come on, love, the night shifters will be here soon for their breakfast rolls! You know how they love their hot rolls.'

Biting her lip, she tried to ignore the irritation in Charlie's voice. She knew he was exhausted after baking and tending the ovens most of the night and needed his rest – he lived on four hours' sleep a night – but his recent short temper shocked her. She turned to face him, wondering whether to tell him about the disappointing arrival of her monthlies, her eyes taking a moment to readjust to the darkness in the shop. With a sigh, she decided against it. However tender she was towards him recently, it was as if he had locked the door to his heart and thrown away the key into a dark pond. Audrey felt she had waded into that pond and was tangled in the weeds.

Charlie, using a hessian sack to protect his hands against the heat, placed the tray of hot baked goods onto the service counter and then wiped his brow with his handkerchief. He managed a tired smile. His dark hair and eyelashes were powdered with flour and his shirtsleeves were rolled up to expose muscular arms. The job of a baker was hard physical work. Charlie had young Albert helping out with deliveries and his uncle John, a proud, semi-retired baker with a belly as big as a bloomer, working alongside him part-time, but John was fifty-nine now, with joints that creaked like old floorboards.

'Oven temperature's fallen enough for the rock cakes,' Charlie said, picking up the long-handled wooden peel that he used to put cakes into the oven. 'I'll put them in. Don't forget Mrs Common's order is to be kept behind the counter for her until she comes in at midday,' he continued, rolling his shoulders to release the knots. 'The tins'll need scraping, coke brought in and I'll need to do that paperwork today. The Ministry of Food want every bag of flour and every ounce of fat accounted for.'

Charlie stifled a yawn and rubbed his eyes with his thumbs.

'We'll be counting out the currants to go in the rock cakes soon!' Audrey said, only half-joking. 'You should get some rest Charlie, you're tired.'

'Don't fuss, there's nothing wrong with me except that the day's not long enough!' he said. 'Did you hear on the wireless that they want men to join the Local Defence Volunteers? They need any man aged between seventeen and sixty-five. I could join if John does a few more hours here at night.'

'You can't take on any more, Charlie, you're breaking your back in here already,' Audrey said, gently pushing the ginger cat, Marmalade, off the counter where he'd left floury paw prints. She flicked through her order book. 'Do you know I've had three more orders for wedding cakes. Trouble is, thanks to rationing, I don't have anywhere near enough icing sugar to ice them. I'm going to have to get creative and use something else. I've heard some confectioners are making moulds from plaster of Paris, would you believe?'

Charlie didn't reply. He disappeared through the floral-patterned curtains that covered the entrance to the small, stifling hot bake-house out back, leaving her alone in the shop, an anxious crease across her forehead.

She patted Marmalade's head and sighed. When war was declared, Charlie had immediately gone to the recruiting station and tried to join up, only to be informed that his occupation as head baker was 'reserved' and that he had important food production duties to attend to at home. Audrey was quietly relieved, but when she'd intimated as much to Charlie he had sternly told her: 'I'm willing to put my life on the line for peace. I would go if I could.'

Audrey wanted to point out there was nothing peaceful about war, but doubted if Charlie would ever talk to her about his feelings of frustration. He was a man best left to his own devices when he had something on his mind, channelling his feelings into his bread. He'd always vowed you could tell which baker had made what bread and you could taste his temperament in each loaf. The mood Charlie had been in recently, customers would likely break their teeth on the crust.

Glancing at the clock, Audrey ran through what she had to do, as Maggie, the young girl who helped in the shop, would arrive at 8 a.m. She stood for a moment, hands on her hips, feeling a familiar sense of pride. The shop, though small in size and modest in yield, always looked chocolate-box beautiful and smelled divine. With the golden loaves lined up in the window and a big wicker basket piled with rolls, alongside cake stands and wooden trays displaying Swiss rolls and delicate jam tarts, it wasn't like the fancy big bakeries in the centre of Bournemouth, but it had for years served the immediate community with a lovely crust. Charlie knew his cast-iron oven inside out and had mastered the perfect dough to make a light and porous bread – some customers said they wouldn't eat anything else but Barton's bread. Compliments didn't come much higher than that.

Straightening the price tickets, Audrey felt a sense of determination about the day ahead. With Hitler obsessed with wreaking havoc on the world, it was easy to feel helpless, but she was trying her best to help keep up morale. It was her belief that it was the everyday things, like buying bread, talking to one another and preparing a pie, that kept people sane. If all you did was think about the horrors going on in the world, a person could easily lose their way.

After quickly sweeping away crumbs from the black and white tiled floor with a broom, she glanced through the window, where the word 'BAKERY' had been hand-painted onto the glass in elegant gold lettering by the signwriter, and saw two small noses pressed up against it. Quickly, she grabbed a couple of halfpenny buns from the window display, popped her head out of the shop and dropped them into the boys' hands with a smile and a wink. She heard the voice of her mother-in-law, Pat, in her head as she did so: 'This is a business, not a charity!' But she took no heed. She couldn't see a child go hungry, no matter what.

'Thanks miss!' the boys said, immediately picking apart the warm bread with their little fingers and pushing it into their mouths before scampering off to goodness knows where. She'd seen them jumping on the corrugated-iron roof of an air-raid shelter earlier in the week, making a terrific din – the little ruffians!

'Go well,' she said kindly, a ghost of longing gripping her heart and squeezing it. 'Go well.'

Chapter Two

'There's only one smell I like more than fresh bread,' said Maggie, as she pulled on her spotless white apron and tied it around her twenty-one-inch waist, fluffed up her wavy white-blonde hair, checked her eyebrows (drawn on with the end of a burnt matchstick as advised by *Woman & Home* magazine) and puckered her lips (tinted with beetroot juice), checking her reflection in the back of a silver cake tray, before she began to serve with a radiant smile and a flutter of black lashes. It was hard to believe she was a girl of fifteen who had only just left the local Catholic school – she had the allure and confidence of a woman, a spirited one at that. Most of the customers, especially the men, loved Maggie's charm and optimism – and Uncle John joked that she had more sugar in her than the cakes she served – but the queue now snaked out of the bakery and into the street and Audrey, sensing the impatience of some of the older women in their thick overcoats and sturdy black shoes who spent whole mornings standing in various shop queues for their rations, worked quickly, sorting loaves and boxing cakes and repeating orders, while shaking her head at Maggie in mock despair.

'I dread to think,' she said to Maggie. 'Enlighten us, why don't you?'

'Well it ain't these gas masks,' said Florence, a middle-aged woman at the front of the queue, patting her gas mask case hanging over her shoulder. 'The smell of rubber gets up my nose and turns my stomach. Oven-bottom loaf please Audrey.'

There was a murmur of agreement in the shop. The gas masks were a vital necessity – and everyone had to carry one – but were horrible to put on. One of Audrey's customers had said her daughter was physically sick with claustrophobia when they tried wearing them for a gas attack drill at school. Everyone was supposed to practise wearing them for fifteen minutes a week, and Audrey had been frozen to the spot recently when she'd witnessed the chilling sight of a class of five-year-olds walking across the playground in their masks.

'Is it 4711 cologne?' Florence said, leaning on the counter as if to steady herself. 'I haven't smelled that in months, not since my boys left for military training.'

Audrey gave Flo's hand a brief squeeze. Flo's sons were serving in the Royal Navy but seemed barely old enough to have left home, let alone be in battle.

'It's got to be figgety pudden on Christmas Day when it's snowing outside,' said Mrs Cook, a customer Audrey adored. 'Audrey's figgety pudden at that. I've never tasted another as good and I've tasted a few in my time.'

Audrey beamed at Mrs Cook in acknowledgement of the kind praise. An elderly lady, with a face so deeply lined it held a library of stories, Mrs Cook had been talking about Audrey's Christmas puddings ever since Audrey started making them when she first got a job at the bakery, six years ago. One of her favourite times of the year was Stir-up Sunday, when she made the Christmas puddings to her grandmother's recipe. If she could bottle the delicious aroma of the mixed fruit, nuts, brandy and treacle, she would.

'No,' said Maggie, shaking her head, giving Florence her loaf. 'My favourite smell is… the slag heaps of Barnsley!'

'You daft thing,' said Florence, while the rest of the women in the queue cracked up laughing.

'And why might that be?' Audrey said, turning around to get another loaf from the shelf and placing it on the counter, for the next customer.

'I went to Barnsley as a small child to live for a bit while my ma learned hairdressing,' Maggie said, deftly working while she talked. 'My Aunty Fanny was the sweetest woman on earth. She made home-made lemonade for me and shortbread and let me pick the plums from her tree and sell them out front. And so that smell reminds me of her and those visits. Course she's dead and buried now. Consumption.'

'You're as mad as a brush, Maggie.' Florence shook her head, chuckling, as she turned to leave the shop.

'How's your "vaccee", Flo?' Elizabeth, next in the queue, asked before she left. 'Any lice? Mine's a bed-wetter poor mite. He's frightened of the dark. The washing's going to be the death of me, let alone the war. Oh it's plain drudgery, that's what it is.'

The women in the shop laughed again as Audrey spotted one of her regular ladies, Mrs Collingham, leaning against the shop door frame looking as if she could barely stand. Audrey rushed out from behind the counter and led Mrs Collingham into the shop and onto a chair she kept on hand for the older customers who liked to stop for a natter.

'Maggie,' she said quietly. 'Can you carry on serving for a moment? And can you pass me the Phospherine?'

'Here you go,' said Maggie. 'Blimey, Mrs C, you do look fagged.'

The bottle of Phospherine, which carried the slogan 'makes life worthwhile' on its label, was a tonic that steadied nerves. Audrey knelt down next to Mrs Collingham, offering her the recommended ten drops on the tongue, while Maggie pasted on a bright smile and dealt with the queue. Mrs Collingham was a woman in her late forties, and Audrey knew that her only son, George, a gunner with the Royal Artillery serving with the B.E.F., was overseas and that her husband – George's dad – had been killed in the Great War.

'What can I get you?' she asked, putting a hand gently on Mrs Collingham's arm, after she'd taken the Phospherine. 'Do you need a doctor, or would a nice cup of tea help?'

A hush descended in the bakery and Audrey could feel the concern from the women waiting in the queue.

Mrs Collingham shook her head, but her eyes misted over. 'I can hardly talk about it,' she said in a ragged whisper. 'It's George. I got word of him… and there was a picture of him in the *Echo* last night. Did you see it?'

Audrey shook her head. Mrs Collingham pulled out a crumpled copy of the *Bournemouth Echo* from her bag and showed Audrey the page where her son's photograph was in a row of images of young men's faces under the headline 'THESE LOCAL MEN ARE PRISONERS OF WAR IN GERMANY'. Underneath the image was a short description of each man and where they were being held.

Audrey gasped, grabbing Mrs Collingham's hand tightly.

'It says he's been captured and is in a prisoner of war camp in Germany,' Mrs Collingham continued, telling the other ladies who were listening in. 'I'm scared I'll never see him again, that I'll not hear his cheerful voice or hear him sing silly songs while he makes tea. That I'll never make him another dinner and pour him extra gravy, or give him the bone marrow from a Sunday joint on the handle of a teaspoon – the best bit. How will he cope? He never even wanted to join up! He was shaking like a leaf when those call-up papers came.'

Audrey held onto Mrs Collingham's hand, but the poor woman was openly weeping now, tears splashing down her cheeks and onto her collar. Audrey noticed she'd left a curler in the back of her hair and her heart broke a little while she gently and discreetly removed it. She felt for a clean cotton hanky in her pocket and handed it to her.

'I feel so helpless,' continued Mrs Collingham. 'I can't do a single thing to help him! Oh I'm sorry, I shouldn't be holding you up when you're so busy running your business, I'm sorry ladies…'

'You're not holding us up,' soothed Audrey. 'There will be better days, Mrs Collingham, you have to believe that. George will be thinking of you and that will help him get through. The war can't go on forever. Maggie, pass me two of those buns there. I think Mrs Collingham needs to go home for a sit-down and a rest and have a cup of tea and a bun. Shall I walk you home, Mrs Collingham? Are any of your girls at home?'

Maggie filled a bag with sweet-smelling, warm rock cakes and pushed them into the bottom of Mrs Collingham's basket, along with her order of a loaf.

'They're at work, but honestly, I really must get going to the butcher for my ration, and then I'll have a rest. I don't think I slept at all last night with worrying,' said Mrs Collingham, standing up too quickly and steadying herself on Audrey's arm. 'Oh dear Audrey, I'm a silly old fool…'

The blood drained from Mrs Collingham's face and her skin looked oddly sweaty, then bright red blood suddenly started to ooze from her nostrils. Audrey grabbed her arm and guided her back to the chair, feeling in her pocket for another hanky. She gave it to Mrs Collingham to soak up the blood and the women in the shop came closer, gathering around Mrs Collingham, offering more hankies and words of comfort.

'Maggie, can you go over the road and fetch Mrs Short from the stationers,' said Audrey. 'She used to be a nurse.'

'Oh there's no need,' said Mrs Collingham faintly. 'Don't bother the woman on my behalf.'

'Please let me through,' said a voice from the bakery doorway. 'I can help.'

At the sound of the woman's voice, Audrey looked up to see a young woman, at once familiar and yet strange. Her red hair beautifully pinned up and carrying a budgie cage and a small brown suitcase, her bright blue eyes darted from Audrey to Mrs Collingham. Audrey's eyes widened into perfect circles.

'Pinch the top of your nose,' said the young woman. 'And lift your chin up. That should stop the flow.'

Mrs Collingham did as she was instructed, and as the bleed slowed, she managed a weak smile and an embarrassed roll of her eyes. Stuffing bloodstained hankies in her handbag, she muttered a stream of apologies.

Finding herself unable to stop staring at the red-haired young woman, think straight or speak, Audrey's heart raced as memories flashed and spun inside her head, like tickets in a tombola drum.

'Audrey?' said the young woman, nervously smiling. 'Do you recognise me? It's your stepsister Lily. Otherwise known as "Copperknob"!'

'Lily!' Audrey said, incredulously. 'Lily, is that really you?'

Chapter Three

The evening before, Lily had journeyed to Bournemouth by train. Hoping to travel clandestinely despite her copper hair, she'd cursed her decision to bring Bertie, her budgie, in his cage; he was attracting her fellow passengers like iron filings to a magnet. But stroking the feathers of the little green and yellow bird was her one comfort in the turmoil she'd found herself in. Leaving London for Bournemouth had been a hastily made plan, snatched out of thin air like catching a fly in her fist, when she found herself in desperate need of escape.

'I'm going to stay with Audrey,' she had decisively told her father, Victor, and stepmother, Daphne. 'She's expecting me, and it's all arranged. You can't change my mind.'

Audrey wasn't expecting her, indeed she had no clue that Lily was coming, but Lily had needed to think on her feet. So, while Lily had packed clothes and her latest Agatha Christie novel, her stepmother and father had waited downstairs, silently fuming, her father refusing to speak to her, but pushing a ten-bob note into her hand before she left. Now, Lily thought of the letter she'd hurriedly scribbled and posted before she left London and her stomach sank. Her words in black ink on white paper meant there was no going back. She had been so sure she was doing the right thing – but now she was riddled with doubt.

'Don't look back,' she told herself, as the train had stopped at towns en route to Bournemouth and she fought the urge to disembark, tempted by the possibility of starting afresh in a town where she didn't know a single soul. But something kept her seated – whether that was faith or fear she wasn't sure.

'Where's a pretty girl like you travelling to at this hour?' an older gentleman sharing her carriage had asked, when she'd helped put his suitcase in the storage rack.

'Bournemouth,' she'd said, with as much confidence as she could muster. 'I'm staying with a relative to help with the evacuees for a little while. Doing my bit for the war effort.' Her cheeks fired with the lie and, as she averted her eyes from the man's gaze, she wished he would stop looking at her. Her stepmother, Daphne, had told her that good looks were a curse and a blessing in equal measure your whole life but so far they had only been a curse.

With her locks styled into what the *Daily Mirror* called the 'Gas Mask Curl', with a centre parting for the strap and curls either side, she was beautiful, if unconventionally so. Between her two front teeth was a gap almost wide enough to slot a penny, and she had skin so pale it was almost translucent. In a very bright light the thin blue veins on her eyelids were visible, like contour lines on an Ordnance Survey map.

Anyway, it was brains more than beauty that mattered to Lily – not that her brains had helped much in the horrible row she'd had with her father. In fact the answering back had only made it worse. She trembled at the memory of his attack, lifting her hand to just above her left eye where he had struck with the back of his hand, his wedding band nicking her skin. A violent purple bruise had bloomed around the cut and she was going to have to lie about how she got that too. Should anyone ask, she would say she had fallen over in the blackout. It was a genuine problem in the city. Despite the posters warning people to 'Look Out in the Blackout', a lot of milk bottles had been kicked over, let alone the car accidents.

'Ah of course,' the gentleman replied. 'A reception area isn't it, Bournemouth? A lot of children evacuated from Southampton too, poor things must wonder what's happening to them. That town must be teeming with children. Good job there's a beach, though it's probably off limits now, what with that lunatic Hitler on the horizon. Good luck to you, miss. Good luck to us all.'

Chugging through the New Forest in the fading light, where wild ponies and deer sheltered in the trees, Lily had watched the landscape change before eventually reaching the coastal town of Bournemouth where the air smelled of hot fish and chip suppers sprinkled with salt and vinegar. This was the first time she'd been so far away from home alone. A moment she had previously yearned for, it was not at all how she'd imagined it would be.

Scribbled on a scrap piece of paper were two addresses, one of a bed and breakfast where she was booked for a night and the other, Audrey's address. Though she had written to Audrey a handful of times, trying her best to keep in touch, she hadn't seen her in six years, not since their stepfamily had been snapped in two like the fingers of a Rowntree's Kit Kat Chocolate Crisp bar. Shifting uncomfortably in her seat at the memory of the day Audrey and William left home and never returned, she sighed regretfully. Now was she following in their footsteps?

Oh it was a fine mess all right, she'd thought miserably, looking down at her heeled lace-up shoes and polka-dot day dress that seemed to belong to a different life. Only two months ago she was employed doing important war work, as a typist at the Ministry of Information headquarters in the city. When the war had broken out, her father had got her the job with a cricketing acquaintance of his, a twenty-five-year-old Assistant Publicity Officer called Henry Bateman, who worked on various propaganda poster campaigns. Henry had eaten with Lily in the work canteen several times and lavished her with words such as 'potential', 'smart', 'bright future' and 'capable'. He'd bought her tickets to see the new Technicolor, *21 Days Together,* a film about a secret love affair starring Vivien Leigh and Laurence Olivier, guiding her to her seat with his hand on the small of her back, and loaned her Agatha Christie paperbacks that she'd devoured. Out of all the girls in the office, it was seventeen-year-old Lily he asked for an opinion when the artists' illustrations for the campaign posters arrived at the office in beautiful black portfolio cases. Making comments like 'eye-catching' and 'strong' made her chest puff with pride and her chin lift a modicum higher than it perhaps should have done. He had made her feel special and admired, loved even, but all that elevation had all too quickly come crashing down. She swallowed at the memory of Henry's treacherous words that crushed her after their working relationship had become something far more intimate. *You are a distraction to the war effort.* Waves of panic rolled over her at the thought of the secret she carried.

Lily, don't you dare think about that now, she instructed herself.

'Bournemouth Central,' the guard had called, as the journey finally came to an end. With clammy hands and a pounding head, Lily climbed from the train carrying her case, birdcage and gas mask box. Thus far she had been buoyed on by a fierce determination not to crumble in the face of the mess she'd got herself into, but in her heart she carried debilitating fear. Her plan depended on Audrey welcoming her into her life, giving Lily time to work out what to do – but would her stepsister be so accommodating?

'Good girls dance and sing through all difficulties,' she muttered, the motto she'd long ago learned in the Girl Guides, as she moved along the unlit station platform.

Outside the station, the streets were completely dark. In blackout it was an offence even to strike a match and there were no signposts at all – she'd heard all road signs had been removed or painted out to confuse enemy parachutists. It was silent too, since the Control of Noises Order had been introduced. She stood still in the quiet night, trying to get her bearings by the light of the moon, when torchlight flashed into her face. She blinked and shielded her eyes.

'You need to be careful in blackout, darlin',' an elderly man in uniform told her. 'There's been some awful accidents, people tripping over and getting run down by motorcars, or some halfwits even falling into the river! You ought to have a luminous band or luminous button badge on your coat. Don't you have a torch?'

He was kindly and gave Lily his spare torch with a home-made tissue paper cover, so she'd set off in the darkness with the muted torchlight dancing along the kerb, following the white line that had been painted on to the edge of the pavement to compensate for no street lighting, and avoiding the trees that also wore belts of white paint. Fear fingered her spine, a sensation that someone was following her making the blood rush into her ears. At one point she called out in a quavering voice, 'Is anyone there?' into the quiet, but there was no reply.

Later, relieved to be in her room at the bed and breakfast, she sat on the single bed and kicked off her shoes. She had no idea what the next day would bring, or how Audrey would receive her after all these years, but at least she was away from London and her father's critical glare. Still fully dressed, with Bertie in his cage beside her, Lily lay on the bed in darkness, not daring to think of what she'd left behind or what turmoil might lie ahead. Or of the letter she'd written in a moment of furious indignation, silently winging its way like an enemy parachutist into Henry Bateman's life.

Now, Audrey held open her arms and pulled Lily firmly into her chest.

'Copperknob!' she exclaimed, laughing at the memory of Lily's nickname. 'It's really you!'

The sweet scent and silkiness of her stepsister's hair against her cheek brought memories of their life in Balham, south London, flooding back. Audrey had spent hours brushing and plaiting Lily's hair in the bedroom of their terraced house when Lily was a young girl, telling adventure stories – all with a flame-haired heroine – while eating bread smothered with Golden Shred. When their parents had married, soon after Audrey's father, Don, had died of tubercular meningitis, Audrey had immediately adored Lily's spirit – and loved Lily as her own sister. She could never understand how Lily's father, Victor, in contrast, could be so very cruel and do everything in his power to alienate her and William. Once Audrey's mother, Daphne, was his wife, he'd made it absolutely clear that he wanted to eradicate the memory of Don from their lives. He treated Daphne like a pet, never letting her off her leash, and it hadn't taken long for Daphne to acquiesce and to put his wishes over those of her children. That was deeply hurtful, but Audrey knew it didn't do her any good to dwell. She'd sworn to herself that when she had a family of her own, she would always remain fiercely loyal to her children, no matter what. Not that she'd had the opportunity to shower love on a child yet.

'Yes,' replied Lily, interrupting Audrey's thoughts. 'It's really me.'

Audrey held Lily out at arm's length to take her in. Lily had grown into a feminine and lovely young woman, with a neat waist and slender ankles. She had an unconventional but beautiful face and, Audrey noted, tried to smile with her lips closed to conceal the gap between her two front teeth – but when she did smile properly it was as if the lights had been switched on in a dark room. Her intelligent eyes were the palest blue and framed with thick black lashes. Her skin was porcelain pale, and her copper hair reminded Audrey of the orange frosting on her marmalade cake. Tucking a strand gently behind Lily's ear, Audrey noticed an ugly bruise next to her eye.

'Your eye is bruised... have you been hurt?' she asked, frowning. 'Is Mother... and your father... goodness, has something happened?'

When war was declared, Audrey had written to Daphne to tell her that William was joining up, but Daphne never wrote back and, hard as it was, Audrey just had to accept that her mother obviously didn't want to be involved in her children's lives. Lily shook her head.

'Your mother is in good health,' she said. 'I tripped over in the blackout. I needed to see you. I...'

Audrey frowned as Lily struggled to finish her sentence, her eyes sliding to her shoes. Despite having brains, the girl was a terrible liar and always had been. She noticed something – guilt at her lie perhaps – cast shadows over Lily's pretty features. She would find out more later, when they were alone.

'Where are you staying?' Audrey asked, changing the subject. 'You must stay here with us. We live above the shop. We have room.'

'Thank you,' started Lily, but was interrupted.

'Uh-oh, Audrey,' called Maggie from behind the counter. 'Pat's on the warpath! Can you feel the ground shaking under those sturdy brogues? Pat should be on the front line – Jerry would run a mile!'

Audrey stifled a laugh and pulled a face at Maggie, watching her five foot nothing, but mighty as a giant, mother-in-law march into the shop and stand with her hands on her hips, her ancient fur stole draped over her shoulder.

'Audrey Barton,' said Pat, lifting her chin. 'I do believe your queue is halfway down the street. Our friends and neighbours are waiting with their baskets and bellies empty. You'll be the talk of the town!'

Audrey was used to this kind of intrusion and it didn't faze her. Even if she'd swilled the shop clean and polished the floor on her hands and knees until it was spotless and her fingers bled, Pat would kick at a crate, dispense crumbs and not be able to resist clicking her tongue. 'I'm sure they have more important things to discuss, Pat,' quipped Audrey, quickly resuming her post behind the counter. 'My stepsister Lily has just arrived and Mrs Collingham felt poorly. I couldn't very well ignore them.'

Looking down her nose at the budgie cage, Pat nodded once at Lily but obviously had something more important on her mind. She cleared her throat and then addressed the queue. Pat relished being at the heart of things and though she ran the drapers, with Fran, one of her two daughters, Charlie's eldest sister, she made sure to call in to each shop on the street at least once a day to give a report on what was going on, despite the government's insistence that 'loose lips sink ships' and that one should 'keep a still tongue in a wise head'. Charlie often made gentle fun of her, asking: 'Who needs the wireless when there's Mother?'

'Ladies, I've just been informed that all our services are needed at the local schools,' Pat said now, suddenly serious. 'You might know that our troops have been battling the German army on the northern coast of France. Well, the situation has become very grave indeed, so thousands of soldiers have been evacuated from the beaches at Dunkirk under heavy shellfire, and have been billeted here. The men have been arriving in Bournemouth by train with nothing but the clothes they've worn in battle. I've been told that some men stood in the sea shoulder-deep for hours being attacked from the air, while waiting to be evacuated. Warships and boats of all kinds were apparently sailed over from our shores to help rescue the men, but it seems there have been many thousands of lives lost…'

Pat paused to take a breath and to wipe her eyes with her hanky. The women in the shop stood frozen to the spot. Because of a media blackout, news of the situation in Dunkirk, where in a procedure called 'Operation Dynamo' Allied soldiers were being evacuated from the beaches after being trapped by the German army, was only just coming in, so it had been virtually impossible to know what was really happening.

'During their train journey here, people have gathered at wayside crossings to fling chocolate and cigarettes and cheer the soldiers on, but their morale is low, they're desperately hungry, exhausted and some are wounded,' she continued, her voice faltering. 'The Mayor of Bournemouth was on the wireless asking families to take a soldier in for a few days, for respite during their short leave. You've a spare room here, haven't you Audrey? I've already offered my house, I have two empty bedrooms for goodness sake.'

The women in the queue spoke amongst themselves, worrying about loved ones, or devising ways to help.

Pat clapped her hands together, standing taller and increasing her volume. 'Any woman with any time on her hands,' she said, 'should get to the school and offer to help. They're going to need homes in the coming days – clothes, warmth, kindness – and I'll wager, bread for sandwiches, Audrey.'

'Of course,' said Audrey, calculating what she could throw together quickly. 'I'll arrange sandwiches and cakes, we have socks and trousers and Charlie has spare boots… there's a stack of hessian sacks we can take down and I'll offer accommodation.'

'We should take those boys some postcards,' said Mrs Collingham, standing now, wearing a determined expression. 'Then they can send a note home to reassure their families they're safe… and if there are French soldiers here, they'll need someone who speaks French.'

'I can speak a little French,' piped up Lily. 'I can help translate.'

Audrey smiled at Lily, whose very presence surprised her, let alone her ability to speak French. Despite the handful of letters she'd received over the years they'd been apart, there was so much about her she didn't know. How William would love to see her. *William.*

Oh goodness, what if…? thought Audrey. What if William was one of those soldiers at Dunkirk? What if her dear brother was one of those left on the beaches or in the sea being mercilessly attacked? She knew he was overseas, in France somewhere. Momentarily she felt too weak to speak.

'We will welcome a soldier here,' said Audrey, finding her voice. 'My door is open to anyone in need.'

'I can stay somewhere else if you need the room,' Lily began, but Audrey raised her hand to silence her.

'You'll do nothing of the sort,' she said. 'We can accommodate you and a soldier, even if I have to sleep on the floor. We'll go to the school shortly with supplies. In the meantime, why don't you put on an apron and help me serve this queue? Might as well get stuck in now you're here. You're family after all!'

Chapter Four

Elsie pedalled so fast along the promenade her calf muscles burned. To onlookers, she was a blur against the sky and sea, like a smudge on a painting.

'Oi slow down!' yelled the pony-ride man at Boscombe Pier when she flew past him. 'You nearly knocked out m' pony!'

'Codswallop!' she yelled in reply, wishing she hadn't worn her red knitted cardigan over her uniform of black knee-length dress, stockings and black smart shoes, but there was no time to stop and unbutton. She was thirteen minutes late (and counting) for her shift in the Needlework Department at Beales Department Store, and had already been warned twice about her punctuality.

When pressed for a reason for her lateness, she would blame the mechanical failings of her ancient Raleigh bicycle. How could she explain the truth? That her mother, Violet, whose legs were growing weaker by the day, but who was too pig-headed to ask the doctor for proper treatment for her condition, insisted on carrying on in the house with the aid of her cane as if she were still perfectly able. Today, washday Monday, when her list of household chores was as long as her arm, the porridge had been spilled over the red kitchen floor tiles, taking the porcelain milk jug and sugar ration with it. Elsie had no choice but to clean it up and salvage what she could of the sugar, while her mother thumped the kitchen table in bitter frustration, making the teacups dance in their saucers.

'Do not pity me!' she declared, her cheeks flaming red. 'Pity will kill me, not these legs!'

'I don't pity you, Mother!' Elsie retorted. 'I only wish you would let me knuckle down and help more. Or that you would speak to a doctor!'

'He has better things to worry about now the war's on,' she said. 'I'll not waste his time. Leave that be, you have a job to get to. We can't do without your earnings.'

Elsie had looked around the kitchen of their small home in Avenue Road, Southbourne, in dismay. With a house to run and Elsie's ten-year-old twin sisters June and Joyce to look after, her mother clearly needed more help – the legs of the kitchen table were uneven and made steady with folded newspaper, the curtain on the window of the back door had come away from the hooks, the chairs sagged in the middle and a gigantic pile of washing waited to be washed and pegged out to dry on the clothes line in the garden. But whatever Elsie tried to do to help – and she did whatever she could when she wasn't working – Violet warned her off, taking the offer as a criticism of her abilities.

'Leave her, flower,' soothed her father, Angelo, taking Elsie aside before he left for work at the barbershop, a fresh egg (laid by their family chicken) in each pocket of his jacket for his favourite customer. 'Violet can make her own mind up in her own time.'

Now, Elsie's thighs ached as she headed up Bath Road (a hill so steep that when the bus was packed the driver would sometimes ask passengers to get off, walk up the hill and meet him again at the top), towards the Bath Hotel, a beautiful white building that stood overlooking the sea like one of Audrey's intricately iced celebration cakes. Elsie yanked on her brakes and came to an abrupt stop at the quite incredible sight of hundreds of soldiers approaching, in a swift-moving cloud of khaki brown.

'Good grief,' she said. 'What's this?'

Everyone on the street stopped to watch the spectacle. A young woman pushing a pram and holding the hand of a small child waved her hanky at the men, and a man wearing a soft cap and leaning on a stick called out, 'Welcome home, boys.' Then he turned to Elsie to explain: 'They're evacuees from Dunkirk. They were in the sea waiting to be rescued by our boats for hours. That water must have been colder than the hinges of hell! T'others didn't get that far, poor blighters.' The man shook his head. 'As if we didn't have a gutful of this in the Great War.'

'They look like they've been to hell and back,' Elsie said, climbing off her bicycle, the creased skirt of her dress fluttering against her legs, tendrils of her raven hair sticking to her damp forehead. Her mother would throw her hands in the air in horror at the sight of her eldest daughter, but Elsie was too busy staring at the soldiers to care. For all the news in the *Bournemouth Echo* and on the wireless and the thousands of military personnel in the town, this sight made war tangible. These men were exhausted. Their faces were covered with dirt or dried blood, their uniforms shabby. Some had blankets thrown over their shoulders, or makeshift bandages wrapped around their limbs, or strapped over their eyes. Several limped along using sticks to help them walk, or leaned against another man's shoulder. Many still wore their protective tin helmets and some were without any kitbag at all.

'I'll bet that was exactly what Dunkirk was like,' the old man said. 'Hell!'

Women ran from the front doors of the houses and businesses on the road, bursting out of their doors like the tiny model figures of a decorative weather vane, offering armfuls of items to the troops. Player's cigarettes, Cadbury's chocolate bars, Palmolive soap, razors, sleeping bags – even hot baths and beds.

'We've landed in paradise,' she heard one young soldier say, accepting a half bottle of Johnnie Walker whisky produced from the pocket of a grandma's housecoat, as seagulls squawked and swooped above as if in fanfare.

And then, as she searched the faces of the soldiers as they passed her, Elsie froze when she glimpsed a familiar set of shoulders and caught sight of a jaw that could only belong to one man. A man who could play a tune on his mouth harp more mournful and beautiful than she'd ever heard. With her heart furiously pounding in her chest, Elsie strained to get a better look, but just as quickly as he was in view, he was swallowed by the crowd.

'William?' she called in disbelief, letting go of her bicycle's handlebars and, as it crashed to the pavement, trampling over the spinning wheels to join the soldiers.

'Excuse me,' she said, squeezing in through the men, the pungent smell of unwashed bodies assailing her, pausing to wolf-whistle to get his attention.

Soldiers turned to face her as she whistled, then pushed through the crowd, their expressions quizzical. The crowd of men allowed her through before closing in around her again until she was entirely surrounded by uniforms, as if they were the flesh and she were the red beating heart. Almost within reach now, she trembled; she could just about see William, his strong shoulders even broader than she remembered, his neck dirty and sunburned. Finally she was close enough to touch him. He had his back towards her and was moving swiftly forward, so she grabbed his arm with her fingers, her eyes blurry with tears.

'William!' she exclaimed, her face exploding into a tearful smile. But as the man turned, she staggered backwards. The man, though identical to William in stature and with the same strong jawline, was a complete stranger. Close up, he looked nothing like the man she loved. Her hand flew to her mouth as she retreated from him in embarrassment, utterly crushed by disappointment.

'I'm sorry, miss,' he said. 'My name isn't William.'

'Bet you wish it was William,' his mate said. 'If the shoe fits…'

The man smiled kindly at Elsie as she stood frozen, unable to speak. 'Looks like you've had a shock, miss,' he said gently. 'What's William's surname? Maybe I know him.'

'Private William Allen, 2nd Dorsets,' Elsie said shakily, but the soldier shook his head.

'I'm sorry, I don't know him, but thousands of men were evacuated and have been sent all over. You should have seen what it was like when we first got to the docks – people working flat out to give us tea, food and a space to rest. They didn't have enough tin mugs for us all to have a cuppa – when we left the station the railway man shouted "sling 'em out", so we threw the mugs out the window. It was raining mugs!'

'Rather them than bullets,' said his mate.

The soldier and his friend smiled at one another, in a stunned sort of way – and Elsie shivered, lost for words. She nodded in thanks and turned to go back to her bicycle, her entire body shaking. The old man she'd talked to picked up her bike for her, and gave her a gentle pat on her shoulder.

'This war is hard on everyone, home and away,' he said. 'Keep your chin up, darlin', you never know what tomorrow will bring.'

She smiled a weak smile and felt for the ring William had given to her. Rather than wear it on her finger, she'd strung it onto a necklace around her neck, waiting for him to propose to her in person and place the ring onto her finger himself. She missed William so much – she physically ached with longing for his arms to be around her – but there was nothing she could do about it. Those pre-war bicycle rides to Highcliffe Castle, eating cream horns from Barton's on a blanket in the dunes, were a dim and distant memory. She shook her head at her stupidity at thinking she'd seen William.

'Daft cow,' she admonished herself. 'Now I better get on and get to work, else I won't have a job to go to.'

She cycled on to Beales Department Store on Old Christchurch Road, feeling hollow.

'Morning,' she mumbled to the other girls already manning their counters, as she drifted past the rails of satin overblouses, printed silk dresses and velvet gowns in the Womenswear Department. She staggered through to Needlework, pinning her hair back up into place as she moved, and forced herself to adopt the shop-assistant smile. What had she been thinking? It would have been some sort of miracle for William to be standing there in the street just yards away from her, she told herself – the impossible daydream of a girl in love.

Chapter Five

Audrey stood at the door of a classroom in Bournemouth School turned rest centre, carrying a basket piled high with hastily prepared fish paste, cheese and beetroot doorstep sandwiches, rock cakes and buns, and took a sharp intake of breath.

'Lily,' she said quietly. 'Would you look at this?'

The school was packed with camp beds and trestle tables, and brimming with volunteers who were tending to dishevelled soldiers dropping with fatigue. Some men waiting in the school's corridors were standing in their underpants, cigarette in mouth, pulling on donated, clean trousers, their old dirty uniforms discarded at their feet and being labelled and bundled up by volunteers for washing and darning. Others were flat out on their backs, with local women lifting cups of tea to their lips. Shafts of bright sunshine shone in through the floor-to-ceiling windows, filling the room with golden sunlight and casting a heavenly light onto some of the men's faces. Voluntary networks and first aiders worked alongside townspeople, trying to help the soldiers who had been starved of sleep and food, surviving on iron rations alone.

'Well done Bournemouth,' Audrey said proudly, turning again to Lily, whose eyes were fixed on a soldier in a French uniform sitting by a door that had been opened to a grassy courtyard. Following her stare, Audrey saw that the soldier had thrown a crust of bread to a squirrel and was watching it innocently scamper across the grass. A small, sad smile played on his lips and was mirrored on Lily's lips – as if she shared exactly what the young soldier was thinking. 'Why don't you talk to that young man?' Audrey suggested. 'He looks like he could use a friend. Offer him one of these sandwiches. You know a little French, don't you? I'm going to speak to one of the Bournemouth War Service Organisation ladies to offer up a room and some home-cooked meals for a few nights.'

'No,' said Lily, suddenly blushing, 'I better not, I might get the French wrong… and… he wouldn't want to talk to me after what he's been through.'

Audrey put her hand on Lily's arm, to reassure her. 'Put your fears aside Lily,' she said. 'These young men are away from their homes and loved ones. They have witnessed the deaths of their friends and nearly been killed themselves. They need our welcome. I will talk to the organiser then come to find you.'

'You're right,' said Lily apologetically. 'What am I thinking of?'

She gathered herself together and approached the soldier. Audrey watched a smile break out over the soldier's face as Lily spoke in French and shook his hand. She observed him turn out his pockets and sand pour out of them and was pleased to see the two young people share a small surprised laugh. Audrey marvelled at people's ability to laugh, even in the bleakest times. A nurse then approached Lily and, after a short discussion, handed her a bowl filled with steaming liquid and some white cloths. Lily glanced back at Audrey, gave her a small nod, then knelt by the French soldier's chair and gently unlaced his boots, before slowly and carefully peeling off his threadbare socks that seemed to be embedded in his toes. The muscles in the soldier's cheeks clenched as he clearly fought back tears as Lily carefully bathed his feet. The interaction was so tender and touching that, not for the first time that afternoon, Audrey felt overcome with emotion and immense pride as she battled to keep from crying. Lily, on the other hand, was doing a wonderful job of smiling encouragingly, gently bathing the soldier's feet and speaking softly in what sounded to Audrey's ears like fluent French. It seemed to Audrey that Lily had arrived in town just in time – like Fate herself had played a hand.

'Well done Lily,' she said quietly under her breath. 'Well done you.'

'Someone's dream just came true,' Elsie whispered to Audrey when she joined her at the emergency rest centre in Bournemouth School after her shift at Beales. One of the Dunkirk evacuees, a private from Westbourne who had been coincidentally billeted to his home town of Bournemouth, was being literally smothered in love by no fewer than eleven women and children – his wife, mother, sisters and daughters. The smiles on the women's faces as they held onto his arms and ruffled his hair and kissed him – unadulterated joy – were a picture.

'I know,' said Audrey, squeezing Elsie's hand. Though it was a long shot, they'd both been hoping and praying for the same thing: that their beloved William would be there. 'No sign,' Audrey said gently. 'I've checked with the register here. But just because he's not here, it doesn't mean he's not safe somewhere else.'

Elsie nodded and forced herself to brighten. There was plenty of helping to be done here anyway, so at least she could make herself useful. And in some small way, helping another soldier felt like helping William.

'I came as soon as my shift was over to see if I could do anything,' said Elsie, looking around and taking in the hive of activity. 'But that dragon boss of mine made me stay on, to make up for the fact I was late this morning and that I dared to have a toilet break. Do you know she counts how many breaks we all take? She should get a job in the army!'

'She sounds a bit like Pat,' said Audrey, with a chuckle. 'Pat was in the bakery this morning berating me for having a queue outside. Thing is, my stepsister Lily just turned up out of the blue. She's over there, the pretty young girl with the red curls helping the French soldier. I haven't seen her in years, not since William and I left home. I haven't had a minute spare to find out why she's here.'

Elsie followed Audrey's gaze and saw Lily and a young soldier deep in conversation. She felt a pang of something over their clear connection – a craving to be able to talk to William in the same way.

'They look like they've known each other years! So, is your mother here too?' Elsie asked, but Audrey shook her head.

'Not on your life,' she replied. 'My mother is glued to my stepfather's side and nothing can prise her away from him. Anyway, Elsie, would you help me hand out these sandwiches? These men look like they could do with meat stews and dumplings, but these doorsteps will fill a gap.'

The rest of the afternoon passed quickly and before Audrey returned to the bakery with Lily and the young French solider, Jacques, she invited Elsie over for tea the following week, to celebrate her birthday.

It was late when Elsie climbed onto her bike, with tired legs, and started the journey home. Seeing the soldiers in such a bad way made Elsie fear the worst for William's chances, but with every turn of her pedals she tried to push those negative thoughts away. She would never give up hope. Could never give up hope.

Cycling towards Southbourne, she turned her thoughts to what would be waiting at home. Her mother would have prepared dinner, probably hotpot with cabbage, and would now be having five minutes on her chair in the garden swapping gossip over the fence with the neighbour as both women, never wanting to be idle, sat in their housecoats and headscarves, knitting for the Forces. Her younger twin sisters, June and Joyce, would be skipping in the street or practising their handstands against the wall before running in for the story on *Children's Hour* and her papa, Angelo, after a long day at the barbershop, would be reading his newspaper, shaking his head in dismay at world affairs and talking at the wireless all through the BBC Home Service news. She adored her family but she desperately missed William. What she would give to go to a dance at the Pavilion with him, or have a night at the pictures, the two of them walking hand in hand through the pine trees in the Lower Gardens afterwards, gazing up at the stars and spotting the constellations. Just ordinary things. Ordinariness. Who would have thought that was what she would long for?

Approaching the front door of her family's house, Elsie heard her sisters singing 'Ten Green Bottles' in the backyard, the smell of boiled potatoes greeting her nose. She picked two daffodils from the front garden, to give to her mother.

'Hello, I'm back,' she called, entering the house and hanging up her gas mask case on the coat hook in the hallway. She walked through to the kitchen and stopped dead at the door when she saw her mother waiting for her at the kitchen table, where instead of finding the table laid for dinner as it usually was at this time, she saw an envelope propped up against the teapot. Her stomach filled with wet sand and the daffodils slipped from her grip.

'It's for you,' said her mother gently, reaching her hand out to Elsie. 'My dear girl, come and sit down.'

Chapter Six

Lily tried not to peek as Jacques, stripped to the waist, rubbed his hair dry with a towel after a hot bath back at the bakery. But what she did see of his body secretly enraptured her. His back, shoulders and arms were pitted with cuts and bruises, but his skin was olive brown and, she imagined, would be soft as petals to touch. Clean-shaven and rejuvenated by plenty of cups of sweet tea, Jacques had scrubbed up well. He also had one of those dazzling smiles that, when directed at Lily, made her feel as if he'd just handed her a beautifully wrapped gift. Jacques took a drag from his cigarette, given to him by Charlie, half closing his eyes in pleasure as he exhaled. Delicious smells of home-cooked food emanated from the bakery and in the distance, the sea glittered in the afternoon sunlight.

Lily crossed her arms over her chest and blinked, feeling disorientated. Yesterday she had left London in a panic, carrying a secret as explosive as a grenade. Today she was in Audrey's backyard with a very attractive French solider, struggling not to feel shy in his presence. She couldn't keep up with her own emotions that seemed to explode inside her like firecrackers.

'The grazes are from the barbed wire,' Jacques explained in fluent English, gesturing to his wounds. 'There was wire in the sea and on the beach. The rescuers were determined though. Some even came on canoes because the bigger boats couldn't get any closer to the beach. The water was too shallow. I owe those brave people my life.'

He tried to reach his back in order to rub on some Germolene, but couldn't stretch that far.

'Audrey gave me this ointment,' he said, looking at her from under thick eyelashes. 'Would you mind…?'

Lily blushed, but smiled and nodded, remembering that, in this situation, she was the next best thing to a nurse. Her fingers shook slightly as, using balls of cotton wool, she dabbed the cream on the wounds, trying to ignore the broad reach of his shoulders and his tapered waist. His wounds must have been so sore, but he didn't flinch. Watching him as he stared out towards the sea, she thought of him as the type of man who suited the outdoors, who liked to be close to nature. She wondered what on earth he had seen on the front line. Before she had time to think it through, the question had left her lips.

'What was it like over there?' she asked quietly, as he carefully pulled on the shirt lent to him by Charlie. 'I mean… sorry, maybe I should not ask that. You won't want to talk about that.'

Elsie blushed even more as Jacques turned to face her, a quizzical expression on his face. He smiled.

'It was like a bad dream, the worst bad dream you can imagine,' he said, in his gentle French accent. 'It was opposite to everything I have ever believed about how men should behave. It was the darkest day of my life and now, suddenly, I am here. Safe for a few hours, days.'

Lily smiled kindly and nodded in recognition. Jacques took a seat on a wooden bench and indicated that she should join him and the two of them sat in silence for a few moments, their legs almost touching, the warm sun on their faces.

'What about you?' he said, finishing his cigarette. 'Tell me about you.'

Lily held her hands up in the air and let them drop back down by her side, shaking her head. There was something about Jacques that made her want to open up to him, but she knew she couldn't possibly. He was there to recuperate, not listen to her silly, self-inflicted problems. She shrugged and smiled, as if there was nothing to tell.

'What did you do before the war?' Lily asked instead.

'I was working with my father,' Jacques said. 'He is a printer and so I was his apprentice, but I also like to draw, so he'd allow me to take off for a couple of days, to see new things and draw them. I thought joining up would be an extension of that, a chance to travel and see more of the world with my best friend.'

His eyes darkened before he went on to tell her the dreadful story of his best friend's death on the beach at Dunkirk. By the end of it Lily was in tears.

'My mother cried when I told her I was going to fight,' he said. 'Now I know why. And you? Where is your mother?'

'She's dead,' said Lily, wiping her eyes and feeling Jacques study her mouth as she spoke. 'She died when I was four. I have a photograph of her, but it's faded. It's quite hard to remember what she looked like, though my father says we're exactly the same. Red hair. Gappy teeth. Pale as milk.'

Lily laughed at her own expense, but Jacques touched her arm and gave it a gentle squeeze. 'I'm sorry,' he said. 'You must miss her.'

Again, Lily's eyes filled with tears and she tutted in annoyance at herself. He touched her hand and smiled. Feeling his gentle concern, she rapidly blinked the tears away and turned from Jacques' gaze to compose herself. For a distraction, she grabbed a tin of mints from her pocket, offered Jacques one and popped one onto her own tongue. They smiled at one another.

'Jacques! Lily!' called Audrey suddenly from the kitchen window. They leapt from their seats, as if caught doing something forbidden. 'Dinner!'

'This,' said Audrey, placing an enormous slice of steaming rabbit pie onto Jacques' plate and a generous portion of stuffed marrow and peas alongside, 'will put some hairs on your chest.'

Jacques and Lily took a seat at the round dining table, with Audrey, Charlie and Uncle John. They were in the best room, the dining room, where the walls were decorated in floral wallpaper and the fireplace surrounded with forest green tiles, and a small cabinet of silver snuffboxes and cigarette cases was displayed, a collection passed down through Charlie's family. To mark the occasion, Audrey had put out the best napkins, candlesticks and crockery (nothing so lovely as a set table), filled a small glass vase with water and picked sweet peas from the patch of flowers that hadn't been turned to vegetable growing – and baked the biggest pie she could with the ingredients available. A ration-friendly version of bread pudding waited in the kitchen to be served up when the dinner plates had been scraped clean.

'I hope you like it,' she said, nervously smiling. Having Lily arrive at the bakery today was enough of a surprise, but now she had Jacques here too and she wanted, more than anything, for them both to feel welcome. And though it was a bit of a squeeze at the table, with elbows and knees bumping, Audrey felt driven – compelled even – to look after Jacques to the very best of her ability. If William was out there somewhere, staying in a stranger's home and putting a brave face on his loneliness, she desperately hoped they would treat him in the same way and help him forget the horror of war, if only for a few hours.

'Bon appétit!' she said, using the sum of her French vocabulary in one go.

Charlie raised his eyebrows, a smile playing on his lips.

'Merci beaucoup,' Jacques said with his gentle French accent. 'It smells delicious. Thank you very much.'

'The proof of the pudding is in the tasting, as they say,' Audrey said with a quick smile, hoping that Jacques was as content as he seemed, though doubting it somehow as he sat, dressed in a spare set of Charlie's clothes, eating foreign food, with his own family and home hundreds of miles away.

'Uncle John,' she said, serving John, who was having dinner with them that evening before he and Charlie started back in the bakehouse, then Charlie and Lily, with a handsome wedge of pie, marrow and fresh peas.

'Beautiful bit-an'-drap,' said John, closing his eyes and breathing in the scent of the rich rabbit meat that drifted from the pie.

'Perfect crust,' said Charlie, tapping the crust with his fork. 'Long time since we've had a pie.'

'This is potato pastry,' said Audrey. 'It's a new way of making pastry saving on fat. Pat told me about it. Full of good ideas, she is. What was the other one? Fudge made with stale crusts. That was it.'

'Nowt so queer as folk,' said John. 'And especially not Pat. I should know, she's my sister.'

Charlie laughed. He was always jovial around John, and Audrey was pleased she'd invited him for dinner. She hated the thought of him eating alone in his house since his wife Hazel had died last summer, or probably not eating very much at all if his empty larder was anything to go by.

Everyone tucked into the food, with the exception of Lily, who held her fork limply over the meal in front of her, spearing a bit of pastry and nibbling a tiny crumb before hastily drinking water from her glass. Audrey frowned.

'Everything okay, Lily?' she asked.

'Did you say it's rabbit?' asked Lily, her skin going a shade paler.

John put down his fork and burst out laughing, his mouth still half full of pie. 'He didn't go by the name Peter, and weren't wearin' a velvet blue jacket or shoes,' he laughed, 'if that's what you're askin'.'

Charlie roared with laughter and Jacques looked bemused, but smiled all the same. Audrey felt a giggle bubbling up inside of her, but realised that Lily was not amused.

'Stop it, John,' snapped Audrey, before turning to Lily. 'Rabbit isn't on the meat ration, so I thought we'd get a better dinner for us all out of it. If you don't like it, I'm sure one of the men will eat your portion and I can give you more vegetables?'

Before she'd had time to reply, John reached over the table and helped himself to Lily's portion, still laughing. This time his laugh became a hacking cough and it took Audrey patting him on the back to make him stop.

'You should get that cough checked,' Audrey said. 'Have you seen the doctor about it? I can't think the flour helps, though I know you wash the dust from your throat with beer often enough.'

'My cough is my business, Audrey Barton. You mind your own,' he said, winking. 'Don't be afeared of me, young Lily, I'm just playin'.'

'I'm not afraid,' Lily replied, confidently. 'The pie looks nice, it's just I have been off my food lately. I'm sorry to be rude.'

'It is the best thing I have tasted in months,' said Jacques, his fork halfway to his mouth.

'Ark a'ee,' said John, grinning, pointing his fork at Jacques. 'There'll be seconds for you, lad.'

'With manners like that you can stay as long as you like,' Audrey joked, then, lowering her voice, added 'You could certainly teach Uncle John here a thing or two.'

'What have I ever done to you?' John said, with fake incredulity. The table erupted into laughter again and Audrey glanced at Jacques to see if he was following the conversation.

'I'd like to help in some way if I could,' said Jacques. 'In the bakery perhaps?'

'We can always use an extra pair of hands,' said Charlie, nodding. 'Lily, if you're visitin' for any length of time, you would be useful serving in the shop, and Jacques, you could help bring in the coke or shift a few bags of flour to save John's old legs—'

'Less of the old,' said John. 'I'm not ready for the knacker's yard just yet.'

'But Jacques should take the opportunity to rest while he's here,' interrupted Audrey, nudging Charlie under the table. 'We can manage the bakery, Charlie, without leaning on this soldier's shoulders? He's already done enough.'

Charlie put his hands down flat on the table, pushing out his chair. 'I'll not lean on anyone. That is not what I was saying,' he barked. 'The young man asked what he could do to help and I gave him a straight answer. There's nothing worse than feeling like you're no use to anyone, is there lad? Nothing worse. Excuse me, I have work to do.'

Charlie stood up abruptly.

'There's bread pudding, love,' Audrey called after him, but he stalked out and left an awkward silence hanging like a pungent smell in the room. Audrey sighed, inwardly chastising herself for inadvertently ruffling Charlie's feathers. Honestly, her husband was so bad-tempered these days! She heaped more vegetables onto Jacques and John's plates, smiling cheerily to compensate for Charlie's mood. 'Don't mind Charlie,' she said, then addressing Jacques, 'I think you should have some fun while you can, that's all I'm saying. Lily and you could go dancing on the pier if your feet are up to it. Do you both good, I'm sure. And it might be the last chance – I've heard the Royal Engineers are soon going to be blowing up the piers to prevent Hitler and his cronies landing on our shores.'

'I would like that,' said Jacques. 'If you would like to come too, Lily?'

Lily, who was clearly struggling to eat anything, even her vegetables, nodded. Audrey noticed the blush creeping up Lily's cheek whenever Jacques spoke to her. It was obvious there was a spark between them – and there was no denying that Jacques was a handsome lad. Now he'd had a bath, his dark hair was swept back from his forehead, revealing bright, striking blue eyes – similar in shade to Lily's – an olive complexion and full lips. He had the quiet air of someone who could hold his own wherever he went. It would do both of them good to enjoy each other's company, and take each other's minds off things, rather than listen to the evening news on the wireless, which was the routine, but was usually depressing.

'I think we're done here, so why don't you two get ready?' she said to Lily and Jacques after pudding. 'I've got a yellow dress needs wearing, Lily, if you want to borrow it? I never get a chance these days.'

Lily and Jacques exchanged hesitant glances and quickly broke into smiles.

'I must first write to my family,' Jacques said. 'Excuse me. Thank you for dinner.'

'I will help do the dishes,' said Lily.

'And I,' said John, 'will be in the flour loft to shift that flour. It ain't goin' t' move on it's own.'

'Watch your back, John!' Audrey called after him, as the flour sacks weighed twice as much as him.

'Stop fussin',' he boomed back. 'I've been carrying those sacks on me back for forty years and I ain't about to stop!'

Audrey held up the 2/- glass bottle of Quix liquid washer and carefully poured a few drops into the sink, while Lily waited by her side, tea towel in hand.

'Supposed to get sixty bowlfuls out of this,' she said, replacing the lid. 'More like half that!'

One look at Audrey's warm kitchen proved to Lily that her stepsister never slept. Not only was she working flat out in the bakery, the kitchen shelves were yet more evidence of Audrey's industry. Lily scanned the handwritten labels on the numerous glass jars – there were salted beans and cauliflower, pickled cucumber, carrot jam and apple chutney, which Lily assumed she was laying down in case rationing got worse. Atop the stove was a pan of carrot, turnip and beetroot tops and a small pot of nutmeg. On the table rested some of Audrey's cake baking equipment – brass weighing scales and baking tins, a flour douser and recipes written in a notebook in Audrey's neat handwriting. It was open on a page for 'Cut And Come Again Cake' and underneath she had written 'recommended by Mrs King'.

Lily was struck by what a homely home Audrey had created. The only missing component was four rosy-cheeked little children sitting around the table, waiting to be fed like baby birds in a nest.

'Expect you're wondering where all the books are?' said Audrey, elbow-deep in suds. 'We haven't got time for reading stories with running a bakery like this. We work all hours. The ovens are lit Sunday night and stay lit until the following Sunday morning, so there's no time for much else. I remember you always had your nose in a book. You always had brains, and of course your father had enough books to fill a library!'

Lily nodded, not wanting to think about her father.

'What's this?' she asked instead, picking up a huge saucepan filled with dozens of scraps of soap. 'You're not baking with soap, are you?'

Audrey smiled. 'Funny you should say that,' she said. 'I'm making a soap cake, but not for eating. I've collected all the unusable bits of soap from the customers and I'll boil this up, then set it in a tin. When it's cold I'll slice it up and give everyone a decent piece of soap. Waste not, want not.'

'Good idea,' Lily said. 'Looks like you've been busy.'

Lily thought of her parents' home, which Audrey's estranged mother kept minimally decorated and devoid of clutter, apart from the bookshelves stacked with her father's books. It was poles apart from Audrey's comforting kitchen, where every surface was filled with things to look at and the walls were peppered with recipes torn from newspapers and magazines. Even the windowsill was busy with flowerpots, biscuit tins and jars holding a collection of screws, keys and oddities.

'I prefer to be working,' Audrey said. 'Keeps my mind off the war and fretting about William. I so hoped we'd have heard from him by now... but less of that and more of you. It's so good to see you.'

She grabbed Lily's hand and gave it a squeeze, beaming at her.

'How *is* my mother?' Audrey asked, tentatively. 'How has she been?'

Lily saw sadness in Audrey's expression and she wished she could give her the news that she wanted – that Daphne had talked about Audrey and William, that she clearly missed them both. In truth, Daphne was intensely private and seemed to exist solely for Victor and for keeping the house in order. Lily knew Daphne wasn't happy though – the bottles of gin she kept on top of the kitchen cupboard were a telltale sign of her dissatisfaction.

'She's been busy helping with Father's accounting business,' said Lily, diplomatically. 'Doing the books.'

Audrey gave Lily a knowing, sideways glance and sighed. 'And what about Jacques?' she said, quickly changing the subject. 'He's a lovely young man, isn't he? He told me his father is a printer in the south of France and that he has three sisters. He asked me about you, Lily – he seems quite taken with you, I have to say.'

Audrey raised her eyebrows in playful question but, feeling her cheeks colour, Lily shook her head.

'He's very nice,' she said, her mind drifting to the sight of him shirtless outside. 'But I'm sure he has a sweetheart back at home. That's who he'll be writing to now. I'm not looking for love, Audrey, though I know people think it's odd for me to not want to be married the minute I turn eighteen.'

Lily's words came out more harshly than she intended.

'That might be so, but there's no harm in you two becoming friends, is there?' Audrey said, slightly taken aback as she looked more closely at her step-sister. 'Lily, are you feeling right? You're very pale and you hardly ate anything at dinner.'

'I'm sorry,' Lily said, blushing. 'I don't have much of an appetite.'

'Is it this war? I know it turns my stomach,' Audrey asked. 'Or is there anything else wrong? You know you're welcome to go over to Old Reg and use his telephone to speak to your father at any time, should you wish to. He does know you're here, doesn't he?'

Lily looked at the floor and pushed a tiny bit of grit around with the toe of her shoe. Thinking of her father filled her with a dizzying set of emotions. Her entire life he'd watched her like a hawk. He insisted on the best education, didn't allow her to court boys and disapproved of her passion for American jazz swing bands. When Benny Goodman came to London and her friends went to watch him in concert, he banned her from going. She'd tried to climb out her bedroom window, but he caught her and so she had to content herself with listening to the wireless, closing her eyes and imagining. Gosh how she'd yearned for freedom over the years, imagining visiting the far-flung places she read about in books, but now without his close attention, she felt strangely out of control.

'I told them I was coming to see you,' said Lily, hurriedly. 'And that I hoped to stay with you, to get reacquainted with you. After all, you're my stepsister…'

'I imagine that went down well,' said Audrey, with a quick smile. 'Are you feeling poorly? You're green about the gills.'

Audrey frowned when she held a hand up to Lily's forehead to feel her temperature.

Lily's stomach clenched and her palms sweated under Audrey's scrutiny, gentle and concerned as it was. Lily felt she was losing track of the truth and the anxiety she'd so far managed to suppress that day was bubbling to the surface. She had to talk to Audrey about why she'd come. It wasn't fair to just arrive and not offer any explanation. She opened her mouth to speak, but quickly faltered. How should she begin? Lily put the pan she had dried up onto the board by the Belfast sink and felt her shoulders sag.

'What is it?' Audrey asked gently, sitting down on the kitchen chair and patting the chair next to her. 'Has something happened at home? Is this something to do with your bruised eye?'

Lily raised her eyes to the ceiling to halt the tears, but her lip quivered and her shoulders trembled as she broke down into tears. She couldn't hold them in for a moment longer.

'Oh no, don't cry,' said Audrey, gently holding Lily in her arms. Beyond the steamy kitchen window, the sun was sinking low in the sky, casting long shadows across the walls. 'What's wrong?'

Being in the warm kitchen with Audrey made Lily want to confess everything, to open up her heart and let out all the feelings she'd been bottling up these last weeks. 'I shouldn't have come here like this, but I didn't know what else to do,' she said. 'I couldn't stay at home with my father breathing down my neck. I needed time to think.'

Tears were streaming down Lily's cheeks now and Audrey handed her a hanky, to wipe them away.

'You can tell me anything,' Audrey said, holding Lily at arm's length and looking her in the eye.

Lily's lip quivered as she recalled the first time she'd given in to Henry Bateman's attention. He'd been showing her the artist's drawings for the new 'Whispers of War' poster campaign to encourage the public not to gossip, and as usual, she had felt honoured to be seeing the artwork proofs and felt that Henry valued her opinion. After working late one evening, the two of them alone in the office, he had confided in her that he had volunteered to join the RAF, and that he would be recommending that she take on a more senior role after he left. Lily was flattered and delighted, but upset that he was leaving. They had grown close and she admired him.

'I've become very fond of you,' he had gone on to say. 'And I'm running out of time to show you how I really feel.'

She'd sensed he wanted to kiss her and, emboldened by his praise, had impulsively leaned into him, planting her lips on his, her entire body blazing with excitement. Though in the back of her mind she was shocked by her bold action and knew it should all stop there and then, Henry looked at her with such desire, she felt strangely empowered, not to mention intrigued.

After quickly locking the door and assuring her he had taken precautions, Henry told her he wanted to make love to her. It was Lily's first time and though she knew she shouldn't be partaking in the act – heavens, they were not even officially a couple – she had happily consented.

She had floated on air afterwards and when it happened once more, two days later, raised the issue of their relationship status. Were they now officially a couple? Was this love?

'I have a fiancée,' he responded. 'Her name is Helen and we have known each other since we were children. We will be married in a matter of months. I should never have let this happen. This all must stop.'

Lily had felt crushed and ashamed, not knowing what to think or how to process what had happened. The predominant feelings she was left with were emptiness and confusion. Then, a few days after shattering her heart, Henry had told Lily he had to let her go, telling her she was 'a distraction to the war effort'. Lily had been stunned. When he told her to collect her things and not to come back, she hadn't been able to move.

'But I love my job,' she'd stuttered. 'You told me I had a bright future ahead of me. My father will kill me!'

'You should have thought about that,' he had said, so coldly she shivered.

Now, in her mind's eye, she saw the pool of fountain pen ink, like blue blood, spreading across the desk and spoiling his paperwork after she'd tipped over his ink in anger. But the ink seemed minor revenge for how ruthlessly she had been discarded. What about her promotion? What about her promising future? What about her reputation?

Worse, when she reached home, after the dismissal, she discovered that Henry had got to her father first – informing his cricketing friend that there had been an unfortunate incident with Lily and an office junior behaving inappropriately together and that, under the circumstances, Henry had no choice but to let Lily go. He assured Victor he'd been 'discreet' about it but that, with all the important work they did at the office, everyone had to stay absolutely focused on the job. Victor had been furious with Lily, and had not let her out of his sight for weeks and weeks. When Lily confronted him with the truth one day, calling Henry Bateman a cruel liar who had treated him like a fool, Victor had lashed out and hit Lily, telling her that she was 'twisting the truth'. Victor had never been violent towards her before and it had shocked them both. It was then that Lily had made a hasty plan to come to Bournemouth, to see Audrey.

Lily trembled, digging her fingernails into her palms as she thought about the fact that nobody, apart from Henry, knew the worst of this whole situation and the real reason she'd fled from London. Though her father was unspeakably disappointed in her conduct, he didn't know the half of it. She gulped as she admitted the truth to herself: her monthly visitor was late. Two months late. Henry, the cheat, had lied about taking precautions.

'I trusted someone I shouldn't have trusted,' she told Audrey. 'I did something I regret… if only I had thought through what I was doing, but I didn't. I was too hot-headed.'

Lily stared at her shoes, too ashamed to look Audrey in the eye.

'Everyone does things they regret,' Audrey said sadly. 'It's part of life.'

At that moment, there was a loud hammering on the bakery door and the sound of Elsie's voice calling Audrey's name. Seconds later the door flew open and Elsie appeared, her face flushed pink, her curly black hair sticking up from her head in a wild bush, as if she had run the whole way. In her hand she clutched a white envelope that she waved around in the air, like a flag.

'Audrey!' Elsie exclaimed. 'I came straight here!'

'What is it?' Audrey said nervously, lifting her hand to her throat.

'It's William,' Elsie said, collapsing into joyous, noisy laughter. 'He's safe. He's written. He's got compassionate leave and wants us to get married.'

'Married?' exclaimed Audrey. 'Oh Elsie, that's wonderful.'

As Audrey and Elsie clasped hands and celebrated together, Audrey looked over Elsie's shoulder at Lily, who smiled apologetically, dried her eyes and slipped out of the room. Her problems, no matter that they felt as enormous as one of the barrage balloons floating on the London skyline, could wait.

Jacques had lied. He was not writing to his family. He had moved the sacks of flour for John while the old man was in the privy, and was now sitting on the rickety chair at the small desk in his attic room, writing to Lily, so that when he left the Bartons' home to return to service, he could tell her in writing what he could not find the courage to say out loud.

In one corner of the room there were several crates of apples drying out for use in pies over the winter, filling the room with a delicious sweet aroma, a smell Jacques thought he would remember forever. Looking out of the small window, the sky blazing with a breathtaking pink and orange sunset, Jacques was struck by the contrast between where he had found himself, here in the heart of this comforting bakery, and where he had come from in the battlefields.

Blinking in the buttery pink light, he thought carefully about how he should best write this, most important, letter. These last few days had utterly changed his outlook on life. He felt he had come away from the bloody battle in France by the skin of his teeth. The death and destruction he'd witnessed plagued his every thought. Even when he closed his eyes, the atrocious scenes played out on the insides of his eyelids: the low-diving bombers, the armoured cars and the sounds of artillery fire ripping into his brain; the pure desolation he and his fellow soldiers had felt on realising they were trapped by Hitler's army; the hunger, dehydration and rotting wounds; the missiles at Dunkirk, dropped on the beaches and into the sea to try to prevent the men getting to the rescue boats. Jacques could not make sense of the sheer scale of inhumanity he'd witnessed, or why he, and not so many others, had survived.

He squeezed his fist around the brass button he was holding – a button from the uniform of his lifelong best friend, Jean Gaudet, who, aged eighteen, had been shot in the back as he ran towards the sea. Thinking of Jean's body, left on the beach in the ungainly position in which he fell, brought tears flooding into Jacques' eyes, silently running down his nose and blotting the writing paper before him.

Jean had been a raconteur who loved a good time. He enjoyed music, singing and dancing and found so much to laugh about. When they were boys, his mother used to say that Jean laughed out loud in his sleep. There was nobody else quite like him, and now he was gone, leaving a huge void in his wake.

Jacques wiped at his tears with the side of his hand. He had tried to revive Jean amidst the chaos, but it was no use. His superior had ordered all surviving men – by roaring at the top of his lungs with almost mythical force – to get into the sea and onto one of the small, overloaded rowing boats out to a ship, or else die. Jacques had tried to drag Jean's body with him, but he was a well-built man and Jacques was too weak from dehydration and hunger. In trying to pull him, Jacques had ripped a button off Jean's uniform. He knew how pathetic it would seem, but he had vowed to Jean to give the button to his mother when he returned to their village.

Jacques closed his eyes for a moment, his stomach cramping and aching with the awful thought of that prospect. *Why did you survive*, Jean's mother would want to know. *And not my precious son?*

The only person who might be able to take away all this pain and indescribable guilt was Lily. From the moment Jacques had laid eyes on her in the school rest centre, he had known that his heart was in her hands. Just when he thought his world was shrouded in darkness forever more, Lily's beautiful face and gentle ways had made him realise that it was possible to rediscover hope. There was something about the soft way she had bathed his feet with her pale, delicate fingers that had rendered him almost speechless – and from that moment on she only had to look at him for his insides to be filled with molten lava, for his mouth to dry up and his palms to turn clammy.

She was beautiful, with hair the colour of autumn, but it was her nature and grace that had lassoed his heart. Little things about her fascinated him: the tiny peppermints she popped into her mouth, taken from a small round tin she kept in her pocket. The delight that lit up her face when she made observations about her budgie, Bertie: 'I sometimes think he is studying me, rather than the other way around,' she had quipped. Her description of the volunteers at the school as a 'colony of honey bees', and the way she tried to cover the gap between her teeth with her lips when she smiled, all squeezed his heart.

There were so many things! It was the way she nodded encouragingly when he talked in English, the patience with which she'd listened to him and, perhaps most intriguingly, the air of vulnerability that she carried close to her chest. In a time when everyone, men and women alike, was having to be as tough as old leather boots in the harsh face of war, Lily's vulnerability felt to him like a precious and delicate rare thing that he wanted to hold in his hands and protect. He wanted her to confide in him as he had confided in her.

The only trouble was, he thought, glancing up from his letter and out of the window, startled by the sight of a fat seagull on the roof, he had very little time to convince her of how he felt. He would try, he determined, to begin to win Lily's heart. If there was anything that he'd learned from the loss of his dearest friend at Dunkirk and the horror of what he'd witnessed, where so many thousands of young men lost their lives, it was this: that those men left standing should rage against the evils of the war and live and love as passionately and boldly as any man could. He owed it to Jean, his best friend, to grasp hold of love and never let go. He started his letter, *Ma chérie Lily...*, an escaped tear blurring his ink.

Chapter Seven

'This won't do!' said Audrey later that same evening, crossly throwing down the wooden spoon on the kitchen table. Since Elsie's news about her and William's impromptu wedding in a matter of weeks, there was one thing on Audrey's mind – the wedding cake! With a strong belief in there being no time like the present, she was in the kitchen experimenting. The actual fruit cake itself was no problem. Twice a year she made a batch of fruit cakes ready for celebration cake orders and there were still a few in store. But the icing was another matter. Chastising herself for not keeping back more icing sugar these last few months, she folded her arms and frowned at the hopeless white icing substitute she'd made from water, caster sugar and milk powder. Normally Audrey would make intricate iced toppings for wedding cakes – sugar paste flowers and pearl piping – but this substitute would sink and soak into the cake, unless she put it on minutes before the cake was to be served.

'I'm going to have to think of something else,' she muttered.

She wrinkled her nose, going through the alternative ideas for icing, and came to the same conclusion as many other bakers and confectioners. A cardboard or plaster of Paris mould would have to cover the cake, and she would bake some other treats to make the buffet as special as possible. The carrot cake she'd recently tried might be an idea, using honey instead of sugar for sweetness; it had sold well in the shop, everyone taken with the idea that carrots help you see in the dark.

Eat plenty of carrots to help you see in the blackout, Audrey recalled the Ministry of Food leaflet she had read. *Fighting the war with carrot cake!*

With a bit of imagination there were ways to get around the lack of ingredients the war had presented her with. Ever since she was a small girl, when her grandmother taught her the art of baking in her tiny south London kitchen, she'd loved experimenting with ingredients and tinkering with recipes. If she was completely still and quiet for a moment, which admittedly she wasn't very often, Audrey could recall a cherished memory of standing barefoot on a polished wooden chair, so she was tall enough to reach her grandmother's kitchen table, always piled with well-used cookery books and attended to by her grandfather sucking on his pipe, and the sound of her grandmother's sing-song voice advising her on how best to bake a sponge cake. 'Do not rush baking; measure, sift and fold with a gentle touch,' she used to say. 'And never open the oven during cooking, and remember that a person eats with her eyes *and* her mouth.'

When – if – she were ever able to have children of her own, Audrey would pass on her grandmother's baking secrets. Privately envisaging, for the umpteenth time, the kitchen table surrounded by numerous of hers and Charlie's children, Audrey was struck by a terrible loneliness. 'It's no good giving in to melancholy,' she told herself sternly, shaking her head at her own self-indulgence.

Storing the mock icing in a bowl for using as a filling in a sponge or fairy cakes for the shop, she closed her eyes for a moment, trying to sort through her overcrowded mind. In the background was the sound of Charlie and John working in the bakehouse: the clang of tins and muffled conversation as they worked, debating various military operations.

Gosh, there was so much to do. But William and Elsie's wedding was the main concern. She smiled to herself and sighed, so utterly relieved that William was safe and excited that he would soon be at home with her again, at the table having tea and cake, and playing his mouth harp. Wanting to make their wedding memorable and not a rushed affair, Audrey vowed to do everything in her power to make it special. She had offered to help Elsie with the special marriage licence, flowers, the venue, invitations and Elsie's dress… There was all that to think of – and then there was Lily.

Audrey paused to take off her apron, frowning as she tried to iron out her deep concerns about Lily. Hoping she and Jacques were able to enjoy themselves at the dance, she thought of her stepsister unable to eat her pie, the bruises on her face and her tears of regret at something she'd done. Whatever the matter was, Lily needed a friend and, as far as Audrey was concerned, Lily could stay on for as long as she liked, though she must talk it through with Charlie. Thinking of her husband, she remembered his irritable mood earlier and decided she must clear the air. They were a good team and were well used to tackling problems together, even if sometimes lately it felt that their marriage was more a game of tug of war than a union.

The bakery was a higgledy-piggledy building on the corner of Fisherman's Road, inherited by Charlie from his Uncle Eric, Pat's brother, who had opened the shop in 1920. The ground floor was devoted to the business and the upstairs – accessed by a door at the side of the property and a flight of stairs from behind the shop – to family life. Beyond the shopfront was a storeroom and a small cake-making and cooling room, and behind that the brick bakehouse, a split-storey building with the coal-fired ovens at one end and the dough trough and table at the other. On the upper level was the flour loft where the sacks of flour were rigged up to pour down a chute when Charlie needed it. The bakery's layout was Uncle Eric's design and there were marks of him everywhere, including up on the wall a sepia photograph of him wearing a white hat and long white apron that almost touched the floor, which Audrey now regarded while Charlie worked. There was another of his wife, Edith, also in a white apron, sitting near the fire with a cup of tea in her hands, glasses balanced on the tip of her nose.

Audrey smiled at Charlie's ancestors, knowing what hard-working people they had been.

'Charlie?' she asked gently.

'Can't stop now,' he said, without looking up from his mixing. 'First twenty minutes are the most important or the mixture will go lumpy.'

'You know you look just like your Uncle Eric,' she said, watching him mix the flour, yeast, salt and water, making the dough for tomorrow's bread. 'You were cut from the same cloth, or should I say cut from the same dough.'

Audrey watched the muscles in Charlie's strong arms and shoulders flex as he worked. This was just the first step. After the yeast had done its job, Charlie would heave the dough out of the trough and cut it into pieces, weigh, hand-mould it and finally put it into tins to prove before baking.

'Brought you some tea,' she said, placing the cup on the windowsill. 'Have you got a minute to talk? About William and Elsie's wedding, and a few other things.'

'I have,' he said flatly. 'Talk away.'

Audrey sighed inwardly. Charlie was still smarting from earlier. Sometimes she wished he'd just rage and shout and get his bad mood off his chest rather than stringing it out for days on end.

'Sorry if I said the wrong thing at dinner,' she began. 'I wanted Jacques to feel he could have a bit of fun while he's here. He's only a young lad, and goodness knows what he's seen in battle. Thought he could do with enjoying a band, or having a dance. Something simple. That's all.'

Charlie stopped to take a drink, looking at her over the rim of his cup, his eyes alert and his face glistening with sweat.

'Nothing for you to get your knickers in a twist about, love,' she said, with a mischievous glint in her eye. He gave a gentle laugh.

'I know,' he said kindly, leaning against a flour sack, his apron dusted over with flour. 'I'm a grumpy sod, I know that. It's this war.

I can't get my head around it. Earlier today I read an eyewitness account in the paper about the Nazi bombs in Paris. There were weeping mothers searching the streets for their sons and daughters, picking through the debris, trying to find their babies who had been buried under rubble. Babies! Will that Nazi bully stop at nothing? I wish I could get my hands on him. I'd wring his evil neck with my bare hands.'

'Oh Charlie, that's devastating,' Audrey said, shaking her head. 'The poor children are the innocents, and what'll they grow up thinking about the world? That it's a cruel place where lives don't matter.'

Charlie nodded in agreement and sipped his tea.

'I can't help feeling that I should be doing more,' Charlie said, putting down his cup and rolling down his sleeves. 'Not leaving the awful battle to William, Jacques and the rest of the poor young beggars who are out there facing heaven knows what. I know they're the youngest and the fittest, but they've hardly lived, those lads. I was polishing my father's medals earlier and I felt I should be honouring him by doing active service just as he did in the Great War – and what am I doing? You can't fight a war with bread and cakes.'

'But you can fight hunger,' Audrey replied. 'That's what we're doing. People depend on our bread. Do you not feel proud of that? I know I do.'

'I am incredibly proud of this bakery,' he said, his voice deep and serious. 'It's everything to me and I strive to be the best baker I can be and serve our customers well, just as my uncle did. But when I read what's going on, I'm torn, Audrey. I'm torn in half.'

Audrey heard the catch in Charlie's voice and ached with concern and love. He rarely opened up like this. She stood close to Charlie and rested her hand on his strong back, which emanated heat. When he turned, she wrapped her arms around him and rested her head on his chest, silently cursing the war. For a moment, his tense body relaxed and he held her close and they enjoyed a few seconds of complete, warm togetherness.

'Not interrupting anything am I?' asked John, appearing with the coal for the ovens, his face streaked with black. 'If you want me gone, just say so. I can do a good disappearing trick.'

'No, John, we've a lot to do, the hotel's weekend order needs sorting,' said Charlie, releasing Audrey and pecking her on the cheek, then frowning. 'What was it you wanted to talk to me about, love?'

Audrey collected her thoughts and paused, comparing what was on her mind to those poor mothers in Paris hysterically searching and digging for their treasured, innocent babies in the bricks and rubble. It was beyond belief.

'Nothing that can't wait,' she said resolutely.

Weary now, after a day on her feet and with a head full of jobs that needed doing and days not long enough to do them all in, Audrey retired to bed, where, in the dark room, she pulled up a tiny corner of the blackout blind and peered out of the window, from which she could see the sea, shimmering with silver moonlight. The street below was deserted, apart from the neighbourhood fox slinking through the streets, and the ARP warden patrolling for chinks of light escaping from the neighbourhood's curtains. Though the blackout beginning and end times were published in the *Echo* every day, there were still a lot of people who forgot to pull down their blinds. 'Put that light out!' was a regular cry from the wardens late at night and there was a one-pound fine for ignoring him.

Audrey stared at the ocean and strained to see the piers in the distance. Both of the beautifully ornate piers at Bournemouth and Boscombe Beach, which held so many memories for the townspeople and holidaymakers, would be partially blown up in a few days' time to avoid night-time enemy landings. A shiver ran down her spine at the prospect.

Yawning, Audrey was about to turn in when she saw Lily and Jacques walking towards the bakery, returning from their evening out. Jacques walked straight and tall, cutting a slim, smart figure, while Lily seemed bird-like and even younger than her years by his side. Their expressions were serious, as if they were deep in conversation and, Audrey noticed, their hands brushed against each other as they moved along the pavement.

Feeling guilty for spying on them, she tried and failed to tear her eyes away when Jacques stopped near a cherry blossom tree with branches laden with pink flowers that resembled giant powder-puffs, and picked a bloom. Jacques gave Lily the flowers and took her hand. They faced one another, and for a long moment, Lily left her hand in his. Audrey suspected, by her posture, that Lily was apologising, but then Jacques lifted his finger to her lips to silence her and, lowering his head slightly, he gently kissed her. Lily, clearly finding it impossible to move, kissed him back before suddenly pulling away, lifting her hands to her cheeks, in confusion or embarrassment, and turning towards the bakery with Jacques following close behind.

Aware that she was holding her breath, Audrey let go of the blind and stepped away from the window, blinking in the darkness, her heart pounding. She heard the door of the bakery open and close, the muffled voices of Jacques and Lily, then footsteps up the stairs, one after the other, to each of their separate bedrooms. One hand on the bedroom doorknob, Audrey listened intently, feeling sure she could hear the sound of crying coming from Lily's room, which was next to her own. Jacques was in the attic room above and she could hear the sound of his footsteps pacing the floorboards.

Lighting a candle and carrying it out into the hallway, she knocked gently on Lily's door. 'It's Audrey,' she whispered. 'Can I come in?'

Chapter Eight

Earlier that night, Lily had briefly forgotten her troubles. For a short while, she felt light with unexpected happiness, enjoying the excitement of her adventure. Here she was, a seventeen-year-old girl in a seaside town on the arm of a handsome French soldier. She had borrowed a yellow crepe rayon dress from Audrey, along with shoes that were a little too big, but with cotton wool stuffed into the toes to make them fit. Walking towards Bournemouth pier, through the heavily scented pine trees and pink rhododendron bushes, past a handful of children fishing in the stream and groups of older folk listening to Bournemouth Military Band playing in the bandstand, she thought the beach resort beautiful and, though it was obvious that there was a war on, with beach huts once used for storing swimming suits now storing decontamination suits, she did her best to push the war from her mind. She also had a feeling that though she and Jacques barely knew one another, they had made a deep connection. Putting her anxiety, her secret and the war firmly aside, Lily was determined to live in the moment, *for* the moment. Tomorrow she would face her problems once again. Tomorrow she would face reality.

Listening to a three-piece swing band with Jacques, at the dance on Bournemouth Pier, it was as if she'd been transported to another world. The place was brimming with young local girls and servicemen stationed in Bournemouth. There were accents from north, south, east and west, as the men and women had come from all over, and this thrilled Lily. If they were all adrift, here in Bournemouth, tonight they had found common purpose in capturing a moment to forget their troubles and enjoy being young. Sitting next to Jacques, sipping on a lemonade shot through with whisky from his hip flask, and moving her shoulders to the music, her eyes fixed on an airman who was causing a stir at the centre of the dance floor, his arms and legs moving so fast to the music he resembled a human spinning top.

'He's letting off some steam!' she commented as the crowd broke out into rowdy applause.

When the airman slowed down, his expression was wild and his face glistening with sweat. He seemed surprised to find himself where he was and fell into the arms of a waiting girl. Lily glanced at Jacques to share a smile and ask him if he wanted to dance, to find him busy with a pencil and a small sketching pad.

'What are you doing?' she asked, struck again by his brooding good looks.

'Drawing,' he said, his dark eyes twinkling.

She leaned over to peer at the sketch of her profile, captivated by the dancers on the dance floor. This was the first time she'd ever seen a drawing of herself and she couldn't stop staring. He'd captured the best version of her perfectly.

'Drawing is my favorite, what do you say, er... hobby,' he said, giving her a slow grin. 'Here, I'll sign it for you in case I am famous one day.'

He signed the sketch with his name and added a kiss, then ripped it from his pad and handed it to her. She held it, admiring the pretty woman that he'd drawn as if she was someone else, a girl with a bright future ahead of her instead of... instead of... a girl who had messed up her life, she thought darkly. Suddenly, as the reality of her situation returned to the forefront of her mind, the energy and excitement drained out of her. The music, laughter and heat made her feel queasy. The many faces around her blurred. She focused on Jacques.

'Thank you,' she told him. 'It's amazing. You're really good. You have real talent.'

Jacques gave her an incredible smile and once again she felt he'd handed her a gift – a bouquet of crimson roses with velvety, perfumed petals.

'Do you have a sweetheart?' he asked quietly.

Lily tore her eyes from him and returned her gaze to the couples spinning across the floor, the girls with skirts flying so high you could almost see their undies. She shook her head. 'No,' she said quietly. 'I don't.'

Jacques reached for her hand and gently laced his fingers in hers. 'A few days ago, I was in some kind of living hell,' he said. 'Now, here with you, I feel I am in heaven.'

They locked eyes, but remembering her situation she pulled back her hand. What was she thinking of? She shouldn't, couldn't, be here with Jacques.

'I'm sorry,' she said.

'Shall we go outside?' he said.

They wound their way through the crowds and out into the open air, where despite a brisk wind the skies were still light and blue and seemingly endless. Lily held on to the barrier at the edge of the pier and, watching the sea swell and crash against the wrought-iron pier supports, felt light-headed.

Jacques suddenly leapt up onto the barrier and took a few steps, his arms outstretched as if on a tightrope. She looked at his face, expecting him to be smiling, but his expression was deadly serious.

'Jacques!' she shouted. 'What are you doing?'

'Come up here!' he said, fixing her with an intense stare.

'No,' said Lily incredulously, but she was enthralled by him.

'Come on!' he convinced her.

Oh why not? she thought, accepting his hand and climbing up onto the rail. Balancing with her arms outstretched, she felt her spirits lift sky-high. They stared at one another.

'Lily,' he said, 'I survived. Out of so many men, I survived. Why me and not one of the others? Why?'

'I… I… don't know, Jacques,' she said. 'You were lucky.'

'No,' he said. 'There's more to it than that. It cannot be chance or luck. My life must have been spared for a purpose. I think this was meant to happen. I think I was supposed to meet you.'

Lily closed her eyes and shook her head in confusion. Quickly, she climbed down from the barrier, holding a hand to her forehead. The evening suddenly felt unreal and Jacques' mood dangerously intense.

He jumped down off the barrier and faced her.

'You're an angel,' he said.

'I'm no angel Jacques. I'm really not,' she whispered. 'Don't say such things, you hardly know me.'

'To me you are,' he said, staring at her with such tenderness in his eyes she longed to grab his hands and return to the dance and lose herself in the music, carefree and wild. But, as much as it pained her, she shook her head firmly and started heading towards the bus stop.

'I'm not who you think I am,' she said, the sound of the crashing waves drowning out her words.

Now, still wearing the yellow dress and shoes and clutching the cherry blossom in her hand, Lily was curled up on the bed. The skin around her eyes was blotchy from crying and her eye make-up had run down her cheeks and over her top lip. Her copper hair, previously carefully pinned in waves, was flat and damp from the humid weather and tears. Audrey wanted to scoop her up in her arms as if she was the eleven-year-old-girl she once knew so well, but Lily was now a young woman. Instead, she carefully took the flower from her hand, gave her a hanky and sat down gently next to her on the bed.

Lily lifted her head and gave an apologetic smile and, suddenly shivery with cold, sat up, tucking her legs under the crochet bed-blanket and holding the hanky up to her nose.

'Are you going to tell me what's wrong?' said Audrey, placing the candle by Lily's bed, watching shadows flicker and dance across her face.

'I'm sorry,' Lily whispered, holding the palms of her hands upwards. 'You have more than enough going on.'

'If we're comparing,' said Audrey, 'it looks to me like you have the lion's share of things going on.'

The corners of Lily's mouth lifted a little. She took a deep, raggedy breath and started to talk, slowly at first.

Audrey bit the inside of her cheek as she listened.

'I was doing war work for the Ministry of Information, as a typist,' Lily began. 'I worked for Daddy's cricketing friend, a man called Henry Bateman, in the Home Publicity Division, and for a while my job made me feel like I was involved with something really important. Daddy was so proud of me. He said that all his hard work educating me in good schools had paid off because while other girls my age were waiting to get married, I had an important job where I could use my mind. It's what he'd always wanted… it's what *I'd* always wanted.'

Audrey nodded, encouraging her to continue.

'I loved working at the Ministry. Daddy has always been so protective of me, choosing my school and my hobbies, even the books I read, but when war was declared it was as if he realised I could do something useful, and so this felt like a new, exciting chapter where I could find out who I was.' Lily's lip wobbled as she paused. 'But it didn't last long,' she added.

'Go on,' said Audrey.

'The trouble is, I got carried away with myself and I just wanted to know what it felt like to be a woman and, well, I ruined it all.'

In a low whisper, Lily told Audrey how Henry Bateman had promised her a promotion, told her he was going to join up and that he had feelings for her, and that then things had gone much too far. About how much she hated herself for being impetuous and careless and for not thinking about her future. How she had wanted to be the woman Henry had implied she was – sophisticated, independent and desirable. That she'd believed he cared for her.

'Then he told me that he was engaged to be married and a few days later said he had to let me go,' Lily said. 'I was so shocked I threw ink on his desk, then I just left and didn't go back. I felt such a fool, especially because by the time I got home, he had already been in touch with my father and made up a lie about me. I didn't even try to tell Daddy the truth at first. For weeks he wouldn't let me out of his sight, but one morning, when I couldn't stand it any longer, I told him the truth about his friend Henry Bateman. We rowed horribly and that was when I decided I needed to get away.'

'So you needed some thinking time?' Audrey asked, but Lily shook her head, a guilty expression on her face.

'It's more than that. The worst thing in all of this, and the reason I had to leave London,' she said, her voice breaking and lips quivering, 'is that I am pregnant! I don't want to have Henry's baby! I hate Henry after how he treated me! I've never wanted a baby!'

In spite of herself, a vision of the Parisian mothers searching for their babies in the bombed-out streets of the French capital flashed into Audrey's mind. She felt a rush of anger at Lily's carelessness.

'You should have thought of that!' she burst out, before she could control herself. 'You're not daft! In fact you're extremely clever.'

Lily looked utterly crushed. She hung her head in shame.

'I know,' she said in a whisper, keeping her eyes lowered. 'I know what a fool I've been. I thought Henry had taken precautions, he said as much, but I'm a fool to have trusted him…'

Audrey closed her eyes and scrunched up her face, cross with herself for speaking before thinking.

'I'm sorry,' she said quietly, reaching for Lily's hand and holding it in hers. 'Really, I'm sorry, I shouldn't have said that. Does my mother know about the pregnancy?'

'No,' said Lily. 'I can't possibly tell her or my father. I have to protect Daddy from the truth. He can never know about this. I imagined, somehow, I would give up the baby for adoption and then one day I could go back home and he'd be none the wiser. To be honest, I don't know what to think, or feel, or do.'

'Does anyone know?' asked Audrey.

Lily stared at her hands. 'I wrote to Henry before I came here,' she said. 'I thought I was doing the right thing, setting him straight, but now I'm not convinced. I doubt he'll care and it doesn't really matter because it's down to me to decide what to do. I can't ignore it any longer. I'm beginning to show a little bit.'

Lily stood up gingerly and flattened her dress against her body. A very small protrusion was visible. Audrey mulled over this news. She couldn't admit to Lily that hearing her say she didn't want a child, when Audrey had so desperately wanted one for the last five years, was torture. Of course she understood why Lily didn't want to be pregnant under such circumstances, but after all Audrey had been through – month after month of disappointment for the entirety of her marriage – her frustration had got the better of her. Lily leaned her head against the wall.

'So did you tell Jacques tonight?' Audrey said. 'Is that why you're upset?'

'No,' said Lily. 'I couldn't say anything. I really like him, but how can I have feelings for another man so soon after being involved with Henry? What kind of person am I?'

'Oh Lily,' said Audrey, affected by her stepsister's innocence. 'You're so young and it's the war, it makes people...'

'Reckless?' said Lily. 'Stupid?'

'I don't know,' said Audrey, shaking her head. 'Make decisions they wouldn't normally make. Act in a way they wouldn't normally.

Time doesn't have the same meaning any more. People feel there are no guarantees, that they might not see tomorrow.'

Lily began to cry again and Audrey put her arms around her stepsister, stroking her hair. Though she acted as if she was perfectly calm, inside Audrey was in turmoil. She'd witnessed what could happen when a girl got pregnant out of wedlock – how they were looked down upon. Audrey couldn't begin to imagine what Charlie's mother, Pat, would make of having Lily in the bakery as she started to show, let alone half of the older customers who wouldn't be able to keep their opinions to themselves – though she knew plenty had some eye-watering secrets of their own.

'I'm here for you,' Audrey said. 'And you know you can stay with us.'

Audrey meant what she said. There was no way on this earth she was going to let her stepsister suffer alone.

'What about Jacques?' asked Lily. 'He must think I'm a cold fish. I like him so much, yet how can I explain the truth? What would he think of me? I know he likes me, but I can't lead him on!'

'He knows you are a good person,' Audrey said. 'Jacques will leave in a few days and return to France. Until then, be his friend. Now is not the right time to be getting mixed up with another lad.'

Lily nodded and Audrey hugged her stepsister once more before bidding her goodnight.

Opening the door to her own bedroom, Audrey's head ached. Henry Bateman had a lot to answer for, but this was also partly Victor's fault for wrapping Lily up in cotton wool for so long. And why hadn't Daphne equipped Lily better in the ways of men? No wonder she had got into trouble at the first sign of male attention!

Audrey undressed, put on a slip and climbed into bed, where she lay, wide awake, staring at the ceiling and mulling over Lily's situation. How must it feel to be pregnant by a man you had good reason to despise? A man whose heart belonged to another woman?

Hours crept by, with a thousand thoughts fighting for Audrey's attention. When it was almost time to get up again and a milky dawn slipped through the edges of the blackout blind, a seed of an idea popped into her head. It was outlandish and ridiculous and Charlie would never accept it, let alone Lily, but the idea, like wasps buzzing around an open jar of strawberry jam, would not leave her alone.

Chapter Nine

Two days later and the idea continued to dominate Audrey's thoughts, making her feel thoroughly distracted. The more she considered it, privately studying the idea like a beautiful shell she'd discovered on the beach and turning it every which way in her mind, the more she fell in love with it.

What if she adopted Lily's baby? Wouldn't that be the perfect solution to everyone's problems?

'Bag of stales for a penny!' Maggie proclaimed, interrupting Audrey's thoughts, as they sold the 'stales' at the end of another busy day. The stales were always popular with the customers, who would make fairy toast, wheatmealies and summer pudding out of them. But, as Audrey bagged them up for Maggie, she found it impossible to concentrate.

Glancing at the clock on the wall of the shop, she wondered how Lily was getting on at the appointment she had booked for her with the doctor. After doing some discreet research, she'd discovered that Lily, as an expectant mother, would be entitled to a green ration book instead of the standard buff-coloured one given to adults, which meant additional allowances of milk, fruit, meat and vitamins. There'd be extra clothing coupons, cod liver oil and medicine bottles of orange juice too, once the baby was born, depending of course on what Lily wanted to do. Whatever her decision, Audrey would do all she could to support Lily, and as much as she would privately cherish the opportunity to adopt the child herself, she would also be careful not to influence Lily in her delicate state.

'Lord have mercy on me!' Elizabeth suddenly burst out, as she came into the shop with her small evacuee boy in tow, a dear little thing, no more than two years old. The boy was screaming blue murder, his cheeks bright red and fists pummelling the air. 'I won't bring you out again if you cause a row.' Elizabeth scowled, wagging a finger in his face. 'Now that's enough, child. I wish I'd never taken you on, you're a bad egg!'

Audrey frowned. There was no need for that kind of talk. She abandoned the bags of stales and walked out from behind the counter and knelt down by the small boy. Wrapped up in a knitted cardigan, he was probably too hot. That, or he was teething.

'Can I pick him up?' she said. Elizabeth nodded and rolled her eyes, but Audrey didn't take any notice. She picked up the child and held him on her hip as she leaned against the counter. 'What's your name then?'

'Bob,' growled Elizabeth. 'I should get paid double to be looking after him. Lord knows what kind of family he's from. I wouldn't be surprised if they never claim him back!'

Audrey gave her a hard look.

'Maggie, give me one of those hard crusts, will you?' she said. 'I remember my niece Pearl's cheeks looked like this when she was teething. She loved to chew on a stale crust.'

She handed the boy the crust and he immediately thrust it into his mouth to soothe his gums. His tears ceased and Elizabeth looked at first relieved and then put out.

'Well if it isn't flamin' Florence Nightingale!' she said.

Audrey stroked the child's cheek and handed him back to Elizabeth.

Not Florence Nightingale, Audrey thought but didn't say. *Just a woman who thinks you should be kind to children in your care.*

'Magic touch,' she said with a self-effacing laugh, then, on seeing Elizabeth's disgruntled face, shook her head. 'I'm only joking with you.'

'You know what, Audrey?' said Elizabeth. 'I heard today that they need more billets for evacuee children who are due to arrive this week. If you're so good with kiddies, why don't you offer to take one in? See how you like it!'

Elizabeth turned on her heel and left the shop without her usual order of stales.

'Do you know what,' said Audrey to herself, watching Elizabeth drag the poor child down the road faster than his little feet could carry him, 'I will.'

Out the back of the shop Charlie was busy whitewashing the bakehouse walls. He had a handkerchief over his mouth to protect his lungs, and a cloth in his hand to coat the walls. He was fanatical about keeping the bakery in good repair and free from cockroaches.

'Charlie love…' Audrey began, wondering how best to explain Lily's pregnancy and the idea that wouldn't leave her alone, as well as talk to him about taking in an evacuee. Before she could get any further, he interrupted.

'There you are!' he said, flustered. 'Jacques got his orders to leave tonight. They're being posted somewhere else. He's getting his things together now.'

'Tonight?' Audrey said, astonished. 'Already? That wasn't much respite, was it? Could he not stay a bit longer?'

'He's still on active service,' Charlie said. 'He's got no choice.'

The sound of footsteps silenced her and she turned to see that Jacques was standing in the doorway, dressed in his uniform that she had patched up, washed, starched and pressed.

'I just want to say thank you,' he said. 'You have been so kind.'

'Wait a moment,' she said, feeling her throat thicken with emotion.

Quickly she dashed into the bakery storeroom and opened the door to the basement where the tea chests held the fruit cakes she'd made months earlier. After the rush of weddings, there were only three left. She pulled one out, breathing in the rich aroma of dried fruits, wrapped it up in a piece of cloth and brown paper and tied a string around it, before running up the steps to where Jacques was waiting.

'I know Lily would want to say goodbye,' said Audrey, panicking. 'But she's… running an errand. Please, take this fruit cake with you. It will last well. Share it with the men. There's little dried fruit getting through on the ships, so it might be the last you'll taste in a while.'

Jacques smiled, accepted the cake and briefly hugged Audrey. He held out a letter. 'Would you give Lily this for me please?' he said, handing it to her. 'Tell her I will see her again. And thank you, for this cake, for everything.'

Audrey pulled Jacques in for another hug, keeping a smile on her face despite the worry she felt inside, and Charlie shook his hand and slapped him on the back, wishing him luck. Before he walked away up the street, he lifted his hand in a final farewell and Audrey found tears were slipping down her cheeks.

'Oh for goodness sake,' she admonished herself, turning to face Charlie. 'We'll miss him, won't we?'

'We will,' said Charlie. 'He's a fine young man.'

'Charlie,' said Audrey, after quickly blowing her nose, 'I think we should…'

'You think we should what?' asked Charlie, returning to whitewashing the walls.

Audrey sighed. It wasn't the right time to talk to him about Lily's pregnancy and her idea to adopt the baby. She had to pick the right moment.

'I think we should take in an evacuee,' she said. 'They're looking for billets. We have the room Jacques had and I can easily look after one, or even two children, here.'

'Aren't you busy enough?' Charlie asked, stopping what he was doing for a second. 'What with the shop, Lily arriving and William's wedding coming up?'

Her eyes flicked up to meet Charlie's and when she shook her head and shrugged, he smiled lovingly.

'Audrey Barton,' Charlie said, with a laugh, 'you're only happy when you're busy.'

'I would never want to be idle,' she said, kissing his cheek, then glancing down, remembering the letter in her hand. 'I'll just take this to Lily's room.'

Her legs felt like dead weights as she took the stairs to Lily's room. Where would Jacques be sent now? Out of the frying pan and into the fire? What horror would he be confronted with, as if he hadn't seen enough? In Lily's room, she reached over the bed to put the letter on her pillow and saw the sketch, leaning against the lamp, that Jacques had made of Lily. Enraptured, she stared at it, smiling at the precision in his art. It looked exactly like Lily. What a talent he had!

'Oh,' she said, as a gust of wind from the open bedroom window blew the letter from the pillow onto the floorboards. As it fluttered down, the letter fell open, revealing Jacques' curly handwriting. Picking it up slowly, her heart began to thud. She knew she shouldn't, but Audrey could not resist scanning the words. 'Oh gracious me,' she whispered, reading Jacques's tender words. It was a love letter like no other she had ever read. She stood quickly, steadying herself against the wall, unable to stop reading his gloriously passionate words. *I've met the girl I want to be my wife. You are the reason for me to survive this war. I will return for you.*

Audrey sat down heavily on the bed, her hand over her mouth. Her heart broke for Jacques, having all these feelings for Lily but having to leave so soon. And for Lily, who hadn't told him about her predicament. Thoughts rushed through her mind. Was Jacques' declaration just one thing too many for Lily to think about? Lily herself admitted how impulsive and hot-headed she was, and what if her decision about the baby was influenced by a desire to be with Jacques but one that she would later regret? And wasn't it doubtful that Jacques would feel the same about her once he knew she was pregnant? It could all end in awful heartbreak, just when Lily needed to keep a steady head.

On hearing the back door open and close as Lily arrived back from her doctor's appointment, Audrey made a decision she would live to regret. Closing her eyes for a moment, she sucked in her breath and pushed the letter into her apron pocket. Dashing into the kitchen, she slipped it into the bureau drawer with other important paperwork, for safekeeping. Audrey had to protect Lily. Her stepsister's life was complicated enough, what with Henry Bateman, an unwanted pregnancy and the pressures of her father hanging in the air. Audrey would keep the letter safe until Lily's mind was clearer.

Back in her bedroom, after returning and hearing that Jacques had gone, Lily released Bertie from his cage and watched the budgie flutter around the room, exercising his fragile wings.

'Oh Bertie,' she said. 'I missed him by minutes. I didn't even get to say goodbye.'

With the top of her fingertip, she very gently stroked Bertie's head, tears of frustration stinging her eyes.

'He'll never know how much I liked him,' she said, quietly. 'Perhaps it's better that way. He'd never like me if he knew the truth.'

Staring at the drawing Jacques had made of her, she was relieved she had this small memento of him, that she would cherish forever. Pushing her melancholic thoughts aside, she reflected on the appointment where the doctor had told her about the Free Church Home for Unmarried Mothers in Bournemouth, where she could stay until the baby was born and adopted. Or — and the doctor seemed to think this would be a better idea — she could accept Audrey's help and stay on with her.

'Audrey and Charlie are good people,' he had said. 'It's worth remembering that many uncles and aunts bring up their nephews or nieces as if they were their own babies. This town is full of families who have made unofficial adoptions, let nobody tell you otherwise. And I can tell you the numbers of babies born out of wedlock will rocket during this war. I saw it all the first time round with the Great War. When men think they're going to their deaths, I'm afraid young people often throw caution to the wind.'

She regarded the Ministry of Health leaflets for expectant mothers he'd given her as if they belonged to a different person. Lily didn't know how to feel about adoption, unofficial or otherwise. Her plan before she came to Bournemouth started and stopped at her stepsister's front door with the feeling that Audrey would be able to help her. Having to make an actual decision about what to do with the baby was another thing altogether. Would Audrey really be willing to take on the baby as the doctor suggested? How could Lily ever ask such a question? And, if Audrey was willing, would it be more difficult for Lily to walk away and get on with her life than if a stranger adopted the baby? Lily longed to be able to forget about the pregnancy altogether and eradicate Henry from her history. But that could never be. She was trapped and now, the one glimmer of light and hope in her life, Jacques, had gone forever without her even saying goodbye. Letting out a deep sigh, her eyes followed Bertie.

'Come on Bertie,' she said, holding out her finger for the bird to perch on. 'Back in your cage.'

Chapter Ten

'Gracious me, look at all these little lost souls, it's like an auction!' said Audrey, arriving at the receiving centre for child evacuees to be greeted with the sight of dozens of newly arrived children, with large luggage labels bearing their name, home address and school, tied or safety-pinned to their coats, being 'selected' by local residents. 'I wish I could take them all home with me.'

The Evacuation Officer looked up from her paperwork. 'You must be mad,' she muttered, handing Audrey a form to complete. 'Choose wisely.'

Audrey had stayed true to her promise to offer a home to an evacuee and had registered with the Evacuation Officer, offering up the attic room in the bakery. Audrey observed in silence, though she felt the urge to talk to every child she saw, taking in the scene that she knew she'd remember until her dying day. There was a row of tin baths, in which young nurses were bathing toddlers, and a line of older children were having their hair checked over for lice by a bespectacled nit-nurse and their skin for impetigo by another nurse. Other children stood waiting, holding their gas mask boxes or sitting on their small suitcases, some with their belongings in brown paper parcels or clutching toy dolls and one or two with tennis racquets. Though excited chatter buzzed through the room like a swarm of bees, several of the younger children were crying or looked close to tears and one boy had his arm firmly clamped around his younger sister's shoulders and an expression on his face that said: we come as a package or not at all. It reminded her of William and herself after their father died – they stuck together like glue. The thought made her miss William with a force so great she felt quite faint.

'Hello,' she said to the children, moving around the room. 'Hello, welcome to Bournemouth.'

Audrey's heart ached for the poor little darlings – and for their families having to make the decision to let them go. Listening in to snippets of conversation, she was horrified to find that while some local women were being gentle and reassuring towards the bewildered children, others were choosing the evacuees for how healthy, strong or useful they seemed. 'I need a boy who can do the jobs around the house that I don't want to do', 'I'd want more than 10/6 to look after that one!' 'There's fleas jumping off that filthy girl, what was her mother thinking?'

Audrey trembled and flushed with shame at what she heard.

'This war is turning some women's hearts to stone,' she said to one mean-looking woman who stood in front of a small girl and called her the 'scrag end' because nobody was picking her. 'Shame on you.'

Desperate to compensate for the woman's cruel words, she knelt down in front of the 'scrag end', a small girl of around six years old whose large luggage label said Mary Lintin, and held out her hand in greeting.

'I'm Audrey Barton,' she said. 'How do you do?'

The girl wore a hat and a thick coat, despite the warm weather, and held a paper bag with her emergency rations inside. Her brown hair was cut up to her ears, by the look of it in haste, and with a not-very-straight fringe. By her mother no doubt, Audrey thought, quietly imagining the poor woman's distress at having to bid farewell to her little girl. She was a sad-looking thing and gave no smile, nor did she offer her hand, though her cheeks were pink with heat and nerves.

'Hello Mary. What's your dolly's name?' Audrey asked gently.

Mary cast her brown eyes down to the floor, and kept her head bowed. She gripped the doll so hard her knuckles turned white.

'Would you like to take your coat off?' Audrey asked, but the girl shook her head. 'Do you have any brothers or sisters here with you, Mary?' she tried instead. 'Or friends from your school?'

Mary took a sharp intake of breath and for a second she glanced up, arresting Audrey with huge liquid brown eyes like bowls of melted chocolate. She shook her head before returning her stare to the floor. Audrey instantly and instinctively wanted to hold and protect Mary and, gently taking her by the hand, she explained that she was going to look after her for a little while.

Once the paperwork was filled out and notice of Audrey's details recorded to be sent to Mary's mother, she walked Mary home to the bakery, showing her the local landmarks as they went, eventually reaching Fisherman's Road, where the sea was in full view. Mary stood for a moment, apparently mesmerised by the great expanse of water topped with pale blue sky and drawn across with a yellow stripe of gorse. She gripped Audrey's hand tightly and Audrey knelt by her side.

'Have you ever seen the sea before?' she asked.

Mary said nothing, but remained transfixed by the sea.

'We'll have to teach you to swim,' Audrey said. 'But probably in the River Stour since we're not allowed on the beach at the moment. The river's pretty too, with swans and ducks and kingfishers. Oh and it's my brother's wedding soon, with dancing and biscuits and lemonade. You'll enjoy that, I'm sure.'

Realising she was jabbering and Mary hadn't said a word, Audrey stopped talking. Perhaps the little girl just wanted a little peace and quiet.

Not that it lasted long. Maggie, Lily and Pat, who had popped in to see Charlie, fussed around Mary the minute she walked through the door. There was something magnetic about the child's enormous eyes and worried expression.

'This is for you,' Maggie said, giving Mary a jam tart in a paper bag. Mary made a small nod in thanks and Maggie affectionately ruffled the hair on the top of Mary's head.

'And this is where we make the bread,' Audrey told Mary, showing her the bakehouse. 'Every night we make a dough and in the early morning we bake the loaves. Do you like bread?'

Even Charlie did his best to welcome the little girl. 'I hope so!' he said, with a big smile. 'Our Coburgs are the best in the town. First lesson in baking, Mary: do you know how to tell if a loaf is perfect?'

Mary gave a small shake of her head.

Charlie picked up half a loaf and handed it to her. 'Sliced open, the inside should be very slightly yellow in colour and springy to touch,' he said. 'The crust should have a rich, brownish yellow tint, not too light and not too dark, exactly as this one. Above all, it should taste delicious.'

Mary nodded but didn't say anything. Wondering whether she was overwhelmed by everyone's attention, Audrey held on to her hand and showed her up to her bedroom. 'And this is your room,' said Audrey. 'All the best people stay in this room. You can see the sea out of that window. Sometimes a seagull sits on this sill. I call him Captain Stan, but you can change his name. He won't mind.'

Mary made another small nod.

'You'll be wanting to speak to your mother, I should think,' Audrey said. 'She'll get a letter with this address, but you can speak to her too, if you like.'

Audrey stood back and regarded the little girl, who looked to her like she had been completely buttoned up, and that the real Mary Lintin was locked inside somewhere like a beautiful, shining conker in its spiky shell. It was only when she left her in the bedroom to unpack her things and she was making her way back downstairs towards the shop that she realised she hadn't heard Mary utter a single word all day. Not even 'hello'.

It'll be nerves, Audrey assumed, immediately plotting ways to help the little girl, suddenly in the care of a complete stranger and living within a busy bakery, relax into her new life. Thinking of the cake orders she had to get on with, she was struck by inspiration. *Baking!* she thought suddenly, smiling to herself. *That'll do it.*

Chapter Eleven

'Then you fold in the flour like this,' Audrey said to Mary, gently showing the little girl how to make a chocolate cake. 'We don't make many of these since rationing, so now they seem even more delicious. Let's get this one in the oven, shall we?'

To help Mary settle in and while she was waiting for her school place to be arranged, Audrey had set about giving Mary easy tasks to do in the bakery, which she seemed to enjoy. It quickly became clear she wasn't going to speak and despite wanting to ask her directly why, Audrey instinctively knew to avoid the subject completely and that, in her own time, Mary would open up. In the meantime they would muddle through somehow.

Watching her now, as she helped Maggie stack freshly baked loaves like building blocks in the shop window, her little arms filled with the hot bread, Audrey tried to read her expression, but found it to be guarded. It was as if Mary's body was there in the bakery, but her mind was elsewhere.

'What I'd give for an orange,' said Maggie, pausing from stacking to straighten her embroidered white Barton's Bakery cap. 'Old Reg has a crateful out front today but they're just for the kiddies. He's even got a sign up: "oranges for children only". Mary, that means you can have one!'

Mary smiled up from under her fringe. In the last few days little smiles had crept onto her face, much to Audrey's delight.

'Children *and* expectant mothers, I believe,' added Audrey, before regretting her words, biting her lip and stealing a glance at Lily, whose cheeks flushed pink. Audrey reminded herself that she must find time to speak to Lily about how her doctor's appointment went, and to talk to her about her idea. Since Mary had arrived and Audrey had so desperately wanted her to feel comfortable at the bakery, she'd hardly had a moment spare.

'It's almost worth it!' said Maggie, collapsing into laughter. 'Oh Audrey, could we listen to *Music While You Work* on the wireless today? I know it's for the munitions girls working long hours in the factories, but I reckon it would help the day go with more of a swing. What do you think, Mary?'

A little nod from the child. Audrey grinned at her.

'After Charlie's had his nap, yes, and as long as you won't be singing along.' Audrey smiled. 'We don't want our windows shattering.'

''S'all right,' Maggie said, pointing at criss-cross tape over the shopfront. 'The windows are stuck over with bombproof tape. I think they'll withstand my soprano!'

Audrey laughed, grateful for Maggie's upbeat manner. With the conflict worsening overseas, and Lily's secret dilemma rumbling like distant thunder in the background, they needed all the laughs they could get. Now, Italian dictator Benito Mussolini had declared war on Britain and France and, days later, despite the best efforts of British and French troops, German soldiers had marched into the French capital, parading on the Champs Elysees, observed by horrified Parisians. Charlie hadn't been able to stomach his breakfast after hearing the news that France had capitulated.

The customers wanted to talk of little else. 'Can you imagine them coming here, marching up the High Street in their long black boots?' asked Flo, ordering a portion of bread pudding. 'I keep waking up in the night thinking they're already here.'

'Never,' said Maggie, pinging open the cash till and scooping out Flo's change. 'You heard what Mr Churchill says: we shall never surrender!'

'He's got some good lines, that one,' said Flo. 'Anyway, Audrey, at least you have William and Elsie's wedding to cheer you on, eh? Nice to have something to look forward to?'

Audrey, sorting out customer orders, alongside Lily who was helping in the bakery, was unusually quiet today. She'd been up half the night worrying about the news of France. How must the French people be feeling – Jacques and his family? Germany had invaded Poland, Denmark, Norway, the Low Countries and now France. Would it be Britain next?

'I've also got this bag of icing sugar for you, to help with William and Elsie's cake because I know it's hard to get hold of these days, even for bakers,' said Flo, handing over a small jar of white sugar.

Audrey snapped out of her thoughts, injecting life into her smile and eyes.

'Oh you're a kind sort,' she said to Flo. 'The sale of iced cakes has been totally banned by Lord Woolton, so this is a real prize. Thank you.'

'There's plenty more collecting who are planning to do the same,' Flo said, moving in a bit closer to Audrey and lowering her voice. 'How's the little girl? Pat says she doesn't speak. Is she a halfwit?'

'No!' said Audrey, hoping Mary hadn't heard. 'She's just not speaking at the moment. I'm sure it's to do with being away from home. Can't be easy for the children, can it?'

'Poor lamb,' said Flo. 'Oh, and have you heard about Crowne's Bakery?'

'No,' said Audrey, her ears pricking up. Crowne's was a bakery on the other side of Bournemouth that had always sold the most exquisite cakes. 'What about them?'

'They're still selling meringues and iced buns and iced wedding cakes,' she said, dropping her voice. 'Under the counter, if you know what I mean. Mr Crowne says he'll do anything to get his customers what they want. He says he's got special means.'

Flo tapped her nose and lowered her voice to an almost whisper.

'Apparently,' she said, shiftily moving her eyes from left to right, 'he meets up with other bakers from Hampshire and Wiltshire in a field in the middle of the night and they swap ingredients. If he's got too much butter, he'll swap it for a box of sugar and so on. Crafty ain't it? Clever, some might say.'

Audrey sighed. Flo's eyes were bright with espionage, but if she was looking for a rise she wasn't going to get one.

'Might land him in hot water if he's not careful,' said Audrey steadily. 'One of the grocers got a huge fine for selling sugar "under the counter". He sold it to an undercover inspector who arrested him a minute later!'

'He never did!' said Flo.

'It's true,' said Audrey. 'This woman came in with a sob story of how she needed extra sugar and would he be so kind and so on, and then, when he fell for it, she told him who she *really* was. How can you tell if someone's an inspector or not? There's no way of knowing! They don't come in with an "Inspector" badge on their forehead. Mr Crowne should watch his back and so should his customers.'

Audrey paused and eyed Flo for dramatic effect.

'Yes, well,' said Flo, suddenly flustered. 'I won't be going there o' course, I was just saying it's amazing what goes on in this town! I hope the sugar helps.'

Audrey instantly softened. Touched by Flo's gesture, she popped another bun in with her order. But the talk of Crowne's unscrupulous ways made her cross. Charlie was a stickler for paperwork and keeping the ledger book up to date, but he never minded them being generous to their loyal customers and it was hard enough to balance the books without Crowne's stealing their customers with tempting offers of iced cakes. There were a few Audrey could think of who owed for their bread – Mrs Collingham for one – but Charlie was generous where he could be, knowing she would pay her accounts when she could.

'Their bread's not a patch on yours,' said Flo. 'Besides, it's a bleedin' long walk to Crowne's!'

They both laughed.

'Bless you Flo,' said Audrey. 'Thanks for the sugar. This wedding really will be a community effort. It's all last-minute, but we'll do our best to give them a day to remember.'

'In wartime you have to do *what* you can *while* you can,' said Flo passionately. 'I expect the moment William's said, "I do", and slipped a ring on her finger, he'll be posted out again. War has changed everything and we all just have to adapt. Find happiness where we can, preferably not in the bottom of a bottle of whisky, like my Sidney…' Flo's face fell and her passionate speech petered out.

'Oh Flo,' said Audrey. 'Not again.'

Flo shrugged her shoulders and smiled in resignation, the skin round her eyes crinkling.

'Found him asleep in the yard this morning, near the pig swill bin, didn't I?' said Flo. 'Got the fright of my life. Looked like a corpse. Thought he was dead and gone!'

'You picked a wrong 'un there, Flo,' said Maggie, overhearing.

Flo's lips pursed together and though she tried to give a knowing smile, she looked like the wind had been knocked out of her.

'You don't pick who you love,' Audrey said, despairing at Maggie's tactless comment. 'Love picks you. You don't have any say in the matter.'

Audrey glanced at Lily, whose blush had deepened.

'Talking of love,' continued Maggie, unaware of any feelings she may have hurt. 'Maybe you and me should go to a dance at the Pavilion, Lily, see if we can land ourselves a pilot for a husband? That's one thing I'll say for this war. The local lads have cleared out, but there are some more than decent replacements in town.' Maggie burst into fits of giggles.

'I'm not looking for a husband,' said Lily. 'Thanks anyway.'

'Suit yourself,' said Maggie.

'Maggie,' said Audrey, raising her eyebrows, then turning to face Lily, who was hurriedly undoing her apron, 'still your tongue and serve these ladies please.'

'Can you spare me for a moment?' Lily said, her eyes on something beyond the shop window. 'I need to call into the… chemist.'

Before Audrey could reply, Lily had pushed past the women waiting for bread and was out the door, crossing the road, narrowly missing being run over by a lorry delivering an ice block to the butcher. The driver had to brake hard to miss her. Lily raised her hand in apology and ran over to the café on the corner.

'More haste, less speed,' Audrey said, losing sight of Lily. Five minutes later, she was back, pale as milk.

'You look like you've seen a ghost,' said Maggie. 'Are you all right?'

'Yes,' said Lily, with a smile that appeared suddenly and vanished just as quickly. 'Fine. I just thought… it sounds daft, but I felt that someone was watching me from the café. There's been someone sitting in there this afternoon, a man. It's me being silly of course. I went to check to see if I could recognise anyone in there, but, nobody there of course. I'm seeing things!'

'It's the sea air,' said Maggie. 'You city folk can't cope with it!'

Lily picked up her white cap and dropped it again, her hands clearly shaking. Audrey wanted to ask more questions, but Lily quickly turned to the next customer.

'How can I help you, Mrs Douglas?' she said, regaining her composure. 'Remind me how you like your crust? Oven-bottom is it?'

Chapter Twelve

'How do I look?' Elsie asked her audience with a self-conscious smile, pirouetting in a small circle in the tight space available in Audrey's kitchen. It was the end of another day. The shopkeepers on Fisherman's Road had locked up, calling 'goodnight' to one another, the blackout blinds had been pulled down, the shops swilled out and the signs switched to 'closed'. Gathered around Audrey's kitchen table were Audrey, Maggie, Lily, Pat and one of Charlie's sisters, Fran, with her two small daughters, Pearl and Vivian, having tea for Elsie's birthday and to talk about her wedding plans. Audrey was determined that Mary begin to feel part of the family too, so she was tucked in next to Pearl. The women and children squeezed in around the table, as the kettle boiled on the cast-iron range and Audrey sawed up a Coburg into doorstep wedges, piling them onto a plate, and placed an open pot of strawberry jam next to them. A birthday cake – that Audrey had baked with Mary – was waiting to be cut and was displayed on a plate with a single rose, plucked from the garden, as decoration. She'd also made lemonade with saccharine tablets for the girls and a small Chivers jelly. There was a collective sharp intake of breath as the women admired Elsie in her wedding dress.

'Gracious me, what a beautiful bride,' said Pat. 'You do look a picture.'

Standing with her stocking feet now flat on the cold floor tiles, arms by her side, Elsie laughed at the silent and stunned expressions of the women before her. It made her wonder how rotten she normally looked! The dress Audrey had passed on to her was a simple, mid-length ivory lace number with silk lining, handmade by Pat for Audrey's wedding years previous. It had cap sleeves, a row of pearl buttons down the front and a ribbon tie at the waist, as well as matching delicate fingerless lace gloves. Even in bare feet, with her hair cascading over her shoulders and her cheeks ruddy from the cycle ride from work to Audrey's, she felt as if she'd suddenly been transformed from Elsie Russo into Rita Hayworth. Unable to stop smiling, tingling excitement shot up her spine. She would soon be married to William, the man she loved with her whole heart. She felt for the engagement ring, laced onto the chain around her neck. The thought of seeing him again after all these months made her quiver with excitement, though there were nerves too.

'You look like a princess,' said six-year-old Pearl, who had slipped off her mother's lap to attempt to stick a finger into the jam pot, only to have her wrist lightly tapped and be tugged gently away.

Audrey reached to the top of her dresser and got down the tin of boiled sweets and offered them to the children. 'There you go, cherubs,' she said. 'Make it last!'

Pearl carefully took one and stuffed it straight in her mouth with a beautiful smile and a 'fankoo'. Vivian clutched one in her hand, to save until later, and Mary, who Elsie hadn't heard speak a single word since she arrived in Bournemouth, gave a grateful smile and nodded at Audrey, who nodded in return. It seemed the two of them had found a way to communicate without words.

'Thank you!' Fran corrected her daughter. 'It's "thank you", for goodness sake.'

Pearl's big eyes filled with tears and Elsie acted quickly.

'Are you sure I look like a princess?' she said, putting her hands on her hips, sticking out her tongue and crossing her eyes. 'Princess Gargoyle more like!'

Pearl burst into fits of giggles, spitting out her precious sweet but catching it in her hand just in time.

'That's more like the Elsie we know and love!' said Audrey. 'William's going to be speechless when he sees you on your wedding day. You look so pretty.'

There was a murmuring of agreement from the women. Pat stood up from her chair to check the waistline on the dress, her fur stole slipping onto Maggie's seat.

'Can't say the same for your mink stole though, Mrs B,' said Maggie, picking it up and, as if it was a puppet, making its little face move up and down. 'He looks like he's seen better decades!'

'What's it to you, Maggie?' said Pat sternly, snatching the stole back and throwing it over her shoulder. 'I am very attached to my mink. My husband gave it to me before he died. I know he's a little worn, but, well… so am I. Some things don't need commenting on, Maggie. In time perhaps you'll learn that not blurting out the very first thing that pops into your head is a preferable way of conducting yourself. You should take a leaf out of Mary's book. I haven't heard a peep from her.'

It was the turn of Mary's eyes to fill with tears and Audrey quickly grabbed her hand.

'Mary's finding different ways to talk to us,' said Audrey hurriedly. 'Aren't you, sweetheart?'

'I've always thought children should be seen and not heard,' said Pat. 'So I think Mary is very polite indeed. Unlike some, *Maggie.*'

After her little speech, Pat continued to inspect the dress. She yanked at a little spare fabric on the waist, pinching Elsie's skin as she did so. Elsie grimaced silently and Audrey winked at her, suppressing a laugh.

'Sorry Pat,' said Maggie. 'Don't mind me and my big mouth.'

'I don't mind you,' snapped Pat, then turning to Elsie. 'I thought maybe we could take it in half an inch, but I think it fits you like a glove as it is.'

Elsie nodded. Pat was a fearsome woman – the type to give anyone a dressing-down if they crossed her – but she had a kind heart. She stayed quiet while Pat fiddled with the fabric, watching Audrey stand to clear some room on the table and then kneel down to reach into the back of a cupboard in the dresser. As she rummaged, the rows of dinner plates and bowls displayed along the top shelves wobbled precariously.

'Are you delivering a calf, Audrey?' Maggie said.

Audrey chuckled and when she pulled a bottle of rum out of the cupboard, holding it up for all to see, the women clapped.

'Delivered!' she said. 'What do you ladies say to some "milk from the brown cow" while we're blathering? We still need to decide on the food. Sardine sandwiches? Jelly and custard?'

'Milk from the brown cow?' asked Lily, frowning. 'Whatever is that?'

'Tea with a shot of rum,' explained Audrey, with a smile. 'Just what we need.'

'I might be able to get you a leg of something for the wedding,' said Fran, her eyes sliding from left to right. 'Don't ask me where from.'

Elsie had always liked Fran. Her husband was away with the navy, but Fran kept chipper for her little ones and you always felt better for being in her company.

'Where from?' asked Audrey immediately, standing up and pouring a dash of rum into the teacups. 'Not the black market, I hope. I've been hearing too much about that recently. I don't think your mother would approve of that, would you, Pat?'

Pat raised her eyebrows as if considering the question. 'Desperation can make a woman behave out of the ordinary,' she said, busying herself with sticking the pins into the pincushion. 'That's all I'm saying.'

Audrey pulled a shocked face, but said nothing more. She handed Fran a tea with a dash of rum in it. Fran gulped in down in three swallows.

'Needed that! Not the black market no,' she said. 'The Canadians!'

'Oh the Canadians!' said Maggie, pretending to faint. 'They're dreamy.'

'I wouldn't have noticed,' said Fran with a grin, 'but I have done some sewing for the Royal Canadian Air Force boys, and they're certainly generous. Last weekend they gifted me a small joint of beef for doing their uniform repairs in a hurry. I tried to refuse it, but they said they had no use for it and it would spoil if left in their digs.'

'Well what were you to do but accept?' Audrey said, with a sly smile. 'No wonder your girls have roses in their cheeks!'

'Exactly,' said Fran. 'But I can see what's available if you like, Elsie? I'm sure they have access to all sorts.'

'I don't want anything special,' said Elsie, sitting down heavily as if suddenly hit with doubt, her shoulders drooping forward and no longer looking the belle of the ball. 'I mean, nothing too ostentatious. People are struggling so much it wouldn't be right to be showy. Who knows how William will be feeling as well? He didn't say much in his letter at all, but people are not in the mood for celebrating now that France has fallen, along with the rest. Everyone thinks it'll be us next.'

The mood in the room darkened as each of the women considered the prospect of German invasion.

'No war talk,' said Maggie, waving a hand in the air dismissively. 'I'm fagged out with war talk. It makes me wonder what we talked about before. Now it's all Hitler's army and the rationing!'

There was a murmur of agreement in the room.

'Life is for living, Elsie,' said Audrey. 'Now more than ever. I think you should celebrate this wedding as much as you can. We all should.'

The women nodded.

'Makes you look to the past when the future's so uncertain,' said Pat wistfully. 'Makes me think about my dear husband.'

'What was he like?' asked Elsie gently. 'I've not heard you talk about him much.'

'Well I've found much of life is about putting on a brave face, so I don't dwell on the past,' said Pat. 'He was quiet, witty and a hard worker. My family didn't really approve of me marrying Bert, he wasn't well-to-do enough, but I loved him and that was that. Nothing could stop me running up that aisle.'

'How about you, Audrey?' asked Lily, who had so far been quietly sipping her tea. 'I knew you were getting married to Charlie but Father said we couldn't come to the wedding. I was furious with him! What was it like?'

Elsie detected sadness pass over Audrey's face at Lily's admission, but after taking another sip from her drink, in what she'd come to understand as usual Audrey fashion, she brushed it aside.

'Charlie baked me a loaf in the shape of a ring, which he thought very funny,' said Audrey, rolling her eyes, 'But it was lovely. William gave me away. I'd hoped Mother would come and bring you, Lily, of course, but she didn't, so I just had to get on with it… It's a good job Charlie has a bigger family because my side of the church was half empty! So anyway, let's drink to Elsie and William's happiness and to all our absent friends and family.'

Noticing that Mary had snuggled up close to Audrey and was chewing on her thumbnail, which was already bitten to the quick, Elsie wondered why the little girl was silent. She gave her a smile and received a small one in return. She was a sweet little thing.

The rest of the evening passed in a warm glow of friendship, laughter and a sense that, no matter what was happening in the rest of the world, Audrey's kitchen was a sanctuary. At almost midnight, after Charlie had gone back into the bakehouse to knock back the dough, the women were yawning and keen to get into their beds. Elsie hugged Audrey, thanking her for a lovely evening.

'Oh hang on,' said Audrey. 'I've got something for you. I'll give you it now because I'll forget otherwise.'

She opened the dresser drawer and pulled something out, presenting it to Elsie in a paper bag. Elsie opened it and held a black iron horseshoe in her hands.

'It belonged to the old roundsman who used to deliver the bread by horse and cart when Eric, Charlie's uncle, ran the bakery,' she said. 'Story goes, the horse knew where to stop without a word from the roundsman! It's a tradition, for good luck for your marriage. Hang it on your wall and always keep it upright, so the luck doesn't fall out, and be grateful I chose this tradition. You know they used to crumble cake over the bride's head for luck in the old days!'

Elsie pulled a horrified face and both women laughed.

'Thank you,' she said, hugging Audrey. 'I love it.'

Elsie walked out into the quiet, still night. On the coast road, where the heady scent of gorse flower filled the air, she looked up at the great expanse of sky above the ocean and gasped. With the blackout in force, thousands of stars were visible. It was as if someone had scattered handfuls of glitter across a blackboard. She wondered how, with breathtaking sights like this, men like Hitler could make it their life's work to destroy, murder and maim. Did he see something different when he looked up at the sky?

'It's something I'll never understand,' she said to herself, jumping onto her bicycle. She was listening to the creak of her saddle and the turn of her pedals when, seemingly out of nowhere, came the ghastly whine and wail of the air-raid siren. The discordant sound enveloped Elsie and, stopping cycling, she held her hands over her ears, her eyes darting all around her. Suddenly bright white searchlights were sweeping the sky and the drone of enemy aircraft added to the din. Confused for a moment, Elsie stood still before she processed what the siren actually meant. An attack was imminent!

'Take shelter!' shouted an Air Raid Patrol warden, blowing his whistle. 'Take shelter now!'

Heart hammering in her chest, Elsie hesitated, not knowing where to go.

'Come quickly!' shouted an elderly woman from the door of the nearby convalescent home. She was dressed in her nightwear, with her coat over the top. 'We have a shelter. There's space for you, my dear.'

Quickly, with her gas mask slung over her shoulder, Elsie abandoned her bike and ran towards the elderly woman, stumbling as she went.

'You're a sight for sore eyes!' she said, as the old woman showed her to the basement shelter where scores of elderly people, who had obviously all retired for the night hours ago, were finding somewhere to sit. Dressed in their bedclothes, many of them were coughing and spluttering, their lungs shaken by the activity.

'Bloody Jerry!' a little old lady with no teeth, sunken cheeks and purple bags under her eyes spat, as she sat next to Elsie. 'I'd have their guts for garters if I was fifty years younger. I'm Granny Ginny by the way, or Gigi to my friends. Would you like a Koff Candy?'

'Pleased to meet you, Gigi,' said Elsie, gratefully accepting one of the clove-flavoured candies and popping it onto her tongue, taking a moment to catch her breath. She strained to listen for activity outside, imagining the destruction that a Junkers Ju 88 bomber could wreak in a matter of minutes, dumping its bombs like confetti. *Confetti.* Gosh, how distant talk of weddings in Audrey's kitchen seemed now.

Chewing on the inside of her lip so hard it bled, Elsie thought of her bicycle abandoned on the grassy verge. The horseshoe that she'd carefully balanced in the basket would be upside down now, the luck running out and spilling onto the road.

Chapter Thirteen

Minutes earlier, Charlie had dropped the loaf tin he was holding as if it were hot coals.

'She's what?' he exclaimed, wide-eyed. 'Is she engaged to a fella?'

When Elsie and the girls had left the bakery and Lily had gone up to bed, Audrey had decided to seize the moment and break the news about Lily's pregnancy to Charlie. The shot of rum she'd had may have helped inform her decision, but she needed to share the news with her husband before any more time passed. Watching her husband's eyes grow darker as he stood with his hands on his hips, she got the devil in her and wanted to laugh.

'Sshhh,' Audrey said, lifting her finger to her lips and then folding her arms across her chest. 'The father is a man from work and no, she's not engaged, nor is she a widow. The man is engaged to some other woman. Not that he told Lily of course. Such is the unsavoury way of some men. It seems Lily thought it best she left London and—'

'And turn up on our doorstep?' interrupted Charlie, incredulous. 'How's that work then?'

'It's safer here for a start,' said Audrey. 'You can't move for bombs in London.'

Charlie stomped over to the bakery oven, opened the door and hurled some coke into the flames, then slammed shut the door again so hard there was a ringing in Audrey's ears.

'As if we 'aven't got enough on, what with Mary, who seems like she's disturbed!' he said.

'Mary's not disturbed!' protested Audrey. 'There's a reason she doesn't talk, I just don't know what it is yet.'

'Why didn't you tell me about Lily?' continued Charlie. 'I had no idea all of this was goin' on under my own roof!'

'I am telling you now,' said Audrey matter-of-factly. 'And you haven't exactly been easy to talk to lately, Charlie. You've been a different man since the war started, acting like you're the only one suffering while the rest of us hardly notice it.'

Warming to her theme, Audrey glared at Charlie and continued speaking before he could get a word in edgeways. He stared at her open-mouthed.

'And by the way, Lily is my stepsister and *all* the family I'm left with,' she said. 'I know how it is to feel as if your options have run out and you don't know where to turn. You've never been in that situation.'

'That's hardly fair—' started Charlie, but Audrey interjected.

'Remember when I first came to Bournemouth? If it wasn't for your family giving me a job, who knows what I would have done. How can I not help Lily?'

'I—' he tried again, to no avail.

'I will help her, Charlie, and that's that,' Audrey said. 'There's enough bad things going on and people suffering in the world without us making it worse! If you're the same man I fell in love with, you'll open your heart and your mind.'

Audrey's cheeks turned pink and she felt her temper rising.

'There are some things I draw the line at and that's turning this bakery into a home for waifs and strays,' Charlie said, sounding a little deflated.

'Which leads me to my idea,' said Audrey boldly. 'I haven't had time to discuss this with Lily, but if she's willing, I thought she should stay on here once the baby's born so that I can help. I'm the child's aunt, by law, and with us not able to have our own child, it would be smashing to have a new baby about the place. I was even thinking about suggesting perhaps we ad—'

Audrey stopped and looked Charlie in the eye before continuing.

'I was even thinking about us, perhaps, adopting the baby, Charlie. I mean, I know it sounds far-fetched, but if Lily wants to put the baby up for adoption, which she might, there's no way we can let strangers have him or her, is there? It seems like the ideal solution to me.'

Charlie's eyes were perfect circles. 'Ideal solution?' he blustered. 'Lily's illegitimate child is not going to be a replacement for the child we haven't been able to have. We might still have one, or have I failed on that front too? Why doesn't that surprise me! My own wife thinks me a failure!'

He slammed a wooden peel down onto the table in fury.

Audrey stepped back, surprised at the emotion in Charlie's voice.

'Failure?' she said, suddenly softening. 'You've failed at nothing, Charlie. If anyone's failed, it's me. I'm just trying to find a way around this. I can't stand to see Lily feeling all alone. Please, love, just think about it. We could look after that child while Lily would be able to start again somewhere new if she wanted. Something good could come out of it. I'm looking for the good, Charlie, that's all I'm doing. Looking for the good.'

Charlie ran his hands through his hair and let out an exasperated sigh. 'Trouble with you,' he said, 'is that you've got more heart than sense.'

Audrey's racing heart slowed to normal. The worst was over. She'd told Charlie her idea and he hadn't said an outright 'no'.

'So you'll think about it then?' she asked, relieved but feeling overcome with exhaustion. She had to be up before dawn to open the shop. There were buns to bake, cake orders to fulfil.

'My feet are aching so I'm going up, Charlie—' she started. Then the eerie sound of an air-raid siren filled the air. The wail, like a dying animal, made Audrey's skin break out in goosebumps and a shiver shoot up her spine.

Forgetting all about their conversation, Charlie and Audrey stared at one another wordlessly.

'Air raid,' said Audrey, after a few moments. 'We need to get to the shelter. I'll go up and get Mary and Lily. Elsie's only just left, I hope she reached home in time.'

When Audrey got to the bakehouse door, Lily was already there, looking younger than her seventeen years, clutching her gas mask box and Bertie in his cage. Mary was by her side, dressed in her white nightdress, clinging to her dolly.

'I can't leave the ovens,' called Charlie. 'I'm staying here.'

'Dampen them down,' replied Audrey. 'We need to get into the shelter!'

'I can't dampen them down,' Charlie said. 'We'll not have bread tomorrow if I dampen them down.'

'We'll not have a baker tomorrow if you don't come into the shelter!' she cried.

'You three go,' ordered Charlie. 'Now!'

'Oh Charlie!' cried Audrey. 'You really are the most infuriating person! Remind me why I ever agreed to marry you!'

'It'll be a false alarm,' Charlie called after them. 'Go, love. I'm telling you, I'm staying here.'

Muttering under her breath, Audrey grabbed Mary's little hand, feeling instantly protective. Leading Mary and Lily quickly out to the Anderson shelter, the construction half-buried in the ground with spring onions and lettuces growing out of the soil piled on top, pulling Marmalade the cat in as she went, she slammed shut the door, switched on her torch and swept it across the floor. It was made from corrugated-iron sheets with steel plates at either end and they'd put in a bench and two bunks with newspaper as 'mattresses' and sleeping bags for warmth. Though the shelter had been in place for months, this was the first time Audrey had used it for real. Striking a match, she lit one candle, placing it in a clay plant pot and covering it with another clay pot for warmth, and lit another for light.

'Do you think they're coming for us?' said Lily, in a quiet voice. 'Is it our turn?'

Fear dragged sharp fingernails across Audrey's scalp, but she forced herself to be positive for Mary, whose eyes were squeezed tightly shut.

'As Charlie said, it'll probably be a false alarm,' Audrey replied. 'Oh he's a stubborn mule. At least he's got that big table to sit under in there.'

When the siren stopped, there was an awful scratching on the roof: a seagull searching for crusts, no doubt. The bakery backyard was one of their favourite spots.

'What's that noise?' asked Lily, clearly terrified.

'Just seagulls looking for food,' Audrey soothed. 'Those birds never give up, no matter what.'

Audrey perched on the bench next to Lily and Mary and briefly closed her eyes, her entire body on edge in anticipation of what was going to happen next, but not knowing what to expect.

'Have you told Charlie about me?' said Lily quietly.

Audrey nodded, as another explosion sounded in the distance.

'Charlie's got a big heart under all that flour,' she said. 'Don't you worry about anything.' Audrey gripped Lily's hand and gave it a reassuring squeeze. 'Those birds never give up,' she repeated as the seagulls continued to scratch overhead. And neither would she, Audrey thought, as the three of them listened in horror to the sound of machine gun fire rattling through the air, followed by the drone of aircraft and booming explosions. The girls huddled together in the shelter, but with each new noise Mary covered her ears with her hands more tightly and curled over, until her head was in her own lap. Audrey threw Lily a worried glance when Mary began whimpering. It was the first noise she'd heard the girl make.

'Mary love,' Audrey said gently. 'It's okay. We're safe in here. There's no need to worry, sweetheart.'

Mary curled up tighter still until she was in a ball shape and Audrey, crouching down next to her, tried to embrace her, but the little girl's body was soaked through with sweat and she began to rock back and forth, as if trapped in her own troubled world.

'Maybe we should sing?' said Audrey. 'How about "Ten Green Bottles"?'

Audrey and Lily started to sing, to drown out the worrying sounds from the skies above, and slowly, Mary's hands slipped off her ears and into her lap. Eventually, she looked up from under her blunt brown fringe, an expression of sheer terror on her face, fat tears rolling down her cheeks.

Audrey, frowning with concern, reached for Mary's hand. 'Come and sit with me, Mary,' she said, guiding the little girl onto her lap.

Mary climbed onto Audrey's knee and collapsed into her chest, her body as limp as cloth.

'It's okay,' Audrey said, wrapping her arms around the little girl. 'Don't you fret. You're safe.'

They remained like that for some time, Audrey holding her tight, singing softly.

Chapter Fourteen

When the all-clear 'raiders have departed' siren had sounded and the townspeople emerged from their shelters, under-stair cupboards and from under their sturdy kitchen tables, Elsie picked up her bicycle and horseshoe from where she'd abandoned them on the street and had ridden home in the eerie, silent darkness. Trembling, she opened the front door of her home in Avenue Road, just after 2 a.m., to hear raised voices coming from the kitchen. Quietly closing the door, she waited for a moment, trying to recognise the voices.

'But Angelo is an innocent man,' her mother was insisting in a strangled, high-pitched voice. 'He's done nothing wrong. Ask anyone in this neighbourhood and they will only have good things to say about him!'

'I'm not disputing that,' said a male voice she didn't recognise. 'But we are acting upon orders and Italian nationals must—'

'Mother?' Elsie said now, her heartbeat quickening as she entered the kitchen to see two police officers in the room. 'Papa?'

Angelo, who was at the kitchen table with his head in his hands, leapt up to embrace her.

'Thank heavens,' he said, holding his hand on his heart. 'I didn't know where you were and when the air-raid siren sounded I worried.'

'Sorry,' she said. 'I was cycling home and I sheltered at the convalescent home. What's going on? Why are these men here?'

'Miss,' said one of the policemen, who had black bags like suitcases under his eyes, nodding at her a little in acknowledgement of her arrival. The other policeman rudely avoided her eye, and when she looked at him more closely, his cheeks coloured. It was Wilfred Watchman, she realised, a boy who she'd been to school with.

'Wilfred?' she said. 'What's the meaning of this?'

'I'm afraid we have orders to arrest all Italian nationals and escort them to the police station for questioning. As your father is an Italian national, we're here to talk to him,' he said.

Elsie, feeling suddenly sick with fear, looked at her mother's stony face.

'But it's the middle of the night!' said Elsie.

'I know it's late but the raid held us up,' said Wilfred. 'We can't delay.'

'You'll take him into a police station over my dead body,' her mother said defiantly. 'You can't just walk into a house in the middle of the night and arrest an innocent man with no evidence of criminal activity.'

'I'll repeat,' said the other policeman, 'Winston Churchill has ordered we round up all the aliens in this country.'

'Aliens!' said Elsie. 'That's my father you're talking about! He's a human being, just like your father. We're all the same. If more people realised that there are more similarities between us than differences, we'd have less trouble.'

'Violet, Elsie,' Angelo said, gesturing for them to sit down. 'Calm down, please, this is not helping, but you have nothing to fear, gentlemen. I have no sympathies with Mussolini.'

'We're not saying you do,' said the policeman.

'Yes you are!' Violet cried. 'Angelo is a well-respected, law-abiding and decent man. Everyone round here loves him and he'd do anything for this country. He's just been talking about becoming a voluntary member of the parachute spotters!' She turned, wild-eyed, to the policeman. 'I can't go out shopping without someone stopping me to ask how he is. How can you even think about arresting him? He's done nothing wrong.'

Angelo was fighting a losing battle to stay calm – he was a passionate man and never hid his feelings. Now his eyes were liquid.

Elsie couldn't stand to watch her lovely papa break down. She rushed to his chair and threw her arms around his neck.

'What would your father think of you, Wilfred?' Elsie snapped, suddenly remembering that Wilfred's family were regular customers at the barbershop. 'He'd be ashamed of you! At a time when all we have is our integrity and principles, you go and do this.'

'Elsie!' said Angelo. 'There's no need to be rude. Please stop.'

Wilfred looked embarrassed – and so he rightly should, she thought. Her entire body was trembling with anger.

'It's orders, Elsie,' Wilfred said. 'Government orders.'

'Damn those orders,' Elsie shouted. 'And what about us, will you be taking us too? Do you think we're on the side of the Germans too, or is it just my father?'

The realisation had dawned on Elsie that her mother was considered Italian by marriage and so then must she and the twins too. Elsie thought of her sisters asleep in their bed, desperately hoping they hadn't woken up.

'Your mother is registered as an invalid and so can stay put,' said the older policeman calmly. 'You can remain here to look after her and your sisters. If you could get ready, sir, we should be getting to the station.'

'Can it not wait until the morning?' Violet said. 'We've hardly slept.'

'I'm afraid not, madam, we were supposed to have moved on to a different address by now,' said Wilfred. 'Orders are—'

'Yes, yes,' burst out Angelo. 'We know about your orders. Why a man can't think on his own two feet and not take another man's orders without questioning them, I do not know.'

The policemen exchanged frazzled glances and allowed Angelo time to put on his day clothes, then escorted him, in stunned silence, from the house. Out of habit, he ran a comb through his hair and reached for his hat and his smart jacket as if he were going into work.

'Don't fret,' he said, blowing Elsie and Violet a kiss. 'I'll return as soon as I can.'

Violet and Elsie watched from the doorway as Angelo climbed into the police car, shaking their heads in disbelief.

'Shame on you, Wilfred Watchman!' Elsie yelled, not caring about the neighbours. 'Shame on you, you spineless coward!'

The police car quickly pulled away and disappeared into the darkness, Angelo's face a white glow in the back seat, and Elsie slammed shut the front door, not before noticing the net curtains of the houses opposite violently twitching.

'There must be some sort of mistake,' Violet said in despair, as Elsie helped her back through to the kitchen. 'Those men should be ashamed. It cannot be one rule for all, can it? Oh Elsie, what are we going to do? Maybe if I go to the police station in the morning and speak to someone in charge, I can explain there's been a mistake?'

Elsie made tea, but Violet's hands were shaking too much to hold the cup. She poured her mother a brandy from their 'special occasions' bottle and climbed the stairs to the bedroom that she shared with the twins to check they hadn't woken up. They were sleeping soundly. What would she tell them in the morning? How could she explain this to their little faces? Standing in the darkness for a moment, racking her brains for ways to help her papa, Elsie's thoughts went briefly to the evening that she'd enjoyed at Audrey's earlier. How could she even think of getting married while her father was being treated like a criminal?

Back downstairs, putting on a brave face, she poured her mother another nip of brandy, aware that Violet's fight seemed to have slipped out of her. She sat in her chair looking like a deflated balloon. Even though it was almost dawn Elsie busied herself with drying up the cups on the washboard. Violet didn't object.

'Did he take his comb with him?' Violet asked quietly. 'I didn't get time to remind him. He'll need some clean things if he has to go away for any length of time… I'll have to get on with that washing and ironing.'

Violet's words drifted off as she wept quietly into her hand, but then she stopped as quickly as she had started.

'It's no good crying,' she said to herself quietly but firmly. 'No good at all.'

Pushing back her chair and leaning her weight on the kitchen table, Violet tried to stand, but her legs buckled. She sat back down heavily and closed her eyes, thumping her thighs with her fists.

'Useless legs!' she screamed, the fury coming from deep within, her arms flailing around. 'What good am I to anyone?'

Elsie felt the tears welling up in her own eyes, but she battled to blink them away.

'Mother,' she said, holding still Violet's fists, 'you always used to say to me that everything looks better in the morning. I think you should get some sleep. We'll find out more tomorrow, but there's nothing to be done now. Shall I help you to bed? Where is your cane?'

Tucking her arm firmly around Violet's waist, Elsie helped her mother through to her ground-floor bedroom and, instead of going to the bedroom upstairs, lay down on the bed next to her mother with her head on her papa's pillow, blinking in the darkness. She lifted the side of the pillow to her nose and breathed in the fragrance of her father's hair pomade, Brylcreem, which he used religiously. Lifting her head slightly, she looked over at the red and white tub on the dresser.

Eventually, as the song thrush and blackbird burst into song at the first sign of day – a welcome sound after the haunting wail of the siren that seemed to be trapped in Elsie's head – mother and daughter fell into a deep, dreamless sleep.

Chapter Fifteen

The residents of Bournemouth woke bleary-eyed after spending half the night in air-raid shelters to the sombre news that Southampton had been badly hit by the Luftwaffe. A bakery customer with relatives in Southampton reported that enemy bombers had targeted the military port and the railways, and that swathes of the city had been reduced to rubble.

'The big bakery plants might be without water and gas,' Charlie said, sorrowfully shaking his head. 'They'll be leaning heavily on the village bakeries.'

Other parts of the country, exact locations unspecified in the local press but alluded to as the east coast, had taken a beating too – with multiple civilian deaths and injuries. With Southampton being just a few miles up the road, the threat of attack felt terrifyingly close.

Audrey's head was full with worries. She couldn't get poor little Mary's reaction to the siren out of her mind. When, finally, she'd taken Mary to her room, the little girl had refused to sleep in the bed, wanting to curl up under it instead. Because she was so exhausted, Audrey had let her have her way, but how could she let a child in her care sleep on the draughty floorboards for more than one night? It wouldn't do. And when another customer then reported to Audrey that she'd heard from her uncle, who was an ARP warden, that Elsie's father had been arrested overnight for being an Italian national, Audrey was horrified. To add insult to injury, someone had thrown a brick through their front window. It was all desperately unjust, and Audrey wanted to visit Elsie, but the queue of customers waiting for their daily bread and counter goods spilling out onto the street put paid to that idea.

'I'll ask Lily to go on my behalf,' she said to Maggie. 'Let me pop upstairs and ask her to run an errand for me.'

Taking the stairs two at a time, Audrey knocked on Lily's door and opened it to find Lily hastily packing her suitcase, her budgie cage balanced precariously on the bed, her face blotchy and red from crying. The bed had been made up and a note, with Audrey's name on the front, rested on the pillow.

'Lily!' Audrey said, registering the letter, then closing the door behind her. 'What are you doing?'

Lily turned to face Audrey. With dark circles around her eyes and a bright red nose, she looked exhausted.

'I've been thinking all night that I have to leave,' she said, her lip quivering. 'I should never have come. I realise that the reason Charlie didn't come into the shelter was because of me. I have the address for the Free Church Home for Unmarried Mothers. It's on St Albans Avenue. I'll stay there until I've had the baby, then it can be adopted and I can go back to London to get a job.'

'Lily,' said Audrey 'I think—'

'This was a mistake,' Lily interrupted. 'You have enough on your hands with Mary being here. I have spent my whole life wishing I could experience more of the world and I'm not going to give up on all of that now. I won't let this one mistake define the rest of my life.'

Audrey heard Lily's voice crack as she finished speaking.

'Don't go,' said Audrey imploringly. 'Those unmarried mothers' homes are for people whose family won't help them. I don't want you to go. And Charlie wanted to stay with the ovens during the raid, it really wasn't because of you. I promise.'

'I'm going,' Lily said, standing straighter. 'I'm going to make all this go away.'

'No Lily, please,' Audrey soothed, taking the suitcase from Lily's hand and putting it on the floor, then wrapping her arms around her and rubbing her back to calm her trembling. 'I admire your spirit, Lily, but please, calm down. I have a suggestion to make.'

Audrey moved over to the window and opened it, looking out at the sea, which sparkled in the sunlight. The sea always had a calming effect on her.

'I was going to pick the right time to talk to you about this,' she said gently, turning to face Lily. 'But there never seems to be a right time. Charlie and I have not been able to have a child of our own, despite all the trying over the years, so I've told him I will gladly help look after your baby. If you want to consider adoption, I would like you to consider me and Charlie taking the baby on. I would be honoured to care for your child, if that was what you wanted.'

Audrey paused to see how her idea had landed.

'But the main thing is Lily,' she continued, 'we're family. What are families for if they're not for helping one another at times like these? You can work in the bakery for as long as you're able and we can pay you a small wage too.'

'No Audrey, I can't accept a day more of your help,' Lily started.

'You would be helping me, really.' Audrey said softly. 'I need you to do something for me. Could you take some provisions to Elsie and her family please? They've had a shock overnight and I want Elsie to know we're thinking of her. Come on, Lily, chin up. As Pat said: "much of life is about putting on a brave face" despite what's going on inside.'

Lily nodded and stood straighter. 'Thank you Audrey,' she said, her eyes misting over. 'I'll think about what you said. Thank you.'

Audrey smiled at Lily, but felt a wave of fury at Henry Bateman for his careless ways, and a pang of guilt for having not given Lily Jacques' impassioned letter. But with the girl in such a tizzy, would it help? She had enough to contend with, which reminded Audrey of another problem.

'We will have to speak to your father and my mother at some point about you staying on here,' said Audrey, grimacing. Lily's face went two shades paler at the thought. 'But you can leave that to me.'

The feeling that she was being watched never left Lily. With every man she caught in her peripheral vision on her route to Elsie's house wearing a dark hat or coat, her heartbeat quickened. Rationally she knew it was all in her imagination, but if she let her mind run free, she thought that perhaps Henry was following her, or had sent one of his cronies to follow her. After the letter she'd sent him before leaving London, he would surely despise her and probably want rid of her from the face of the earth. Her stomach turned over at the thought of the letter she'd written to Henry: *You have lied and cheated, but there's one truth you can't run away from. I am with child and you are the father.* She'd scribbled the words down in the heat of the moment, in a fit of indignation at the injustice of the situation, wanting to shock and hurt Henry *and* his bride-to-be, without thinking through the consequences, but she was quickly learning that this impetuousness led her into awful trouble. In fact it was becoming a bit of a theme running through her life. Perhaps that was why her father had always been so protective and controlling of her. He had often said: 'You're your mother's daughter,' and for all Lily knew, her mother might have had a reckless streak. Lily had only a hazy memory of her mother, who had died when Lily was four, in childbirth. The baby, Lily's brother, also died. No matter how hard she strained to remember her features, her mother's face was horribly indistinct, but she missed her, or the thought of her, dreadfully.

Passing the imposing St Katherine's Church on Church Road, Lily's eyes rested on an exhausted-looking woman who was sitting on the bench outside the church, giving her baby a bottle of milk. Two small boys and a girl, presumably her other children, sat beside her.

'Sleepless night with the siren an' all so the baby's cried all morning,' the woman said to Lily. 'If I want a bit of peace I have to feed him! Shame Hitler ain't so easy to please!'

'Yes…' muttered Lily with a smile, trying desperately to avert her eyes from the tiny baby, but it was as if her eyes were being magnetised by the baby's fingers and chubby, creased little wrists, its eyes scrunched closed and its little lips sucking at nothing, now the bottle was finished. Hot and cold flushes of terror passed through her, as she tried to contemplate the unbelievable fact that a baby was growing inside her own body – a baby she feared she didn't want and couldn't love.

Continuing, she passed a group of servicemen on a training exercise and was abruptly reminded of the bigger picture. While everyone else was worrying about war, she was worrying about her own problems. She was going to have to be matter-of-fact about it and give the baby up for adoption, to Audrey, if she was definitely willing. There would be nobody better than Audrey to look after a newborn, Lily knew that, and she was incredibly grateful for her offer.

One thing was for sure and though she was aware of how uncaring and cold it sounded, Lily knew she wasn't ready to be a mother, especially when society would treat her like an outcast for being unmarried. So far she was making a proper mess of her own life – how could she be entrusted with the life of another?

With a heavy sigh, she followed the directions to Elsie's home, glancing over her shoulder more than once, again imagining a man trailing behind her, only to discover there was nobody there at all.

Lily knocked on Elsie's front door, which was already ajar. A net curtain had blown through the smashed front window and caught on jagged shards of glass. Must have made an awful mess inside too. Cowards, thought Lily. How – and why – could anyone do such a thing?

'Hello, it's Lily,' she called, entering the dark hallway. 'Elsie? Can I come in?'

'I'm in the front room,' shouted Elsie.

Lily found Elsie on her knees next to a pile of broken glass, scrubbing at the floor rug where the brick, covered in something sticky and black, had crashed through the window, knocking over a side table and taking a lamp with it. With sleeves rolled up and soapy forearms, Elsie pushed her hair out of her eyes to smile up at Lily.

'Can't get this black mark out of the rug,' she said, resuming her scrubbing. 'Goodness knows what it is. Tar or paint or something. It's so sticky.'

'Why would someone throw that through your window?' Lily asked.

'Because they're thick,' said Elsie, putting down the brush and leaning back on her hands. 'My father is Italian so because Mussolini has jumped into bed with Germany, Italian nationals are now social pariahs, or aliens as the policeman called us. He's been arrested and will be interned.'

'That's terrible!' said Lily, horrified. 'You must be in shock.'

'I can't keep up with this war,' said Elsie, shaking her head. 'And now the neighbours will be talking about us like we've done something wrong, like we should be ashamed of our father. It's already started hasn't it, with this brick? I feel like I want to run away this morning!'

'Oh I sympathise with you,' Lily said. 'I know that feeling well.'

'Did you run away from London?' said Elsie, her interest piqued. 'Audrey said she hadn't seen you for six years. I've been dying to ask why you turned up out of the blue like that.'

Elsie smiled at Lily, but Lily blushed furiously, subconsciously touching her pregnant stomach. Elsie's eyes widened into perfect circles.

'You're not...' said Elsie. 'You're not in a fix, are you, Lily?'

'I am,' said Lily quietly.

'Do you have a sweetheart?' asked Elsie.

'You don't want to know,' said Lily, her words barely audible. 'It's a mess.'

'Oh yes I do!' said Elsie. 'Does Audrey know about this?'

Lily nodded slowly, desperately hoping that Elsie wouldn't judge her too harshly.

'I know what you'll think of me,' said Lily, standing straighter as if to face an onslaught. 'I fell under the spell of an unavailable man. Are you shocked?'

Elsie shook her head. 'This war is turning lives upside down,' she said, gently. 'There's nobody who knows that more than me. What will you do?'

'I don't know,' said Lily, her shoulders sagging. 'I think the baby will have to be adopted.'

'Oh,' Elsie said sadly. 'Well if it's going to have a better future with another couple then I suppose that's wise. You could lie though, couldn't you? There are so many girls expecting whose men won't come home from the war. You could pretend to be a war widow.' At the mention of the word 'widow', sadness settled on Elsie's face.

Eager to steer the subject away from adoption and widows, Lily's eyes flew to Elsie's wedding dress, draped over the back of a chair. It was marked with black paint where the brick had brushed against it. 'Is that your dress?' Lily asked.

Elsie nodded, scratching her forehead. Her thumb – that she'd obviously cut on the broken glass – was bleeding through a makeshift bandage.

Lily frowned and picked up the dress, inspecting the damage. 'We can get that off,' she said. 'Audrey's whites gleam. I'll ask her what her secret is.'

Elsie shrugged, taking the dress and throwing it on the table. 'How can I get married anyway, without my father here?' she asked, her expression hopeless. 'I've been told he'll be interned to a prisoner-of-war camp on the Isle of Man. I had a look on the map and it's so far away! Right up in the Irish Sea, on the west coast of all places!' Elsie lowered her voice and gestured towards the downstairs bedroom. 'My mother is in bits, acting like she's been widowed. She poured Papa a cup of tea this morning before she remembered where he was,' Elsie went on. 'She's having a rest now. I'm supposed to be at work this afternoon. There's a display I have to put together of sample garments that need knitting for the Forces, but how can I leave her?' Elsie resumed her scrubbing.

Lily didn't know what to say. She was horrified that the government could treat people this way and lock up innocent men whose families depended on them. It seemed a knee-jerk reaction to a complex issue. She crouched down next to Elsie on the floor and briefly rested her hand on her back, feeling her muscles stiffen under her touch. From the little she knew of Elsie, she'd gleaned that she was a girl with fire in her belly and wouldn't take kindly to pity or moping about.

'Why don't I make us a cup of tea and a sandwich?' Lily said, resolutely. 'Audrey sent some fresh bread and you must be hungry. I'll help you get this sorted out. We could board this hole up until you can replace the glass? When you pull the nets over you'll never know from the inside. Look on the bright side, you won't need to bother with the blackout blind, will you, and we can sort out the dress, replace the lace if necessary.'

Elsie sighed deeply, tucked her hair behind her ears and gave Lily a weary smile. Extending her hand to Elsie, Lily helped pull her to her feet. 'Thank you,' said Elsie. 'You're a pal.'

Chapter Sixteen

'I will never again eat porridge for breakfast,' RAF flying instructor George Meadows told Maggie, taking a bite out of his lardy cake. 'Not now that I have discovered this bakery. My uniform is going to get tight around the middle if I'm not careful though, Maggie.'

He tugged at the waistband of his trousers, which fitted his slim and muscular torso perfectly, and winked at her. He was incredibly handsome; chiselled features, sparkly-eyed, kissable lips.

Maggie dissolved into fits of giggles, while the eyebrows of the older ladies in the queue moved skywards. Maggie didn't care. She was sick to the back teeth of all the worrying around her and the drone of aircraft ahead, and entranced by the RAF airmen in their smart uniforms, some of whom were in barracks in Bournemouth in one of the many hotels requisitioned for army personnel. George Meadows was as medicinal as a strong cup of tea when he strode into the bakery. Just his gigantic smile and the fragrance of the lotion he wore made Maggie feel happy to be alive. All she heard at home from her grandmother, who she lived with in a tiny terraced cottage with her three other younger sisters, was complaints about being penniless, rationing and pessimism about the future. There was even a small bottle of poison waiting on the mantelpiece in readiness for her grandmother to swallow if there was a German invasion.

It wasn't much better at work. Poor Audrey was struggling to stay positive about the wedding since Elsie's dad had been taken to a prisoner-of-war camp and Elsie had been questioning whether she should get married at all. Though he was now 'safely' on the Isle of Man, there'd been sickening news about how a requisitioned cruise-liner, the *Arandora Star*, taking Italian and German internees to Canada, had been torpedoed by a German U-boat just after leaving the Liverpool docks. Eight hundred and five people had lost their lives. Elsie and her mother had taken this news very hard, understandably, but Maggie didn't know how to ease their suffering.

She also knew the bakery secret, that Lily was in a fix, as she'd heard Charlie and Audrey arguing about it. That was juicy gossip, if she was the sort to gossip, but she wasn't.

'How would you like to step out with me some time?' George asked her, in front of a shop full of gaping women. 'We could go for a walk on the promenade, or go to a dance at the Pavilion?'

Maggie enjoyed theatrically winking at the customers. Being a shop girl was sometimes like being an actress.

'I think we know what the answer will be,' said Audrey, smiling up from the accounts book she was writing in.

'I thought you'd never ask!' said Maggie.

George laughed his rich, robust laugh and Maggie grinned. He was exactly the sort of chap she needed to be spending time with. Fun, loud and good-looking.

'You could be my plus-one at a wedding I'm due to go to at the weekend,' said Maggie. 'Could he Audrey? Would Elsie and William be put out?'

Audrey didn't seem to hear. She was scrutinising the accounts book, a frown on her face, shaking her head in confusion.

'Audrey?' repeated Maggie. 'Could I invite George to the wedding?'

Audrey looked up from the book, wearing a distracted expression. 'Of course,' she said, with a smile. 'You'd be welcome, George. Which reminds me. I have some preparations to be getting on with!'

Audrey tried to steady her hand as she balanced the tiny figures of bride and groom onto the top of the wedding cake she'd made, but to no avail.

'What on earth is wrong with me?' she said to the empty kitchen. She had too much to think about, that's what it was. Ever since she'd mentioned her idea to Lily about adopting the baby, she couldn't stop her mind running away with itself. To add to it all, the bakery's accounts didn't seem to add up. Audrey sighed. She'd have to deal with that another time. With the wedding now only a day away, the preparations were getting on top of her. With Elsie in an understandably distracted mood since her father's arrest and the dreadful news of the sinking of the *Arandora Star*, Audrey had carried on with the preparations, knowing Elsie had her hands full at home. Thankfully others had chipped in to help: Old Reg had donated some fancy biscuits for the wedding spread, the photographic dealer had offered to do the wedding photographs, Mr Chester from the cooked meats shop had gifted some ham for sandwiches and the dairy had gifted milk so Audrey could make extra custard tarts. Pat had washed the stain from the dress and made beautiful bunting for the hall, and the florist was doing the bouquet and buttonholes. All they needed now was for William to come home.

William had written a short note to say he would be arriving by train the evening before the wedding. He had given up his rented digs when he joined up, so he would stay at the bakery and Mary would go in with Lily. She'd washed and pressed Charlie's suit, and helped Violet arrange the special marriage licence and book the church. The only thing left to do was finish preparing the food for the 'do' that they'd have in the community hall afterwards. Audrey had planned a simple buffet of finger sandwiches, sausage rolls and a wedding cake topped with the icing sugar friends and neighbours had donated, which, she was delighted to see, was enough for two tiers and some piped decorations.

She tried again to place the figures of bride and groom onto the cake and, finally, she added a small horseshoe for luck and stood back to admire her work.

'They need all the luck they can get,' said Charlie, appearing behind her. 'I saw Mr and Mrs Stringer today when I was doing the rounds with Albert. They got a telegram yesterday – their two boys have both been reported missing at sea. Mrs Stringer is inconsolable, as you can imagine.'

Audrey sat down heavily on the kitchen chair, the wind knocked out of her. 'Oh heavens, Charlie,' she said, shaking her head. 'That's just dreadful. What can we do? I must take them something.'

Audrey thought of the Stringer boys, so full of energy and good cheer and the sort to pass the time of day with anyone and everyone. She couldn't imagine them no longer being a fixture in the neighbourhood.

'I left extra bread for them,' he said, shrugging. 'Though what good that will do, I'm not sure.'

'It's something, Charlie,' said Audrey, moving to the stove to make tea. 'Something is better than nothing. Oh I wish I could put an end to all this madness.'

She turned on the wireless and the couple listened in silence as, in a broadcast to the nation, Neville Chamberlin, who was still a member of Churchill's cabinet, warned that a German attempt to invade Britain by sea and air might be launched at any moment.

'*…Brave men and women will only be braced by the knowledge that we must now rely upon ourselves, under Providence, to win through as we have won through before…*'

When the broadcast was over, Audrey handed Charlie a cup of weak tea – the ration was only 2oz per person per week so they had to make it last.

'Hardly feels like a time to be celebrating, does it?' Charlie said quietly, moving to stand in front of the map he'd fixed to the wall, where he marked out the various battles with pins. He frowned at the map. 'But we'll put a smile on for Elsie and William. It's only the once you get married, after all.'

'Remember when we got married, love?' Audrey said. 'We felt like we had the world at our feet and that we were going to be together forever. What must it feel like for William and Elsie? They have forty-eight hours before he leaves again and then she will have to get on with life not knowing what's going to happen to her new husband. When will it end?'

A cloud passed over the evening sun and the kitchen was thrown into gloom. Audrey felt a dizzying sense of foreboding.

'This wedding means so much,' she said quietly, gathering herself. 'It's a moment to stand together in honour of love, against all this… this… hatred.'

Audrey put a hand over her face, before shaking her head and tutting at herself.

'Come on, girl,' said Charlie, putting an arm over her shoulders. 'We're doing okay. I swear you get softer every day. But that's why I love you.'

Chapter Seventeen

'He's not coming, is he?' said Elsie. Her voice was thin and high, and though the air was warm in the bright midday sun, she visibly trembled. Standing outside St Katherine's Church in Southbourne in her lace wedding dress, clutching her bouquet of pale pink tulips and fern, her hair carefully pinned to frame her face with a band of delicate and fragrant orange blossom fixing it in place, Elsie looked nothing like the happy bride-to-be she was meant to be. Her expression was one of sober anxiety, her skin pale and her shoulders hunched over, as she peered up and down Church Road squinting in the bright light, desperately searching the cloudless horizon for William.

'Let's just give it another fifteen minutes,' said Audrey, her heart sinking into her shoes because they'd already given it another hour and a half. She put an arm around Elsie's shoulders, silently and fervently praying that her brother would arrive, his kitbag slung over his shoulder, his smile wide. But that was beginning to feel like an erroneous hope. Waiting for him like this was torturous and she wasn't even the bride. Goodness knows how Elsie's heart must be faring. The happiest day of her life was rapidly becoming the worst.

Audrey felt more blood run from her face with each passing minute. She had waited at Bournemouth train station the night before, for the train he'd said he'd be on, and then onwards until the middle of the night, hoping that William had missed his train and had caught the next one, or the one after that, but, when he still wasn't on the last train, she'd been forced to return to the bakery in low spirits, willing him to arrive by other means, or even the following morning, as long as he was in time for the wedding. But he still hadn't arrived. She'd gone through every possible reason for him not being there: the travel ban, which made it hard for people to come to the area without good reason, but if marriage wasn't good reason, what was? A lost identity card? Illness? Money? Surely not a change of heart?

'He might have had a sudden posting and not been able to get word to us,' Charlie had said, comforting Audrey. 'I've heard some men have been told they could have three weeks' compassionate leave only to receive a telegram after just a few days, ordering they immediately return to service.'

Now, Audrey smoothed down her practical but pretty baby blue dress, which touched just below her knee and was neatly belted at the waist, and sighed deeply. Her thoughts went to the food she'd arranged earlier, with little Mary's silent but enthusiastic help, waiting on platters on trestle tables at the community hall, the colourful banner exclaiming 'Congratulations!' strung up over the entrance, the gramophone ready, and the bunting hung diagonally from corner to corner over the dance floor. And of the wedding cake, for which she had used so many donations of their friends and neighbours' icing sugar – it would be criminal to let it go to waste.

'Any news from William?' asked Maggie, who looked sensational in her daisy-print dress and silver shoes. Her guest, George Meadows, was charming Maggie and the other guests, but was clearly restless.

Audrey felt the fight drain out of her as she swept her eyes over the guests, all dressed in their finest clothes, the men's shoes shining, the ladies' hats carefully positioned on their hair – they had all gone to so much effort, pleased to have something to celebrate at last.

'Nothing,' she said to Maggie quietly, feeling the deepest regret. Perhaps they should have waited until William had returned from the war for good, when it was over and life had gone back to normal. Perhaps it was a hasty and silly assumption to think that you could organise a celebration in wartime when men's lives were no longer their own?

Audrey forced a smile when Violet, Elsie's mother, interrupted her thoughts. Dressed in a green suit and perfectly turned out, but clearly in discomfort and leaning heavily on her canes, Violet must, Audrey knew, be consumed by anxiety at having lost Angelo to the prisoner-of-war camp. And now this would only make her heartbreak worse.

'You don't think your brother has had a change of heart, do you?' asked Violet, her eyes darting from Audrey to Elsie. 'What with Angelo being arrested? Maybe he doesn't want to be associated with—'

'Never!' interrupted Audrey, shaking her head. 'He doesn't even know about Angelo and I know he would only feel sadness that it's happened. William would do everything in his power to be here. There must be a different sort of problem...'

'I hope he hasn't come to any harm,' said Elsie, nervously. 'There were more raids overnight on the east coast. What if his billet took a hit? I would rather he had changed his mind about marrying me than be suffering in any way.'

The three women looked at one another in despair, observed by the other guests, whose determination to keep positive was rapidly fading. A sense of despondency fell over the wedding party and some guests wondered aloud whether they should stay on and wait or go home.

'All we can do is wait,' Audrey said, folding her arms across her chest defiantly. And though, over the next hour, some of the guests excused themselves, close family and friends waited for two more hours, before finally – and reluctantly – giving up and trailing off home.

'I'm so sorry,' Audrey apologised to every guest, feeling personally responsible for William's absence. 'I'm ever so sorry.'

Though Audrey had wanted to stay with Elsie, Violet didn't think it was a good idea for Elsie to go to the community hall and see the spread that had been prepared for the wedding party and the banners, bunting and balloons. It would only serve to make her feel worse, so Elsie, Violet and her twin sisters went home, defeated and desolate.

'We can't let the food go to waste,' said Audrey to Lily and Mary, linking arms to walk together to the hall. Audrey decided to give the sandwiches and custard tarts to the, very grateful, Children's Society School for Girls and to take the cake back to the bakery, where it sat in two tins on the counter, just in case William appeared. By nightfall, however, there was still no word from him. It was as if he'd disappeared altogether.

'Goodness knows how Elsie feels tonight,' she said to Lily, Pat and Charlie, who were in Audrey's warm kitchen sharing a pot of tea and a sandwich, after Mary had gone to sleep in her little bed on the floor. 'Her father interned and now this – it's too much for the girl to cope with. And where on earth is William? I'm worried sick about him.'

As she lay in bed that night with one ear open in case William arrived, tears slipped down her cheeks and onto her pillow in the darkness. Better to get her disappointment out now in private, because first thing the bakery would be open again – and her customers would be expecting happy news of the wedding. She took a deep, despondent breath, and went to sleep.

Elsie wondered if life could get much worse. Instead of spending the first night of married life together with William, she sat alone in darkness on her single bed in the cramped childhood bedroom that she shared with her sisters, her knees tucked under her chin. Tears streamed down her cheeks. It seemed the heartache of war had penetrated every vestibule of her life. Despite being a loyal, honourable citizen, her papa had been carted away to a camp on the Isle of Man and her wedding had been a disaster. Her white dress hung on the back of the door, and on the windowsill sat an old toffee tin containing her 'something old, something new, something borrowed and something blue' – and the silver sixpence she'd had in her shoe. She had a good mind to hurl it all out of the window.

'Don't be like that,' she told herself, but it was hard to find anything to feel positive about, it really was.

The room was silent apart from the gentle breathing of her sisters, who had done their best to hide their disappointment at not being able to be bridesmaids, and whose yellow hair ribbons and pretty handmade dresses had been carefully folded away in the drawers.

Violet's words ran through her head, that William would not have intentionally let her down, and Elsie told herself that was true – she was just desperately disappointed and worried. That evening she'd listened to the wireless, half expecting there to be news of him, a newsflash explaining his whereabouts, but of course there was no mention. The pain of longing was physical and unbearable and morbid thoughts filled her head. What if William was dead? What if she never saw him again? What if he had decided he didn't love her, or that he had fallen in love with another girl?

She closed her eyes tightly shut and curled up on her bed, waiting for sleep to release her from the day. Tomorrow would be better. Tomorrow she would write to William and try to find out what had happened. She was still and quiet now, her muscles began to relax, and she slipped into a turbulent dream of being unable to open the door of a train at a platform where she needed to get off. A moment later came the dreadful, piercing wail of the air-raid siren and for a second Elsie thought she was dreaming.

Snapping open her eyes, she immediately heard the chilling drone of aircraft directly above, followed by machine-gun fire. Before she'd even had time to move a muscle, a blinding flash of white light and a colossal explosion physically blew her out of bed, followed by the deafening crash of falling timber and windows shattering. Her head buzzed with the excruciating noise and intense heat blasted her face. She was too shocked to scream. Hands over her ears, sitting bolt upright on the floor in the darkness, breathless with panic, Elsie tried to make sense of what was happening. Water was pouring in through the ceiling and her sisters were screaming out hysterically, thick black smoke making it impossible for any of them to see even their hands in front of their faces.

'Don't move,' Elsie warned her sisters, feeling her way across the room to reach their bed. She grasped hold of both girls' hands and pulled them close into her body, feeling their little hearts racing and their bodies trembling. Her own heart pounding in her chest so hard she thought it might burst out of her ribs, Elsie looked upwards through the smoke and gasped. There was a huge hole in the bedroom ceiling and part of the roof was missing. What was left of it had burst into flames that were leaping and ripping through the wreckage of their home at incredible speed. Realising that a high-explosive bomb had been dropped on the house, she tried to remember what the public information leaflets told you to do in event of an attack. What use were the buckets of water and sand downstairs? Their gas masks were unreachable somewhere, their handy torches lost and it was too late to take shelter.

'We're going to die!' wailed the twins.

'We're not going to die,' said Elsie calmly. 'We're going to get out of the house and go to safety.'

Moving cautiously through the house, holding her sisters' hands, Elsie registered that whole walls had collapsed and their destroyed home was suddenly exposed to the outside world like a bizarre version of a doll's house. The Auxiliary Fire Service had arrived, sirens were sounding, but she needed to get her mother and her sisters to safety.

Outside, she heard a man calling, 'Is there anyone in here?'

'Four of us in here!' she yelled back. 'We need help!'

'Elsie?' She heard her mother's weak voice. 'Girls?'

Elsie pushed on through the smoke and debris, aware of flames ripping through their front room, her sisters whimpering. Elsie became aware of a fire warden with a pump and buckets of sand. He was calling out instructions, but Elsie couldn't hear his words. She pushed the girls out towards him, shouting that she was sending out her sisters, and went back for her mother.

'Mother!' she called to Violet, pushing her shoulder against her mother's bedroom door, which was wedged shut. Finally she forced it open and saw Violet had been injured. Her head was bleeding from the impact of ceiling panels that had fallen in.

'Elsie,' she said. 'Help me will you? My legs…'

Cutting her bare feet on broken glass strewn on the floor, Elsie helped lift Violet and support her weight as they staggered through the smoke and debris and out into the street, choking and coughing. A first aider came to their immediate help as firemen tried to control the blaze. Buoyed with adrenalin, Elsie ran next door to help her neighbour, Sidney, who Elsie knew had difficulty breathing.

'Stay away from the property!' commanded a fireman, but Elsie, now followed by the fireman, ran to the back of Sidney's house where she knew he kept his spare key and unlocked the kitchen door to find Sidney collapsed on the floor. She ran towards him.

'What's his name?' said the fireman, now beside her.

'Sidney,' she answered. 'His lungs are weak.'

'Let's get him out,' he said.

Stumbling over a paintbrush and pot of something black and sticky in the darkness, a deeply disturbing realisation cut into Elsie's heart, but she didn't hesitate. She looped her arm around Sidney's frail waist and helped the fireman walk him, barely able to get his breath, out to safety.

Sitting in the ambulance in their nightclothes, Violet and the twins looked helplessly at their home, which was now half-collapsed, smoke billowing from the windows. After escorting Sidney to another ambulance, Elsie joined them in the van, throwing her arms around her family, wanting to hold them tight and never let go, wishing their papa was there to protect them.

'God help us,' Violet said in a stunned voice, holding a bandage to her head wound. 'Everything… all our possessions, our memories, our home… it's gone.'

'I know,' said Elsie, hugging her. 'I'm sorry, I'm sorry.'

The street was now full of people who had come out of their homes, with buckets of sand and blankets and offers of help.

Those families whose homes had been badly damaged were taken to the rest centre at All Saints Hall, where volunteers from the Women's Voluntary Service supplied them with emergency clothing, hot soup, tea and a bed. Elsie collapsed onto a camp bed, but her mind was ablaze with the day's events. As the night wore on, her feelings of anger intensified and Elsie convinced herself that the war was personal.

By dawn she was so filled with fury and frustration that at the first hint of daylight, she walked determinedly towards the cliff top, wearing borrowed shoes that were too big and a wool coat that must have belonged to a woman twice her size. She knew she wasn't supposed to be near the beach at this hour, but she sat on the cliff scrubland regardless, surrounded by the yellow flowering gorse, glaring out at the sea, where scaffolding jutted from the water like a mouthful of ugly black teeth.

The chilly early morning breeze whipped her hair across her face, but Elsie left it there, to mingle with her tears. This morning, more than at any other time in her life, she felt that everything she held dear was under threat: her home, heart, family and liberty – and she was powerless to change anything. When the sun began to rise and glow in the sky like a giant peach, she made a pact. She might not be fighting on the front line, but she would fight on the home front. Whatever she could do to help put an end to this war and get the men she loved back home, she would do it. Her gloves were off.

Chapter Eighteen

When the sun had risen over the sea and military training exercises had started on the beach, Elsie returned home to see the extent of the bomb damage, and to check that the house hadn't been looted. Not that the family had an abundance of jewels and treasures, mind, but there were some precious things she wanted to rescue from the rubble if she could: the family photographs, her wedding dress.

'You wouldn't reckon on it,' a fire warden had told her in the night, 'but some no-good toe-rags around here have been helping themselves during air raids. People leave their front doors open, see. Well, you don't think to lock your front door when there's a raid on, do you?'

Despite it being July, the weather during the last few days had been changeable and today a fierce wind blew in from the Channel, and standing on the pavement outside her house, Elsie felt chilled to the bone. She hardly dared look at the unrecognisable smoky stumps that were left of her home, shaking her head in disbelief at the night's events; how in such a short time everything she held dear could be destroyed. Piles of broken glass and bricks were being removed in a cart, roof slates and tiles were strewn across the pavement and the house stood, open to the street, as if sliced in half, a papered wall with pictures hanging on it, a bizarre sight. A tree had been uprooted and lay on the pavement as if it were just a weed pulled up by a gardener.

We were lucky, she tried to convince herself. *We could very easily have been killed.*

The bomb had actually fallen in between the two houses, making a huge crater in the ground. 'Poor Hitler couldn't even aim straight,' the fire warden had tried to joke. The explosion had destroyed Elsie's house completely and half-destroyed Sidney's home. Blackened beds and wardrobes had fallen into a broken and macabre mess amongst shattered windows, heaps of bricks, plaster and rubble. Chairs lay upturned, burned and broken, blankets and clothes were strewn amidst the wreckage; there was a teddy with its fur burned, and Violet's careful knitting, unravelled and singed. The family photographs Elsie had wanted to rescue had blown along the pavement in the wind like litter. Elsie managed to stamp on one to stop it disappearing. She picked it up. The photograph was of her, William and her sisters in their swimmers on Bournemouth beach. Handwritten on the back was the date: August, 1938. The sight of William, smiling happily into the camera lens, took her breath away. Memories of his voice and touch came flooding into her mind and the disappointment of yesterday swelled in her throat. That picture had been taken during the second month she'd been courting William – the excitement of being in his company was written all over her face. She positively glowed. Now, it felt like a different lifetime.

'Just think,' Elsie whispered. 'We had no idea what was going to happen. No idea.'

Pushing the photograph into her coat pocket, she turned to see several of her neighbours emerging from their homes to inspect the damage, all of them wearing a similar stricken expression. It could just as easily have been them that got hit.

Out of the corner of her eye, she saw Sidney's black cat, Silky, who she often petted in the garden. 'Silky,' Elsie said in a quiet, high voice, calling the cat, who was covered in dust. 'Silky, come here Silky!'

The cat wound his body through her legs, purring loudly. She picked him up, burying her face into his warm coat.

'Oh you poor cat,' she said, sitting down on the edge of the pavement, still clinging to Silky.

'You should charge to view the damage,' said Mrs Eden, the neighbour who lived opposite, gesturing at the crowd who had come to see the wreck. 'Give it to charity.'

'Oh they're all right,' said Elsie, with a shadow of a smile, setting down Silky. 'It's a shock to us all.'

Mrs Eden rested her hand on Elsie's back, to comfort her. 'Come in for some tea,' she said. 'I'm just going to put the bucket on.'

'Thank you, Mrs Eden, but I better get back to my mother and the twins,' said Elsie, wiping her nose on her hanky and managing a smile. 'We'll need to find somewhere to stay. Can you make sure Silky gets some food? I doubt Sidney will be able to get here from the hospital.'

Elsie thought of the pot of spilt black sticky liquid she had found in Sidney's kitchen and shuddered.

'Wait there,' said Mrs Eden, rushing into her house and returning carrying a pair of shoes that were Elsie's size and a beautiful pale pink mac that Elsie knew Mrs Eden kept for best. 'Have these at the very least. They're your size. You'll look a picture in that coat.'

'I'll not take no for an answer,' said Audrey, when Elsie went into the bakery later that day to tell her about the raid.

Leaving Maggie and Lily serving in the shop, Audrey had immediately ushered Elsie upstairs into the kitchen, thrown a blanket over her shoulders and plied her with hot tea and toast and a shot of rum, even though Elsie protested at the attention.

'How dare they bomb you and your innocent little sisters?' Audrey raged, banging down the cups on the table in fury. 'You all could have been killed! If Hitler thinks he can take on this family, he's another think coming. You'll stay here with us and that's that. You can share with Lily. Your sisters and your mother can stay with Pat, so she can have a bedroom on the ground floor. They're only round the corner, you can see them all the time.'

Elsie was touched by Audrey's choice of words. She'd said 'this family' as if Elsie's family were already a part of her own, though the truth was sadly different.

'Don't worry yourself, Audrey,' said Elsie. 'You already have Mary and Lily staying. The people at the rest centre said although we're only supposed to be there for forty-eight hours, people are staying much longer and they'd turn a blind eye if we stayed on—'

Audrey put her hands on her hips, her eyes flaming. 'What, and live out of a suitcase when you can stay here with me?' she said, appalled, then turned to open the window and water the geraniums and the cucumbers growing on the windowsill in quick succession.

'I don't even have a suitcase,' said Elsie, feeling suddenly limp. 'We don't have anything at all.'

Audrey came over to her and put her hands on Elsie's shoulders. 'I can help you replace your things,' she said. 'William would want you here. Charlie will speak to Pat and she'll be happy to welcome Violet and your sisters I'm sure. She's always saying she rattles around that house on her own.'

'What are you signing me up for?' Charlie said, at that very moment entering the kitchen, reaching across the table to kiss Audrey on the cheek. 'Why aren't you out in the shop? We're nearly sold out in there. Hello Elsie. Are you all right?'

Elsie opened her mouth to speak but found herself unable. Exhausted by what had happened that day, she smiled wanly.

'I'll explain it all later,' said Audrey, glancing at Elsie. 'How was your meeting?'

Charlie, who was holding a bunch of paperwork, explained that he'd been to a meeting for the Master Bakers and Confectioners of Bournemouth and the bakers had agreed they were going to put a notice in the newspaper, requesting that all customers settle their accounts as quickly as possible.

'Folk are hard up, that's what it is,' Charlie said, clearly reluctant to criticise or badger his customers. 'But without their payments we bakers will be struggling to pay the wholesalers or the gasworks. We've also heard from the Ministry of Food that from the end of August we'll need to change what loaves we sell.'

'Oh really?' said Audrey, holding on to the back of a chair. 'What do you mean?'

'We're only to bake Coburg, tin, sandwich and Scotch batch,' he said. 'They're limiting the loaves to the more economical shapes, aren't they? If you think about it, with a round loaf, your first slice is small and the slice in the middle the biggest. Ministry of Food want the bread evenly cut, so people have a decent slice each day. Makes sense, but there will be some customers who won't want to give up their cottage loaf—'

'Goodness,' said Audrey. 'Are there to be any other changes?'

'We've swapped some of our delivery customers,' he said. 'So that any bakers who have to drive a long way will have to drive less far and so use less fuel. There's also talk of using a different flour, with added calcium, but we've yet to hear more about that. And then there's the new District Bread Officers. They're to make sure that we're delivering what we say we're delivering but also to make sure if there's a bombing in Poole or Southampton on the gasworks and the big bakeries are put out of action, the smaller bakeries in the surrounding areas can help fulfil the deliveries.'

'Good grief,' said Audrey. 'It's all been so well thought through. Shows what value they put on bread, Charlie.'

'Folk rely on bread,' said Charlie, nodding. 'For some families without two pennies to rub together, it's pretty much all they eat. Bread is the staff of life in war and peace, as Uncle Eric used to say.'

Charlie was interrupted by the wail of the air-raid siren and Elsie leapt to her feet, instantly panicked.

'Again?' she said, her face stricken with terror. 'Quickly. It can happen in seconds.'

'Good lord,' Audrey said. 'Can't a day go by without the war interrupting?'

She slammed her cloth down on the table as the drone of aircraft sounded above.

'If there's anyone in the shop, they'll have to come to the shelter too,' she said. 'Goodness, where's Mary?'

'By the time you've remembered everything there'll be no point in going into the shelter,' said Charlie, refusing to be panicked by the siren. 'I'll be in the bakehouse.'

'I'll find Mary,' said Elsie, her heart pounding as memories of the previous night's attack haunted her. 'There's no time to waste. Mary! Mary love!'

Elsie ran through to the storeroom to look for Mary and, peering through the door of the large cupboard where Audrey kept ingredients, saw Maggie, who was bent over, fiddling with the catch on her gas mask case, with her back to Elsie.

'Maggie!' cried Elsie. 'We should go to the shelter urgently.'

Elsie's voice made Maggie jump and she immediately dropped the gas mask case onto the floor. It landed with a thud, the lid flipping open and sugar spilling onto the floor. Frowning, Elsie peered into the case. Instead of Maggie's gas mask, it was filled with white sugar.

'Maggie?' asked Elsie quizzically. 'What are you doing?'

Maggie's cheeks flushed deep red as she quickly swept the spilt sugar into the case, securing the lid.

'I'm borrowing it and I swear I'll put it back,' she muttered. 'I can explain, but not right now. Please just keep your trap shut for now.'

Confused, Elsie continued out into the courtyard where Mary was standing, trembling. Grabbing Mary's hand, Elsie joined Audrey, Maggie and Lily in the shelter. It was a crush, but Elsie, whose hands were shaking, found a space next to Lily and Mary on the bench, over which Audrey had hung some dried lavender in bunches under the affectionate roll of Charlie's eyes. A box filled with all the bakery's important documents was in the corner, along with a first aid kit and a biscuit tin containing shelter snacks.

'Here, Mary,' said Audrey, handing the little girl some earplugs. 'The ARP are giving these out for free all over town. I think they will help you.'

Mary stuffed them into her ears and for a while everyone stayed quiet, nervously glancing at one another, straining to hear if anything was going to happen. Planes were heard overhead with frequent bursts of firing from anti-aircraft batteries – and then, after a while, it all fell silent. As they waited, breath bated, for the siren that marked the end of the raid, Elsie turned over Maggie's actions in her head. Why would she be borrowing sugar? Should she tell Audrey what she'd seen?

'I didn't get time to lock the bakery door,' said Audrey. 'I hope nobody's got their hands in the till, though if Charlie catches them he'll have their guts for garters!'

Elsie tried to catch Maggie's eye, but Maggie stared defiantly ahead.

Chapter Nineteen

On 10 July, the 'Battle of Britain' – a major air battle fought in the skies above southern England – began, marking a new and terrifying era in the war. Göring's Luftwaffe were relentless in their mission to attack British coastal targets, and the skies above the south coast raged with Hurricanes and Spitfires defending Britain. Though throughout those July weeks the lilies in the Bournemouth Garden pools blossomed profusely and the sun continued to blaze upon the pine-scented promenades, making the sea sparkle as if with fallen stars, the Victorian piers had been partially blown up, the gaily coloured deckchairs outside the beach huts removed and kite-flying banned. No person was allowed on the seashore between dusk and dawn and the drone of aircraft was a horrifyingly familiar sound.

At Elsie and Lily's bedroom window in the bakery, Elsie stood, arms folded defiantly, watching a dogfight play out high up in the distant skies above the Channel. Dressed in her Beales uniform, she tried to imagine what was going on in the minds of the pilots in the cockpits of those RAF fighter planes, tearing through the clouds leaving curly white contrails like signatures in the sky, each new flight potentially their last. It made Elsie think of and miss William dreadfully. He was in her thoughts hundreds, no thousands, of times a day. At night, her dreams took her to a dark lawless place, where William was in pain and suffering terribly. Every morning she felt a sense of relief when, at 5 a.m., the noise of the bakery dragged her from those nightmares, as Audrey joined Charlie in the bakehouse and set about greasing the tins, the clatter of metal resounding through the house.

Now, in her hand she held a letter that had arrived from William that morning. A neighbour had brought it to Barton's Bakery when the postwoman had tried to deliver it to Elsie's former home. Frowning, she ran her tired eyes over his words, for the umpteenth time.

My dear Elsie, it read, *I'm sorry but due to circumstances beyond my control I could not return for the wedding. Forgive me, for I do not wish to hurt you, William.*

Her heart ached with longing to know more. It was William's handwriting and the sentences complete, but the letter seemed full of holes. The tone was bizarrely formal and the letter incredibly short, offering no real explanation for his actions. She knew the government encouraged soldiers and citizens alike not to disclose confidential information in any letters, but this was taking careful wording to another level. The more she read it, the less sense it made and the more devastated she became. The words knocked about in her mind, clashing with one another, taking on new shapes and meanings.

'What if he's met another girl?' she said to Lily. 'Perhaps he's met a girl in the Auxiliary Territorial Service who had been billeted to France, or a nurse in the Military Nursing Service who is really "doing her bit" and not working in a department store like me.'

Elsie's panicked eyes darted around the room, settling on Lily, who was pulling on her dress, which was now snug around her tummy.

Lily shook her head. 'From what I know and remember of William, he's not the sort of person to treat you like that,' she said. 'When he was a boy he was kind and loyal and thoughtful. I saw a different side to him only once, when he lost his temper after he thought the memory of his father was being abused—'

'What happened?' Elsie asked, moving over to Lily's bed and sitting on it next to her. 'He never told me about that.'

Lily started to pull on her stockings, shaking her head. 'Oh I shouldn't have mentioned anything,' she said. 'I don't even know what the details are but—'

Elsie grabbed Lily's forearm, suddenly desperate for any information about the man she loved, even if from his past. Maybe it would give her a clue to what was happening now. 'Come on, Lily,' said Elsie. 'Please. I just want to hear about him.'

Lily sighed and shrugged, tutting at her own indiscretion. 'It's only that the reason he and Audrey left home so suddenly was because William lashed out at Daphne, his mother, my stepmother,' she explained. 'It was odd, because he was normally so mild-mannered and then one evening they all had this big argument. I think it was about his father, Don. Something to do with William wanting to defend the memory of him. I was in bed, so I crept down the stairs and I saw Daphne strike William, then he struck back, hard. My father went ballistic and William struck him too. He was told to leave and never come back. Audrey went with him out of loyalty I suppose. I don't know any more details…'

Elsie listened to the story without making any comment. William had never mentioned any of this. She struggled to imagine William being aggressive and wondered why he hadn't shared this piece of history with her. Whenever she'd asked him about his parents, he said his father, Don, was dead and that his mother, Daphne, lived in London with her new husband. Why would he not explain what had happened to make him leave?

'I suppose he's ashamed about it,' said Lily, reading Elsie's mind. 'He's a gentle person. There must be good reason for him not coming back for the wedding. It'll be to do with his war duties and he wouldn't have been able to write about them in a letter.'

'You're right,' said Elsie. 'I have to trust in the thought that he will get in touch properly when he can. Besides, I've got so much to think about right now, I should focus on other matters. The house needs rebuilding, my mother's condition needs attention and my sisters' lives need to be kept as normal as possible. I need to find more work too as my job in the shop doesn't pay enough.'

Elsie ran through her options. Needing to earn more, she also wanted to be doing something useful to help the war effort, like join the land girls, or go to work in the munitions factory. But with the twins and her mother to look after, she couldn't go too far from home. She needed to sort out more permanent accommodation too. The house had been almost completely destroyed in the raid and though Elsie had applied to the Assistance Board for funds and the Local Authority was due to do repairs, she had no idea when that would happen. She barely had two pennies to rub together and didn't want to take advantage of Audrey's generosity in the longer term. Talking of taking advantage, Elsie suffered a twinge of guilt for not telling Audrey about Maggie borrowing that sugar, but she had sworn she would put it back. Shaking the thought from her head, she concentrated on how she could take control of her own life. If it meant doing different work or having two jobs and working twice as hard, then she'd do it.

'Is there anything in the Situations Vacant pages?' said Elsie, pointing towards the *Bournemouth Echo* that Lily had been reading. Lily picked up the *Echo* and scanned the jobs pages, reading out jobs as she went through.

'Girl needed for domestic duties,' she read. 'Girl needed for domestic duties. Girl needed for…'

'Domestic duties?' said Elsie, raising her eyebrows. 'Anything else a bit more exciting? Spitfire pilot?'

Lily ran her finger down the adverts, until she turned the page and pointed a finger three times on a specific ad. 'How about this?' she said, her expression animated, turning the newspaper around for Elsie to see the ad from Dorset and Hants Transport Office. 'Bus conductorette to work on the buses? Fit, energetic women to fill the shoes of the men who have gone to fight. That would suit you. So would that uniform – it's green. And the pay is £4 a week.'

'Let's have a look,' Elsie said, reaching for the paper and running her eyes down the person specification and job description. She tried to envisage herself working on the buses, punching holes in tickets and taking fares. It was a job traditionally done by men, but she thought she'd be good at it.

Tearing out the advert, she pushed it into her pocket and felt a fire ignite in her belly. Everything might feel like it was upside down, but there was no point moping about. She was going to make it better by getting on with her life. She would concentrate on her family, get herself another job so she could take care of the twins and pay for her mother to visit her papa. Now, it was time for her to be as brave as those fighter pilots weaving through the clouds in the sky, every flight possibly their last.

Chapter Twenty

The beautiful celebration cake that Audrey had made for Elsie and William's wedding had only sat in the window of Barton's Bakery with a handwritten sign that read *'Free to a deserving bride-to-be'* for a matter of hours before Mrs Brookes, a woman she knew who worked in the café as a cleaner, had shyly requested it for her daughter's wedding. Audrey knew that the family struggled to make ends meet and gave it to Mrs Brookes without hesitation, relieved that it no longer stood in the window as a sad reminder of what should have been a beautiful day. The cake had also roused the interest of a reporter at the *Bournemouth Echo* and it had been photographed being cut by the bride and groom and a story published under the headline 'THIS WEDDING CAKE HAS A SECRET INGREDIENT. COMMUNITY SPIRIT!'

Since the newspaper article, Audrey had had numerous enquiries about iced wedding cakes. Each time, she'd had to politely explain to customers that she was no longer allowed to sell iced cakes because of rationing and that the wedding cake in the paper really was a community effort as numerous of her customers had all brought in small donations of icing sugar that they'd had in their kitchen cupboards.

This morning a young woman, beautifully turned out in a white dress with a single navy blue pocket and blue buttons, and a navy hat to match, was the latest to enquire, after seeing the article, which was pinned on a noticeboard in a local hotel. Holding her white gloves in her hand, a handbag balanced on her forearm, she addressed Maggie, delivering plum tones from raspberry-painted lips.

'I hear that you make iced cakes?' she said, fixing Maggie with an authoritative stare.

'Are you one of those inspectors?' replied Maggie. 'Because if you are, we don't need your sort making trouble when all we're trying to do is a day's work—'

'Maggie!' interrupted Audrey, rushing over to speak to the lady.

'Hello.' She smiled. 'I'm Audrey Barton and you probably read the piece in the paper? I made a cake for my brother's wedding last month, but unfortunately he had his leave cut short and couldn't travel here for the wedding. I made the icing from donations from all the guests. I don't sell iced cakes because it's considered a luxury food and Lord Woolton has put a stop to that. We're all tightening our belts, aren't we?'

The woman put her head to one side, regarding Audrey through slightly narrowed eyes. Something about her made Audrey stand up a little straighter.

'Oh that is a shame,' the woman said. 'I'm looking to make an early order for several iced Christmas cakes. I've just been married myself and we had a plaster of Paris mould, with a rather pathetic bit of cake inside, and I want the real thing for Christmas. I know we're all giving up our luxuries, but there are some things I won't do without. I saw the article and thought I'd ask you.'

Audrey realised she was a woman used to getting her own way. 'I can't help you, I'm afraid,' she said. 'Are you from around here?'

'No, I'm from Richmond, London,' the lady asserted, with an expression that said she'd rather die than be from around here. 'I'm here with my husband. We're actually on a substitute honeymoon. Can't exactly go anywhere exciting with the war on! So we thought we'd get some sea air in Bournemouth. Darling? Darling?'

The woman popped her head out of the door and into the street, where she waved to a slim and suave-looking gentleman, dressed in a smart suit. She gestured at him to come into the bakery and he quickly walked over the road. Audrey thought how they stood out a mile as city people. Both of them looked like they wouldn't know a hard day's graft if it slapped them in the face.

'Audrey!' Charlie yelled from the bakehouse. 'Gasworks delivery! Can you come, love?'

She was needed to sign for the coal delivery from the gasworks as Charlie was tied up in the bakehouse grappling with the yeast, which went bananas in the hot weather.

'Lily,' Audrey said. 'Can you take over for a few minutes? The coal man's waiting.'

Audrey left the shop in Lily and Maggie's hands and rushed through to the back door to receive the weekly coal delivery, changing out of her white apron and pulling on an overall as she did. It was always such a messy job. As the curtain fell behind her, she glimpsed the lady coming back into the shop, followed by the handsome young man who looked like he'd just stepped out of a newspaper advert for gentlemen's hats or shaving lotion. The regular customers in the shop were all gawping at him. Audrey laughed, taking an extra look at his fine features herself.

'AUDREY!' yelled Charlie.

'Coming!' she yelled back, dashing to the door.

The woman in white from London came back in to the bakery, with a man following close behind. Lily glanced up from the weighing scales where she was weighing out the raspings – portions of stale crumbs sold for use in thickening stews – about to offer help, when her mouth fell open in surprise, her stomach somersaulted and the colour drained from her face. She clung on to the counter to keep her balance as sweat sprung onto her forehead and above her top lip, her heart drumming so loud she felt sure everyone could hear its march.

Henry Bateman.

'Lily?' said Henry, coughing a little as he spoke, before regaining his composure and introducing her to his wife. 'Lily used to work for me, months ago. Lily, this is my new wife Helen.'

Helen's eyes narrowed as her gaze travelled from Lily to Henry's face, searching their expressions. Detecting Lily's excruciating embarrassment, she looped her arm through Henry's protectively and gave Lily the once-over, a look of displeasure settling on her features.

'How do you do, Lily?' said Helen, offering Lily her fingertips. Lily wiped her hands on her apron and lightly took Helen's fingers, blushing madly as her eyes fell to Lily's pregnant bump. 'I see you are expecting? When are you due?'

Never before had Lily wished so hard that the ground would open up and swallow her into it. There was immediate silence in the shop as everyone opened their ears to hear what was going on. Opening her mouth to speak, Lily found she was completely unable to get the words out.

Maggie, who was watching the situation closely, helped her out. 'Christmas,' she said. 'Ain't that lovely?'

'Yes, December,' stuttered Lily, unable to look Henry in the eye.

'Oh how sweet,' Helen said. 'A Christmas baby. Congratulations. Isn't that nice, Henry? We're hoping for some of our own too, aren't we darling? Is your husband away fighting somewhere? That must be hard.' Not waiting for an answer, she continued: 'Do you want anything to eat, Henry darling? A jam tart? They look a little dry actually.'

'No... no I don't,' said Henry, who was already backing out of the bakery door. 'I think we'll eat in the hotel, dear. Come on, let's go. Good day.'

When they left the shop, Lily stood frozen to the spot as she watched Helen and Henry cross the road. It wasn't until they were out of sight that she breathed again. Had it been Henry following her or was this a coincidence? Had he come to put the frighteners on her? Shaken, she turned to Audrey, who was now back in the shop beside her.

'Did I hear that woman say that my jam tarts look *dry*?' Audrey said, incredulous. 'The gall of some people!'

'One of those jam tarts would have looked good on the front of that white dress she was wearing,' Maggie said. 'I would happily have been the one to throw it too.'

Audrey laughed, but Lily didn't say anything at all.

'Could you spare me for five minutes?' she muttered, already untying her apron. 'I need some air.'

'Are you unwell?' Audrey replied. 'You look terribly pale.'

But Lily was out of the door, half-running towards the sea in the opposite direction to the way Henry and Helen had gone, pulling her cardigan close around her body, her eyes fixed on the pavement, pushing past shoppers until she was out on the cliff with the vast ocean in front of her, her mouth set in a grim line. What would Henry do now that he'd seen her with his own eyes? Why had she ever written that stupid letter? She should have kept the whole thing a secret. How could she be so daft?

Chapter Twenty-One

'I'll feed the chickens,' Lily said that evening, standing and stretching her hands towards the ceiling after she and Audrey had listened to the evening news on the wireless and Mary was asleep. 'I need to cool off. It's always so hot in here, isn't it?'

'You'll be grateful come Christmas,' Audrey said, with a gentle laugh. 'There's a bitterly cold wind comes off the sea during the winter months, but the bakery stays toasty. Some silly clots swim in the sea at Christmas and they turn blue.'

Lily smiled. *Christmas.*

Slowly walking down the stairs, absent-mindedly running her fingertips along the white floral pattern on the dark brown wallpaper as she moved, Lily tried to envisage Christmas when the baby was due. Her own mother had died in childbirth. She swallowed hard at the thought – would she herself even survive this birth? Oh, how she wished none of this was happening and that the prospect of Christmas was just as it always had been – London lit with pretty fairy lights, fir trees in every window, the promise of a brand new year ahead. Now things were very different, especially since Henry Bateman had seen her. She shuddered at the thought of their earlier exchange. Would he tell her father or make up another lie about her? A cold sweat broke out on her forehead.

'Oh!' She yanked open the back door to the backyard, but caught her finger on the lock as she did so. Sucking the blood oozing from her finger, she stood still outside in the cool air for a moment, a dizzying sense of uncertainty gripping her. Without Audrey extending a hand of kindness to her, she didn't know how she would have managed so far. How could she ever repay her?

Scooping the feed from a bucket, she opened the chicken run and tossed the feed down for the chickens. She also filled a small bowl of water for the birds, promising to leave their favourite – a crust soaked in tea – for them tomorrow.

'You birds get forgotten with this war going on,' she said. 'Yet you still sing your songs.'

Thoughts of Henry and the baby tumbled through her mind, distracting her from what she was meant to be doing, and in a bid for freedom one chicken darted out of the run into the backyard and out through the open gate.

'Come back!' Lily called, slamming shut the chicken run before more could run away and following the escapee chicken out onto the street behind the bakery. 'Charlie will never forgive me if I lose you,' Lily said, following the bird onto the grassy area that some of the shopkeepers had turned into an allotment to 'dig for victory'. She picked her way through the rows of leeks, cabbages and potatoes, now growing in abundance, careful not to step on the produce, holding up the skirt of her dress so it didn't catch on any thorns.

Pausing for a moment, she held her hand over her eyes to shield them from the evening sun, searching for the chicken. Just when she thought it was lost for good, she saw its speckled brown feathery legs heading towards the steep steps down to the beach. Running a little, Lily chased the chicken down the steps, cursing it, holding onto the iron handrail as she moved.

'Got you,' she said, grabbing the bird with a firm grip when it had almost reached the bottom of the steps, the beach in close view. 'Were you heading for a swim?'

Turning to climb back up the steps, she glanced at the pale skies above, streaked with vapour trails, and shuddered at the prospect of a formation of enemy planes suddenly appearing on the horizon like a swarm of killer flies. She concentrated on the chicken instead, feeling its tiny heart beating under her grasp. Counting the steps as she headed back towards the bakery, she was halfway up them when a voice ahead startled her.

'Lily,' said the voice.

She saw his shoes first – black and shiny, probably polished by a shoeshine boy. Slowly, she raised her eyes up his suited legs and jacket, settling on his face, which was partially obscured by his black hat, a trail of smoke rising from his lips. She met Henry's glare, trying her hardest not to show the apprehension she felt.

'What do you want, Henry?' she said, the chicken struggling under her arm now, its spindly legs running in thin air. 'Have you been following me?'

She tried to walk past him, but he blocked her way.

'Of course I haven't been following you!' he said.

'Let me pass!' she said, the chicken escaping her clutch in a flurry of feathers.

His eyes were bloodshot and he emanated the stink of alcohol and tobacco smoke.

'About that letter you sent me,' he said, moving his face to within an inch of hers. 'I burned it the minute it arrived! Don't you ever repeat those words to anyone ever again. Do you understand me?'

His words were slurred, and though frightened, Lily glared at him.

'You lied to me,' she said quietly. 'You didn't tell me you were engaged and you said you were going to join up and that's why I… If I'd known the truth, none of this would have happened.'

She had barely finished her sentence when he roared in her face.

'NOTHING HAPPENED!' he shouted, his lips pulled back across his teeth like a growling dog. 'Nothing happened at all. Do you hear me? Do you think I'd ever even look in the direction of a little slip like you? Your father thinks you're something special, but you're no better than any of the other cheap tarts in that office, desperate to impress me to get a new job. Pathetic!'

Lily was speechless. She recollected the compliments he'd given her and the time he'd lavished on explaining the workings of the office to her. Tears threatened to spill, but a red mist was building in front of her eyes.

'That's not true and if nothing happened,' she seethed, 'then how do you explain this baby? It didn't grow itself.'

She knew she was on dangerous ground, but her body pulsed with reckless indignation.

'That,' he said, reaching for his umbrella and jabbing the sharp end into her stomach so hard she doubled over, 'has nothing to do with me. Don't you dare try to ruin my life with your dirty little secret.'

She stood up straight, wanting to cry. Realising there was no point in trying to argue with Henry, who was drunk and potentially violent, she just wanted to get past him and run back to the bakery. Again she tried to move up the steps, but he gripped her shoulders.

'Let me go,' she said. 'Get your hands off me!'

'Not until you admit that baby is nothing to do with me,' he said. 'If Helen found out, I would—'

'You would what?' said Lily. 'I'm sure Helen has every right to know who she has married and what he gets up to behind her back.'

Lily was amazed at herself and though a voice in her head told her to stop being so foolish and instead say the words he wanted to hear, she couldn't stop. Wild with fury, she had to say what she thought, regardless of the consequences. *You're your mother's daughter!*, she heard her father's warning voice boom.

'Shut up!' spat Henry, this time pushing her in the chest.

Lily staggered backwards and the heel of her shoe slipped off the back of the step. Though she tried to steady herself with her hands, there was nothing to grab hold of so she stumbled backwards, her legs twisting beneath her. Angry tears leapt from her eyes as she fell down several steps, finally landing on her bottom, the back of her head whacking against the handrail. Above her she saw an expression of pure horror on Henry's face as he bobbed down the steps towards her. Behind him, in the distance, was Charlie, in his baker's whites.

'I'm sorry Lily, are you hurt…?' Henry said, fear in his eyes and suddenly sounding more like the man she once so admired. 'I didn't mean for you to fall. Please, take this, will you? To help.'

Henry handed her a five-pound note and Lily blinked numbly, stunned by what had just happened, aware of the throbbing in her head and the shooting pain up her back. Tasting blood in her mouth from where she'd bitten down on her tongue, she slowly stood as Henry moved past her. He was closely followed by Charlie who, by grabbing Henry's arm, stopped him in his tracks.

'What have you done, you coward?' Charlie spat.

Henry took a moment to focus on Charlie before shaking off his hand and pushing him in the chest. 'Get your hands off me,' he said. 'You're the coward! Hiding behind your apron strings when you should be fighting for your country!'

Seething, Charlie lifted his fist to thump Henry, but regained his composure just in time. Instead he moved to within an inch of Henry's face and spat out his threat. 'Don't let me see you 'ere again unless you want to end up in my bread ovens,' he said, before turning his attention to Lily and helping her up.

Having twisted her ankle when she fell, she hopped on one foot while Henry marched away in the opposite direction.

Charlie folded Lily's arm around his own and tried to help take her weight so she could climb up the steps, but it was a slow and painful process.

'Carry her up!' came the familiar cry of Audrey's voice, from the top of the steps. Charlie and Lily looked up to see Audrey standing windswept at the top of the cliff, holding the chicken under her arm. Charlie grinned at Lily, lifted her up and carried her like a child in his arms.

'Maybe I should walk, I'm not sure you'll be able—' Lily began, blushing.

'Compared to them flour sacks you're as light as a feather,' Charlie interrupted, easily climbing the steps. 'Let's get you and that flamin' chicken inside.'

Chapter Twenty-Two

'The swine!' said Audrey, squeezing out a cotton wool ball and dabbing antiseptic ointment on the grazes on Lily's legs and arms. 'That no-good swine! I've a mind to take the kettle to his skull. You know we could call the police on him? Did he deliberately push you down the steps, Lily? It's almost as if wanted to have shot of you— God forbid. Keep still, this might sting.'

Lily and Elsie's eyes met and despite the tension in the room, they shared a small secret smile. There was nothing so unlikely as gentle Audrey hitting anyone over the head with a kettle. But the mention of the police made Lily nervous. Yes, Henry had pushed her as she tried to pass him, but she was sure he hadn't meant for her to fall down the steps. That was clear from the fear in his eyes. Besides, he'd obviously had a skinful. Despite how much she now despised Henry, she didn't think he was actually trying to kill her!

'He was terribly drunk,' Lily said. 'I've never seen him like that.'

'Do you think he'll come back?' said Elsie.

Lily flinched as Audrey dabbed more ointment on her cuts and bruises, thankful that the injuries were just superficial. Or so it seemed, anyway. Casting her eyes down to the gentle curve of her body under her dress, she privately fretted. She had recently been amazed to feel the baby somersaulting around in her womb – like a trapeze artist – but since Henry's shove, the baby had been completely still.

'He'll not be round here again,' said Charlie, washing his hands in the sink. 'Makes you wonder what went through his head, what with you expecting an' all. Doesn't bear thinkin' of, does it? I think Audrey has told you that we'll help you, Lily, if you… if you decide, oh you know what I'm sayin'.'

'Thank you,' said Lily. She had been convinced that Charlie resented her presence at the bakery, but tonight he had defended her. 'Thanks for sticking up for me out there.'

'Nothing to thank me for,' he said. 'Anyone with an ounce of decency in their bones would have done the same.'

Audrey put the cotton wool down next to the bowl of water, grabbed Charlie by the hand and pulled him towards her. 'No they wouldn't,' she said, tiptoeing to kiss him on the lips. 'He could have done Lily serious damage if it wasn't for you stepping in. You're a hero.'

'Don't talk rot,' Charlie said, crossly, unwrapping her arms from around him and leaving the room, muttering under his breath, 'I'm no hero.'

Audrey recoiled like a wounded animal, sighed deeply but quickly recovered, busying herself by stuffing the cotton wool into a packet. Lily's heart went out to her stepsister. Though Charlie was evidently a strong and kind man, he had the ability to crush Audrey with just a flick of his tongue. It wasn't that he raised his voice or spoke to her in a stern manner, like her own father did to Daphne, it was something more subtle, as if he silently blamed her for something, but wasn't saying what.

'Let me fill the tin bath with warm water for you, Lily,' Audrey said. 'All the five-inch ration of it!'

'Thanks Audrey,' she said, resting a hand on her bump. 'I can't stop shaking and shivering. Henry was like a different man to the one I knew. So full of anger and hatred.'

'Full of fear more like,' said Audrey, topping up the teapot. 'He doesn't hate you, Lily. In fact he obviously liked you very much at one time. I reckon he's terrified of what he's done and it's soul-crushing guilt that's turned his insides mean and sour. I see it with my Charlie all the time in different ways. When he's needled about something it comes out as about another matter entirely. Men are a riddle, but it doesn't take a genius to work them out.

Henry Bateman is scared stiff his new, stuck-up wife will find out about you and that's about the sum of it.'

Lily shivered again and Elsie took off her cardigan and draped it over her shoulders and poured her another cup of strong tea.

'Thank you,' said Lily, watching her hands tremble as she lifted the cup to her lips.

Henry's cruel words ran through her mind on repeat. *Dirty little secret*. His behaviour made her, for the first time, feel protective of the baby growing inside her and, when she felt it move again, an unfamiliar surge of what she could only guess was maternal love, or relief perhaps, powered through her. Confusing thoughts and emotions plagued her and she pulled Elsie's cardigan tighter over her shoulders.

'Oh blimey,' she said as the five-pound note that Henry had given her fell to the floor. Dropping them onto the table as if the notes were on fire, she shook her head. The presence of the money made her feel even more ashamed, as if she was no better than the street girls who frequented disreputable establishments in certain parts of town.

'What the heck is that?' said Elsie. 'Five pounds? Did he give you this?'

'You'll have to give it away,' said Audrey. 'Donate it to charity. I'm sure the Children's Society would be glad of it.'

'Why don't you keep it as payment for my board,' Lily said. 'That money was owed to me. When Henry sacked me he didn't pay me for all the weeks I'd worked there. I'll not have it myself, but I'd like it if you kept it.'

Audrey refused the money, but Lily decided she would secretly put it in her cash tin, or in the bureau drawer with all her paperwork, for her to find at a later date.

'I'll decide what to do with it tomorrow,' she said, standing shakily on her legs. 'I'm so tired and these bruises are aching.'

In the bath, listening to Audrey and Elsie talking in quiet, serious voices about what had happened that night, Lily inspected the pale skin stretched over her bump, running her finger over the red welts that Henry had left with the pointed end of his umbrella – and where she'd fallen down the stone steps. The Henry she'd seen earlier bore no resemblance to the Henry she had fallen for at the Ministry of Information. 'I'm sorry,' he had said, revealing a flash of his former self. 'I didn't mean to hurt you.'

Lily breathed deeply, trying to make sense of the last few hours, but feeling overcome with tiredness. Drying off and pulling on her underwear, she stopped dead when she noticed a drop of bright red blood in her white undies.

'Oh please God, no,' she said, fresh tears leaping into her eyes.

The doctor ordered complete bed rest for Lily and, as keeper of the doctor's orders, Audrey spent the next few days running up and down the stairs from the shop floor to Lily's bedroom as often as she could be spared from the bakery to keep up her spirit and strength.

'Bought you some hotpot, bread, vitamin A and D,' she said, bringing in a tray of nourishing food and placing it on the side table for Lily who, most days, was sat up in bed gazing out the window deep in thought, or sitting with her pen poised over a writing pad, balls of scrunched-up paper on the floor, her copper hair hanging loose and beautifully contrasting against the white skin of her pale shoulders.

'I need to write to my father and Daphne,' said Lily, showing her carefully written words with lines drawn through them. 'But I can't find the words.'

Though Audrey chose carefully who she told about Lily's condition, news ripped through the neighbourhood like wildfire and the very idea of Audrey's stepsister in trouble, despite her being an unmarried girl, touched some of Bournemouth's bigger hearts. Even Pat brought round a basket of wool and needles, so that Lily could get on with some knitting for the Forces while she lay in bed.

'Can't have you sitting there in bed bone idle,' Pat said, while Audrey winked at Lily. 'There are jobs need doing even when you're laid up.'

Though Lily had rested well, she was in low spirits and confided in Audrey that she was missing her father dreadfully. 'He must be feeling the same,' Audrey told her. 'Why don't I write on your behalf?'

So, Audrey wrote a short letter to Victor and Daphne saying that she was planning to visit London because there was an important family matter they needed to discuss. She gave a date and time for her visit and, taking the letter to the post office, anguish swept through her. The rift between her and Daphne and Victor had gathered momentum over the years, but now Lily needed all of their support. Daphne had used to be a kind, warm-hearted woman who loved William and Audrey, but when her husband died the grief seemed to suffocate her spirit. When she married Victor she changed, and their mother–daughter relationship disintegrated. Perhaps Lily's baby would be the glue to bring them back together. Her family might be badly broken, thought Audrey, but was it beyond mending?

Chapter Twenty-Three

Early August saw the pale skies over the Channel plagued with waves of German raiders attacking the south coast, or dumping their unused bombs after attacking major cities inland on their way back to Germany. There was also the first pamphlet raid on the south coast, where papers containing one of Hitler's speeches, 'A Last Appeal To Reason', fluttered through the air like leaves.

'Rather them than bombs!' Charlie had said, throwing a handful of pamphlets into the fire.

Though the RAF continued to valiantly defend Britain, chasing away enemy planes through the clouds, the air-raid siren frequently wailed its warnings. The businesses on Fisherman's Road did their best to cope with the constant disruptions, some offering their basements as temporary air shelters open to all in the event of a siren. It played havoc with the baking though – whole batches of buns and cakes were spoiled – so it was decided that if Audrey had just put the cakes in the oven when a siren sounded, Charlie would stay by the ovens, using the protection of the strong bakery table as shelter if need be.

'I didn't build that Anderson shelter for it to sit empty,' said Charlie, when Audrey insisted she'd rather stay with him. So Audrey reluctantly used the shelter, often taking ingredients in with her. Grating carrots for the carrot cake mixture was a better use of time than worrying, after all.

Mid-month, when a weariness had set into the bones of the town, a letter came for Audrey, not from Daphne and Victor as she had hoped (and slightly feared), but with a French postmark. Sitting at the kitchen table during a two-minute break, half a sandwich in her mouth, she opened the envelope, which held the hint of an unfamiliar perfume, and scanned the short handwritten note. It was from Jacques' mother. Thanking Audrey and Charlie for the hospitality they had showed Jacques while he was in Bournemouth, of which he had apparently spoken of with great fondness, she wrote that she thought Audrey would want to know – and that Lily should know – that Jacques was missing in action, presumed killed. *'My heart is broken,'* his mother had written in pale blue ink. *'Our family is in ruins.'*

Clutching the letter in her hand, Audrey dropped her sandwich and closed her eyes for a long moment. The normal sounds of the bakery carried on all around her, but she sat in silence, a hard ball of grief sinking deep into the pit of her stomach. *That beautiful boy is dead*, she thought numbly, remembering the startling colour of his eyes: summer skies and swimming pools.

The sound of Lily's laughter in the shop jolted Audrey from her desperate sadness and she quickly pushed the letter back into the envelope and stuffed it into the bureau drawer where she kept her correspondence and where she'd put Jacques' love letter for safekeeping.

Pushing the chair into the table and in a trance-like state, she watered the geraniums and the cucumber plants on the windowsill before walking out into the backyard and staring up at the sky, her hands on her hips. She wasn't a God-fearing woman, but at least if she was, there would be someone to rage and scream at, to shake her fists at in bitter fury. Instead, her sadness about Jacques' loss had to be controlled, just as she had to contain her fears about the safety of dearest William. As with all the women she knew who had lost their husbands, sons, brothers, uncles, cousins, friends and neighbours in this loathsome, detestable war, there was nothing to do and nowhere to go with the pain of loss except bury it deep.

Pushing open the door of the Anderson shelter and closing it behind her, she covered her face as she sobbed silently into a cushion, cursing Hitler and cursing the war. That darling boy was gone. He had loved Lily and she had never known. Audrey had not yet given her his letter.

She snapped up her head when the door opened, to see Charlie's silhouette, his white apron flapping in the breeze, the *Bournemouth Echo* in his hand.

'Audrey?' Charlie asked. 'Whatever's wrong? I was on my way to the privy when I heard you.'

'Oh Charlie,' she said in a whisper, her face red and wet with tears, her hair escaping the pins. 'It's Jacques. He's missing in action, presumed dead. That lovely young boy! His life wiped out... like that.' Audrey clicked her fingers together.

Charlie came into the shelter and sat down heavily on the bench opposite her, shaking his head in shock. He brought the smell of fresh-baked bread with him wherever he went. She leaned over and rested a hand on his knee.

'I can't sit here any longer and do nothing,' he said, pointing to his heart, a tremor in his voice. 'I've too much rage and sorrow in here. We don't know where William is, the Stringer boys are dead, the Collingham lad is a prisoner of war and now Jacques, who was sharing our table not two months ago. Albert will be signing up soon, when he comes of age and he's barely out of school. I can't watch any more of 'em fall, Audrey, I simply can't do it.'

Charlie's mouth contorted with emotion and Audrey's heart broke all over again.

'Charlie love—' she said, but he raised a hand.

'I know what you're going to say,' he said, before standing up. 'And I don't want to hear it just now. Sometimes you... you... suffocate me!'

'But Charlie, I...' she started, her voice faltering.

'I need to get on,' Charlie snapped. 'Dry your eyes.'

Charlie opened the shelter door to find Lily standing outside holding two envelopes. Her face was whiter than white, her entire body trembling. Charlie patted her on the shoulder and walked past into the bakery, leaving Audrey and Lily together. Audrey knew immediately what had happened. Her mouth fell open and she shook her head in dismay.

'Oh Lily,' she started. 'I'm sorry.'

'I went to put the ledger book in the bureau,' Lily said, barely audible. 'And I found these letters. I don't understand. Has Jacques been writing to me? Have I read this right? Is he dead?'

Audrey dried her eyes and extended her arms to Lily, who looked fit to faint. Audrey talked quickly and quietly, desperate for Lily to understand the reasons why she had kept his letter hidden.

'Jacques gave me a letter to give to you when he left the bakery to return to service,' Audrey said, holding Lily's hands. 'I thought you had so much on your mind, with deciding what to do about the baby, that his letter would be too much for you to cope with. He didn't know you were pregnant and you would have had to tell him. I kept it safe and was waiting for the right moment to give it to you. And then the letter came this morning from his mother. I'm so terribly sorry.'

Audrey's voice broke and she frantically studied Lily's face for her response. She expected tears but instead a thunderous expression darkened her features.

'You're just like my father!' Lily cried. 'Keeping me wrapped up in cotton wool! It isn't up to you, Audrey. You're not my mother. I don't even have a mother! If I did I wouldn't be here, like this, my life in tatters!'

Lily fell to her knees in the soil by the shelter, as she broke down into gut-wrenching sobs. Audrey knelt by her, pulling Lily's head into her chest and rocking her back and forth, stroking her hair.

'I'm so sorry,' said Audrey. 'I'm sorry.'

'I didn't even get to say goodbye…' Lily spluttered.

Lily untangled herself from Audrey's grip and moved away, staggering backwards.

'How could you do that?' Lily said. 'The letter wasn't for you… you should never have even read it! Why did you read it?'

'It fell open,' said Audrey quietly. 'I shouldn't have done. I wanted to protect you, Lily. Your young shoulders have so much on them at the moment.'

Lily turned away and Audrey followed her inside, but she ran up the stairs and slammed the door to her bedroom. Meanwhile Maggie was hollering through from the shop floor.

'It's like Picadilly Circus in here,' she yelled. 'Is anyone going to join me?'

Audrey picked up a cup from the kitchen table and hurled it onto the floor, where it smashed into hundreds of tiny pieces.

'Damn it!' said Audrey, wiping the tears from her face with her sleeves, marching downstairs and through into the shop.

When Elsie arrived home, after her first day training as a 'conductorette' with Dorset and Hants Transport, her brain laden with the rulebook she'd had to master that day, she'd found Audrey in the flour loft, sweeping up flour that had escaped from the hessian flour sacks. Audrey's dark blonde hair and navy dress were white with a dusting of flour, her skin pink from the exertion of furiously sweeping. On seeing Elsie, Audrey stopped working and leaned one hand and her chin on the broom handle, smoothing down her apron with the other.

'What's that broom ever done to you?' Elsie asked, smiling at Audrey. 'I could hear you banging it a mile off. Is everything okay? Where's Lily? I was going to ask her and Mary if they'd like to come to visit my mother and the twins with me. I bought a bag of sweets for them to share and they want to hear all the details about the buses. I'll have to omit the wolf whistles and the gaping.' Elsie paused to roll her eyes. 'Honestly, Audrey,' she continued, 'you'd think half the men in Bournemouth had not seen a woman do a day's work before. One of the old boys there kept saying: "Now that the fairer sex have had to go out to work for a living," with his eyes burning a hole in my back. Makes me wonder: do men think that women who are at home working their fingers to the bone in the kitchen and raising families do it as a sort of hobby? I know a few who could set 'em straight!'

Audrey smiled, but Elsie knew right away that something was bothering her. She looked seriously upset. Elsie's thoughts went to Maggie and she vaguely wondered if this had anything to do with her borrowing that sugar? But when Audrey explained about the letter from Jacques' mother, all the while fiddling with the strings of her apron, Elsie saw that her friend was drowning in guilt.

'Lily's put herself to bed,' said Audrey. 'I've made a mess of this one. I thought I was doing the best thing, but I got it very wrong. I can understand why she's feeling broken-hearted.'

Elsie shook her head in dismay. Of course she could understand Lily's anguish over Jacques, but Lily couldn't blame Audrey, who was clearly distraught about his death. Audrey embodied kindness and open-heartedness, Lily surely knew that Audrey would rather die than do anything to hurt those she loved.

'Let me talk to her,' she said to Audrey. 'She has a tendency to wallow.'

Knocking briefly on the door of the bedroom she shared with Lily, Elsie entered the room with a 'Hello' to discover Lily had pulled down the blackout blinds, despite it still being light outside. Sitting in the darkness on her narrow bed and pulling off her work boots, hurling them onto the floor in relief, she waited for Lily to peer out from under the cream blanket. But she didn't. Elsie frowned. Lily's shape was visible, but there was no sound or movement. Her slightly scuffed shoes – brown leather with embossed dots – were neatly positioned on the floor by the bed. On the bedside table was a pot of Snowfire Vanishing Cream foundation and the filigree brooch she sometimes wore.

'Lily?' she said, peering at her outline more closely. When there was no answer, she gently shook the shape under the blanket, which quickly gave way. Yanking back the cover, she saw that pillows lay where she had thought Lily's body was. Crossing the room and opening the blackout blind, she scanned the streets below. Then, checking through the few belongings in her drawer, she realised that Lily had taken Jacques' drawing of her and a change of clothes, but nothing much else. Bertie was still in his cage, nibbling on a small pile of seeds, which Lily must have left for him.

She can't have gone far, she thought, racking her brains for where Lily might have gone in a town she barely knew. Lily was soon going to be a mother – she couldn't just run away when the going got tough. Elsie sighed. Lily had a lot of growing up to do – and quickly – and Elsie wasn't afraid of telling her as much when she found her.

Chapter Twenty-Four

As the last of the day's sun melted into the sea on the horizon, the light on the cliff-top was golden. Elsie enjoyed the warmth of the late sun on her skin as she walked towards Hengistbury Head, the headland where she imagined Lily might be. The day was so clear that the chalky white cliffs of the Needles on the Isle of Wight were pin-sharp and looked close enough to touch. Now though, much of the Isle of Wight was being used for military training. Glancing at the barbed wire on the beaches, she imagined the pre-war sounds of her own family enjoying the sun-soaked beaches, laughing wildly as they played cricket and her mother laid out a picnic, her twin sisters leaping carefree into the waves. Oh how she longed for those days. She was sick to the stomach of this war.

As she approached the Head, where beach huts, now requisitioned for military use, were visible, William floated into Elsie's mind. He was a constant presence in her thoughts; bobbing like a little fishing boat on the waves, far out at sea, unreachable. Pushing her hands into her pockets, she willed him to write to her again, to shed light on his actions. The 'not knowing' where he was or how he was feeling was worse, she thought, than finding out he no longer loved her. The 'not knowing' slowed her down, making her feel as though she had weights attached to her ankles.

'Oh Lily, there you are,' she said quietly, when she saw a flash of Lily's copper hair in the distance, like a flare being shot into the sky.

Finding her sitting on a bench near a wooded area on the Head, Elsie was struck by how pregnant she now looked in the checked maternity smock Audrey had bought her from a charity shop. Though Lily's complexion radiated health, she carried her bump awkwardly, as if it was an unwieldy, heavy parcel she needed to deliver to someone else.

'You didn't get far,' Elsie said, gently. Lily looked up and gave her a small smile.

'No,' she said. 'As usual I didn't have much of a plan. I just wanted to get out of the house. How did you know I'd be here?'

Elsie shrugged and sat down next to her on the bench. 'I know you like it here,' she said. 'And I didn't think you'd gone for good because Bertie was still in our room. Audrey told me what happened. I'm sorry.'

For a moment they sat together in silence watching the seagulls overhead, Elsie waiting for Lily to speak first.

'I was just so shocked,' Lily said eventually. 'I didn't think Audrey would do that sort of thing. And now Jacques is gone and I didn't get to tell him how much I enjoyed meeting him. He's died thinking his words meant nothing to me, that I actively ignored him!'

Elsie reached her hand across to reach for Lily's and gave it a gentle squeeze.

'It's so sad about Jacques,' Elsie said. 'There are no words, really.'

Lily nodded, removed her hand and felt for the letter in her pocket. She held it in the air, towards Elsie. 'Would you like to read his letter?' she asked, her voice trembling. 'I've never received anything like it, nor will I ever again. I knew he liked me, but… Go on, I want you to. Then you'll understand why I feel so wretched.'

Elsie took the letter, leaned back on the wooden bench and began to read. The passion in Jacques' words leapt off the page, clutching her heart and squeezing it. Reaching the end, Elsie held her hand over her mouth to stop herself from crying.

'Oh Lily,' she said. 'I've never read anything like it.'

The pain she felt for Lily and Jacques was genuine and intense, but she couldn't help reflect on her own situation. Reading Jacques' letter only served to make William's recent contact seem all the more vague. She battled to suppress the overwhelming disappointment she felt, taking an exaggerated deep breath, before handing the letter back to Lily.

'Treasure that,' she said. 'He must have felt that elusive thing people talk about and you read about in books – love at first sight.'

Lily nodded and put a hand on her forehead.

'His death,' she said. 'It's made me think differently about life. I realise now I've got to face up to things.'

Elsie nodded and raised her eyebrows, relieved that Lily was seeing sense.

'I do wish I'd done things differently,' Lily said. 'I had a good job and prospects in the city. Then I blew it for a man. I shouldn't have done what I did, but I *wanted* to go through with it. There's something in me, a wilfulness, that I can't keep up with.'

'Rebelliousness more like!' said Elsie. 'There's nothing wrong with being a rebel, but if you're going to take risks you've got to toughen up a bit. Yes, you're in a real fix now, but things are changing because of the war. People's lives have been turned upside down and they are having to adapt. You're no different.'

'Audrey has suggested that she and Charlie adopt the baby,' said Lily, biting her thumbnail. 'And I have just shouted at her, after all she's doing for me—'

'She'll forgive you,' said Elsie. 'Audrey is the kindest person I've ever met. If you were to consider adoption, you could guarantee that child would have a happy life with Audrey and Charlie. You could go back to London if that's what you want, get on with your own life…'

Lily sighed.

'And I'd get that bedroom to myself,' said Elsie, with a mischievous grin.

Lily laughed. 'Is it that bad to share a room with me?' she asked.

Elsie pretended to consider her answer. She scratched her chin and eventually shook her head. 'It's Bertie I have a problem with,' she said. 'He snores!'

Lily laughed again and when Elsie stood and offered Lily her hand, she accepted it. Elsie pulled her up from the bench and the pair linked arms as they walked down the slope of the Head and back towards the bakery.

Later, Audrey cooked a conciliatory tea of bacon, eggs and beans and served it with bread and tea. 'This is to say how sorry I am for earlier,' she said. After frying the bacon, she took out the rashers and heated the beans in the same pan, mingling the bacon fat with the tomato sauce – perfect for dipping bread into for a special treat.

'I'm sorry too,' said Lily. 'I shouldn't have said what I did.'

Later still, while listening to the news on the wireless, Elsie, Lily and Audrey congregated in the kitchen with their knitting. Lily put down her needles and held out her hand over the table towards Audrey, who immediately grasped it, her mouth a wobbly line. Audrey then extended her hand to Elsie, who grabbed it and squeezed her hand too. With a gentle laugh Elsie and Lily joined hands too, so that they formed a small circle of three.

'Listen,' said Audrey. 'I think we should raise a toast to Jacques, don't you?'

Gently releasing their hands, Audrey poured three small shots of brandy and each woman held up their glass to meet the others. The glasses gently clinked together.

'To Jacques,' Lily said.

'To Jacques,' repeated Audrey and Elsie, in unison, falling silent while taking a sip from their glasses.

As the trio let the liquid warm their throats and hearts, the air-raid siren began its awful wail.

'It never ends,' said Audrey, rising from her chair. 'I'll fetch Mary.'

With Mary in her arms, they headed to the shelter. Elsie lit a candle as the boom of distant explosions filled the air and the women and Mary sat wrapped in blankets, quietly talking in the flickering candlelight, while to the north of Bournemouth an RAF pilot was shot down by enemy aircraft. Failing to properly release his parachute, the young pilot careered through the skies to his certain death, another bright light suddenly extinguished.

Chapter Twenty-Five

'I'm not buying a ticket from you,' a woman spat at Elsie, who squared her shoulders, squeezed tight her fists, narrowed her eyes and clenched her jaw, ready for a fight.

Since getting her new job as one of twenty 'conductorettes' on the buses after two weeks of training, to replace the men who had gone to fight, she was learning a lot about the people of Bournemouth. Most were hard-working and polite, but there were some rude folk, she realised, who wanted to make trouble. Well, she thought now, feeling her blood boil, she wasn't having any of it.

'Why not?' Elsie asked, half knowing what was coming next.

The woman took a seat on the bus. 'I know your father is Italian,' she said. 'I know he's been interned as a prisoner of war. As I said, I'm not buying a ticket off you. Plus you girls look daft in them trousers.'

The windows of the buses had been covered so they wouldn't emit light, which gave the woman's face a horrible corpse-like tinge.

'It's the uniform,' said Elsie. 'Now do you want a ticket or not?'

It was poles apart from the feminine black dress she wore in her job at Beales Department Store, but Elsie felt smart in her uniform: a pair of trousers, coat and soft cap in a bright shade of green. She had got used to punching tickets and taking the fares and holding on tight when the bus driver, an old boy called Barry, took a sharp corner at speed, cigarette hanging out the corner of his mouth. She'd learned the routes off by heart and knew where the public air-raid shelters were, since in the event of a raid it was one of her jobs to help lead the passengers to safety.

For the first time since her father was taken away, the failed wedding and the bombing of her home, she felt she was doing something positive. Not only was she doing her bit for the war effort, she was earning enough money to help with the twins and Violet, so that they could slowly piece their lives back together since they had literally been blown apart. Being a conductorette was one of the only jobs where women and men were paid the same wage. She had sent a letter to her father, telling him what she was doing, knowing he'd be proud of her for looking after Violet and the girls. He'd written back saying she was a 'girl after my own heart' and that he was keeping busy in the camp on the Isle of Man, cutting men's hair. 'Even prisoners of war need their hair cut,' he'd written.

'So what have you got to say for yourself?' the woman asked. Some of the other passengers were craning their necks to see what was going on now. It had been a long shift and Elsie was tired out; her feet ached like hell and she was parched.

'Not that it's your business but yes, my father is Italian,' Elsie said, tripping over her words. 'He's on the Isle of Man when he should be here in his home town. Can I get you a ticket?'

'Doesn't that make you an alien too?' the woman said, her eyes boring through her. 'What's an alien doing on my buses taking my money? I can't trust your kind. I read in the paper a load more aliens had been carted off this week on a coach. Why weren't you on it?'

The woman had raised her voice. Passengers were staring wearily at her, clearly wishing she'd be quiet.

'Would you like a ticket?' Elsie repeated, her heart pounding in her chest.

The woman threw her fare on the floor of the bus, so Elsie had to bend over to pick it up.

'Eyetie spy,' the woman hissed.

Elsie's lips tightened into a grimace and she let out an exhausted sigh. People like this made her want to scream at the top of her lungs. There she was working hard, doing long shifts on the buses during the day, trying to earn enough to keep her family in food and clothes, helping passengers to safety when the air-raid siren sounded, and what was this woman doing to help?

'I'll tell you something else,' said the woman. She took a breath to continue but a stranger interjected.

'Seems to me like you've said more than enough, madam,' said a young man with a rich, deep voice like cream and butter. 'Why don't you keep your opinions to yourself? Nobody wants to hear them.'

Elsie turned on her heel to see who had spoken. A young man in uniform owned the voice. With cropped dark hair, shiny brown eyes and perfect white teeth, he was unspeakably dashing.

'Who are you to be telling me what to do?' the woman said, then, as the driver lurched around a tight corner, she bumped her head on the window and shouted out to the driver: 'Watch what you're doing, you lunatic!'

Grumbling and complaining, at the next stop the woman got off the bus, shaking her head in Elsie's direction as it drove away.

'Thank you,' said Elsie, watching the woman out of the window, before turning to the man, 'I was about to try out my right hook.'

'I wouldn't want to be on the receiving end of that,' the man laughed, introducing himself as Flying Officer Jimmy Browne, looking her directly in the eye.

It took her completely off-guard. Elsie's heart did a sudden – and forbidden – leap in her chest.

'I'm tougher than I look,' she said, cursing herself for blushing. Shocked by the fire ripping through her body, she averted her gaze, fiddling with the strap on her ticket machine instead.

'You don't seem like a girl who needs rescuing,' Jimmy said, with a short laugh. 'But that woman was giving me a headache. As if this war isn't headache enough. I'm sorry to hear about your pa. That's tough.'

Elsie smiled and nodded, busying herself with looking out of the blue-painted window. Her heart pounding, she told herself to get a grip. The bus continued up Commercial Road towards Poole

Hill and, feeling Jimmy's eyes still on her, she glanced at him a little crossly. Under his gaze she felt exposed. He looked away, a blush crawling up his cheek now too. He laughed a little and she rolled her eyes at herself and crossed her arms. Whatever this exchange was that was happening between them needed stopping right away. She cleared her throat.

'Going anywhere fancy?' she asked him, trying to sound normal.

'Er, there,' he said, pointing to a photographic studio further up the road. Servicemen would often go to photographic studios and have a postcard-sized photograph taken that they would send to their families. 'My gran will be missing me so I thought I'd send her a reminder I'm still alive and kicking. Want to come with me? It would make a much prettier photograph than me on my own.'

Elsie laughed and shook her head.

'How about fish and chips then?' he persisted. 'You must be hungry. There are singers on at Bobby's restaurant tonight.'

Elsie shook her head again, holding on tight as the bus came to a halt. 'I have a long shift,' she said, smiling.

'This is me!' Jimmy called out, just before he stepped off the bus. 'What's your name?'

'It's Elsie,' she replied. 'My name's Elsie.'

'Goodnight Elsie,' he said, pretending to be in an invisible boxing match, punching the air with a right hook.

As the bus moved off, she cracked up laughing and followed him with her eyes for as long as she could, before he disappeared into the photographic studio.

'Someone's got an admirer,' called out Barry, the driver.

'Don't be soft,' said Elsie, reddening. 'I'm engaged, you know.' *And I should be married*, she thought but didn't say.

For the rest of her shift Jimmy's appreciative and inquisitive stare popped into her mind, making her feel quite guilty. A tiny part of her was intrigued by Jimmy and flattered by his attention. Many girls who had sweethearts abroad still stepped out with other chaps, but she knew it wouldn't be right and would only serve to make her feel William's absence even more strongly. Yes, Jimmy's attention was nice, but it was William she longed for, his loving smile, fair hair and cheekbones sharp as knives. The song of his mouth harp, the curve of his body as he played, the creases by his eyes as he grinned, his gentle touch. Holding hands.

At the end of her long shift, when the buses stopped running at 10.15 p.m., Elsie took in her ticket machine to the depot, to check money and tickets and pay in her takings.

'Any word from your young man lately?' asked Judith, another newbie conductorette. 'William is it?'

'No word,' said Elsie, shaking her head.

'Don't fret,' said Judith, lighting up a cigarette. 'We're all in the same boat. My chap's on the other side of the world and I haven't heard from him in months. I sense he's safe though, somehow. See you tomorrow!'

Setting off back to Audrey's on her bicycle in the still, balmy night, Elsie's legs felt like blocks of lead. Narrowing her eyes to see better in the darkness, she listened out for pedestrians or motorists driving with their lights off, who could suddenly seemingly appear out of nowhere if one wasn't listening properly. She longed to talk to William about how different the town was in blackout, how quiet it seemed, how aware you became of the stars and the moon, of night and day.

'Where are you William?' she whispered into the night, trying to sense if he was safe. 'Where *on earth* are you?'

Chapter Twenty-Six

'Have you heard?' said Pat, blowing into the bakery door in her russet coat like a flurry of autumn leaves. 'About the Shearing lad?'

Everyone in the bakery stopped what they were doing and faced Pat. Lily put down the buns she was holding and put an arm around Mary's shoulder. The girl had taken to helping in the shop before school. Just over a week ago the Shearing lad – a twelve-year-old boy from Moordown in Bournemouth – had been lost at sea on the torpedoed evacuee ship, *City of Benares*, en route to Canada. His parents had just put a death notice in the *Echo* and the whole town shared their grief.

'What is it, Pat?' said Audrey, her hand flat against her throat.

Pat smiled. 'He's safe!' she exclaimed. 'He was found in a lifeboat eight days after the ship had been torpedoed.'

'Eight days!' said Flo. 'It must have been terrifying and so bitterly cold! Gracious me, that's a miracle.'

'I know, it's like he's back from the dead,' said Pat.

Mary pulled away from under Lily's arm and ran out through the back of the bakery. Lily frowned, but remained inside to hear more of the story. Her thoughts went immediately to Jacques. If his body had never been found, was there a tiny glimmer of hope that he could still be alive?

'The boy's parents are overwhelmed of course,' continued Pat. 'His mother apparently stood out in the street late last night and shouted that he was safe to all her neighbours. They were calling out of their windows and doors saying how glad they are! There were six children and forty adults saved, all of them kept going by a young lady who told them stories and massaged their limbs to keep out the cold.'

'Well,' said Mrs Collingham, wiping her eyes, 'I think she deserves a round of applause, whoever that young lady is.'

Mrs Collingham started to clap and soon everyone waiting in the queue was clapping, until the bakery resounded with applause for the Shearing boy and the young lady who had helped keep him and the other stranded passengers alive.

'That'll show Hitler what we're made of,' said Pat.

'Can you believe he's starting on Greece now?' said Mrs Collingham. 'And did you read about Buckingham Palace being bombed? Even the Royal Family can't escape.'

'London's getting it bad all right,' said Flo. 'The East End's had raids every night since the start of September! Whole city is up in flames at night. My sister's friend who works as a nurse up there says they've even bombed schools and hospitals, would you believe?'

The women in the bakery sighed and shook their heads in disbelief.

Lily's hand shook as she prepared Mrs Collingham's bread order. The talk of London had made her worry. What if her father and her stepmother had been victims of a raid? Would she know? It had been months since she'd left London and though she'd written to her father early on and had one reply from him, she hadn't heard word from him in weeks.

'I suppose Londoners have just got to set their teeth and grin and bear it, haven't they?' said Pat, with a resigned shrug. 'We've all got to.'

Elsie came into the bakery, yawning, ready to go to work on the buses.

'Late night, Elsie?' asked Audrey.

'Yes,' she said. 'I was helping serve refreshments to the AFS and I didn't turn in until 2 a.m.'

'You're working so hard,' said Audrey in concern. 'William would be proud of you. Did you hear about the Shearing lad?'

Elsie broke out into a smile and nodded. 'I'm so glad for his family,' she said. She and Audrey briefly held hands, sharing a knowing glance. Lily knew they were both hoping for news of William and ultimately his safe return.

'I'm going to find Mary and tell her it's time for school,' said Lily. 'I'll be back in a minute.'

Outside, there was no sign of Mary.

'Mary?' Lily called, but she wasn't in the backyard and the gate leading out to the pavement was swinging open.

Lily went into the street and held her hand over her eyes to protect them from the glare of the sun, as she scanned the area for Mary.

'Mary?' she called again, walking out towards the overcliff, where she saw Mary sitting in the long grass, poking at the soil with a stick, one sock up to her knee, the other rolled down.

'What is it, Mary?' asked Lily, sitting down on the ground next to her. 'Are you upset?'

Mary shrugged her shoulders and continued to poke at the floor.

Lily sat down in the grass next to the little girl, staring at the soil she was poking with the stick. It had been months since Mary arrived at the bakery and she still hadn't spoken a word, but none of them had pushed her, instead believing she would speak in her own time.

'Do you like it here?' Lily asked and Mary nodded.

'Do you miss your mother?' Mary shrugged again.

'I think there's something going on inside that you probably need to get out,' said Lily. 'Whatever it is, you can tell me when you're ready. Now, what have you got here? I think it's a stag beetle. Isn't it amazing?'

The stag beetle's black shell shone with an almost blue tinge in the sunlight.

'Do you know what stag beetles do?' said Lily. 'They live in a piece of wood for years as larvae before they make a cocoon and transform into adults. Then they come out in summer, just for the summer, like this one and look for a mate. They don't have long to shine, do they? So we should feel extra lucky to have seen one.'

Mary looked up at Lily then, her eyes glassy. Lily felt absolutely sure the little girl was desperate to speak, but that she just couldn't find the words.

Chapter Twenty-Seven

It wasn't safe. Audrey knew that. For weeks now London had been under attack in day and night-time raids, in a campaign known as the 'Blitz', and she had prepared herself for the worst. Charlie had pleaded with her not to go, but despite the travel restrictions she had made her way to the capital, as the need to tell Victor about Lily and see Daphne was pressing heavily upon her.

Making her way along the capital's streets, pulling her blue coat tightly around her and clutching her gas mask case and the Christmas fruit cake wrapped in brown paper, she could hardly believe her eyes. Everywhere she looked there was horrific bomb damage: jagged shells of buildings rising out of flattened debris into the sky like stalagmites, rows upon rows of houses blown apart, parts of houses still standing as if cut open with a carving knife, entire streets decimated and reduced to bricks and rubble and bent girders jutting out at awful angles, people working with shovels and pickaxes or just standing staring, as if frozen in disbelief. Audrey's mouth fell open as she watched a milkman, wearing his white coat, carrying full bottles of milk across a bombsite, still delivering his round despite the ruins and wreckage.

'Mornin',' he called to her with a smile. 'Cool wind, ain't it?'

'Morning,' she said, full of admiration for the milkman's stoicism. 'Good day to you.'

With glass and debris crunching underfoot, she held her breath as she walked towards Balham High Street, south London, where Daphne and Victor lived. With every footstep, her heart broke a hundred times over as the signs of Londoners' determination to carry on, no matter what, became evident. Never more so than in the middle of the high street; early signs of Christmas were creeping into carefully put-together window displays, but in the road outside the shops there was a massive crater, over ten feet deep, where a bomb had struck outside the tube station. Audrey gasped as she tried to process what had happened. Being lifted out of the crater by a giant crane was a London bus. Suspended in mid-air, the bus was a surreal sight, making the ordinarily busy street seem like something from a ghastly dream. Increasingly terrified for her mother's safety, ghosts from years past, the faces of school friends and neighbours leapt into her mind's eye, vying for attention. *Where are you all now?* she thought, biting the side of her cheek until she tasted blood.

Finding Milkwood Street, where her mother and Victor lived, Audrey's heart pounded so hard in her chest she feared it would burst. She scanned the street, a row of terraced two-up, two-down Victorian houses, some of them with pots of colourful flowers in their postage-stamp-size front gardens where the metal gates had been removed, collected for war use.

Audrey was relieved to see that none of the immediate neighbouring houses had suffered a direct hit, though some windows had shattered and were boarded up. Her legs trembled and nausea hit as she approached the front door of the house that she'd lived in for over a year in a stepfamily that was more out of step than in. Lifting her hand to knock on the black-painted door, it was as if she'd frozen solid and was unable to do it.

'Give me strength,' she whispered, worrying she might keel over at any moment. Racked with doubt about her decision to come to London, she was tempted to turn on her heel and run straight back to the train station, but squeezing her eyes shut, she took a deep breath, knocked, stepped back from the door and waited. There were hurried footsteps inside the house, the sound of a key clattering in the lock, and then it quickly opened to reveal Daphne, who looked carefully put together. The sophisticated black dress she wore was not one that Audrey recognised, but it looked brand new, with pretty cream lace collars and cuffs. Was this for Audrey's benefit?

'Audrey,' Daphne said in a choked whisper. An incredulous smile appeared and disappeared on her mother's face in a blink, as she opened the door wider. 'Audrey, come in. You wrote to tell us you were coming, but I didn't know whether you would. I've been sitting here since dawn, waiting for you.'

Daphne ushered Audrey into the dark hallway, where mother and daughter stood opposite one another, apparently not knowing what to do. Audrey longed for her mother to take her in her arms and hold her tight, but in a beat, the moment was lost. It reminded Audrey of the day her father died. Though Audrey had been desperate for her mother's comfort, Daphne had preferred to keep a stiff upper lip.

'I wrote what time I'd be here,' said Audrey. 'It's good to see you, Mother.'

Trying not to cry, she leaned towards Daphne and briefly embraced her, resting her chin on her shoulder. Daphne's thin body trembled with emotion usually pent up and buried deep inside, until she recovered her poise and moved away from Audrey, clasping her hands together in front of her as if she couldn't trust herself not to grab Audrey and never let go.

'Can I ask you a question?' Audrey said quietly. 'Why have you never replied to my letters? I've always written to you with love in my heart.'

Daphne, quickly wiping her eyes, moved across the hall and, with shaking hands, opened a drawer in the bureau, where a bundle of letters were carefully tied together with a length of red ribbon.

'I read them all and I wanted to write back,' she said, her hand at her throat. 'But after what William did and the way you stood by him, I felt perhaps you'd made a choice… I felt…'

Daphne stopped talking and Audrey watched her struggle to put her feelings into words. Staring into the middle distance, she gave up with a small shake of her head and Audrey knew they were both recalling the night that Victor and Daphne insisted William leave the house. There had been a terrible fight, with things said that could never be unsaid and the glass frame of her dead father's photograph crushed under the heel of Victor's shoe, ground into the floor until his face was erased. Then it became physical. Daphne slapped William around the face and he, unbelievably, slapped her back. Victor had thrown William from the house so hard he had fallen spread-eagled onto the road, shouting that he was never allowed to return.

'You must understand why I had to go with William,' said Audrey. 'He's my little brother. I had to look after him. I couldn't stay here.'

'Well there you are then,' said Daphne, defensively. 'You made your choice.'

'But I've written to you numerous times,' Audrey said, her voice cracking. 'I don't think we should hold grudges, especially in these times. Father wouldn't want that, would he?'

Daphne sighed and shook her head. 'I know,' she said, her eyes flicking up. 'I thought about replying but…'

'But Victor said you couldn't?' remarked Audrey. 'How can you let him dictate what you do? Why don't you stand up to him? I've never understood how he's got such a hold over you.'

Daphne looked up at Audrey. She seemed exhausted by the conversation. Perhaps, just as Audrey had done over the years, she had been playing out this scenario for a long time.

'He's never wanted to share me,' said Daphne. 'He wants me all to himself. Ever since William attacked me and Victor and you both left, he considers you disloyal and undeserving of me. He loves me, Audrey.'

Audrey knew she should say *And so do I* to her mother, but a certain stubbornness stopped her from doing so.

'William was fifteen and grieving for his father,' said Audrey. 'You're his mother! You should defend him!'

'William almost broke Victor's jaw,' said Daphne.

Audrey stopped herself from saying that Victor deserved everything he got and that if William hadn't have thrown a punch at Victor after what he said about their father, she would have been sorely tempted.

'But that was because he knew that Victor took you from Father,' said Audrey. 'And then Father died and Victor said we weren't allowed to mention him by name in his house. He was talking about our father, the man you once loved, who loved us and who we loved and who I still miss.'

Audrey's voice cracked and Daphne stared at her hands.

'Victor has a certain idea about the way things should be,' said Daphne, more softly now. 'He doesn't see any use in talking about and dredging up the past. Of course, his heart's truly broken now that Lily has let him down.'

'What did she tell you?' asked Audrey, quickly wiping her eyes with a hanky, glad that the conversation was moving on.

'She said she'd arranged to go and stay with you, which Victor wasn't happy about,' said Daphne. 'Unfortunately we had to hear from her superior at work that she'd been let go for bad behaviour. She had such a good job you know? Victor wouldn't let her out of his sight for weeks but she pushed him and pushed him, until one night Lily suddenly decided she needed to get away…'

At that moment, Victor came into the room and nodded at Audrey, but didn't smile.

'Victor,' said Audrey. 'I wanted to talk to you about Lily, as you know she's staying with me and…'

'Indeed,' he said. 'I am aware.'

Audrey struggled to find the words, suddenly doubting whether she'd done the right thing by coming here. There was something incredibly intimidating about Victor. It was his strict and sombre manner, the way he held his six-foot frame rigidly upright, the dour expression on his face and his crisp, serious tone. Audrey felt her own confidence diminish in his presence.

'I know that Lily is pregnant,' he said, matter-of-factly. 'If that's what you've come running to report.'

'You know?' Audrey asked, aghast. 'How do you know?'

Victor put his hands behind his back and rocked on the balls of his feet, like a policeman. 'I have been down to Bournemouth to check on her, more than once, and it's impossible not to see that she is,' he said.

Audrey reeled. 'You came to Bournemouth but you didn't talk to her?' she said. 'Were you following her? She's been paranoid about someone following her, was it you?'

Victor stared beyond Audrey, through the net curtains and out into the street. 'I wanted to know she was well enough,' he said. 'She's my daughter. Despite how silly she's been, I care for her deeply.'

'Silly?' said Audrey. 'She's a young woman who made a mistake, who needs her family on her side. For goodness sake, you and Mother were together when our father was dying but pretended you weren't! Don't be hypocritical.'

'It wasn't like that,' said Daphne, holding her hand to her forehead. 'Victor comforted me when your father fell ill, that's all.'

Audrey knew that wasn't true. She knew from what she'd seen with her own teenage eyes, but she wasn't about to enter into another confrontation now. She had come here to get some help for Lily, not to go over old ground.

'Lily's going to have the baby at Christmas and I'm here to ask what she dare not,' Audrey said. 'Would you consider supporting her if she came back to London?'

Victor shook his head. 'I will welcome my daughter back,' he said. 'But I will not have that bastard child in my house. This is my house, these are my rules.'

'But she's your daughter and her child will be your grandchild—' said Audrey.

Daphne raised a hand to stop her speaking. 'Audrey, please listen to Victor,' she said, shaking her head.

'These are my rules,' Victor said, turning on his heel, leaving the room and slamming shut the door of his study.

Audrey, physically shaking, glared at Daphne for not standing up to Victor, feeling appalled that her mother couldn't be more gutsy.

'He won't change his mind,' said Daphne.

What about you? Audrey wanted to ask. She hated the fact that she thought her mother weak and useless, that she hadn't even asked how William, her own son, was, let alone how Lily was faring. Her disappointment weighed heavily upon her, but this was wartime, and every day in London could be your last. The people who had lost their lives in the tube station the previous night would never again have the opportunity to see their families. She had to leave Daphne's home on good terms.

'I should go,' Audrey said, moving towards the front door. 'I brought you this fruit cake for Christmas. It's not iced, but with dried fruit and nuts so hard to come by, I thought you would like it. If you change your mind, you are welcome to visit me in Bournemouth. We're a family down there. One that I hope Father would have been proud of and would want to be a part of. Look what he did for you. He gave you his consent to be with Victor when he became ill and learned of your friendship. He didn't make life difficult for you. He loved you too much for that. Can you not extend that understanding to me, William and Lily?'

Daphne's face remained expressionless. She opened the door for Audrey but, just before she left, grabbed Audrey's arm.

'Victor worries about Lily,' Daphne said, her voice tremulous. 'She should know that he loves her.' She retrieved a small parcel from the living room and handed it to Audrey. 'It's from Victor to Lily,' said Daphne. 'He wrapped it up the night she left for Bournemouth. It's a book of poetry. Give it to her for Christmas.'

Audrey travelled home in a state of complete turmoil. By the time she reached Bournemouth she had decided to assign Daphne and Victor a room in her mind that she would leave firmly shut and open only when absolutely necessary. Her priority was the people in Bournemouth, who needed her.

When she arrived back at the bakery, Lily was waiting for her in the kitchen. She poured Audrey a cup of Ovaltine.

'Your father already knew about the baby,' Audrey said calmly. 'He's been down here to check on you, to see for himself that you are safe. I wonder if it's him you think has been following you?'

'What?' Lily answered, horrified. 'Why would he do that and not speak to me? All this time I've been thinking something sinister.'

Audrey sighed and shook her head. She wanted to speak her mind and tell Lily what she really thought about Victor and his moral high ground. But, looking at Lily's sweet face, her red hair tumbling down over her shoulders, she couldn't.

'He loves you,' she said, with a smile. 'He wants you home, but not with your baby in tow. They can't accept your indiscretion, Lily, I'm so sorry.'

'I knew as much,' said Lily.

'I get the feeling he wants to pretend the whole thing isn't happening,' said Audrey, taking a seat at the kitchen table. 'Your father gave me this. He said it's a small gift for Christmas, since you won't be home.'

Lily accepted the parcel with a sad smile and hugged it close to her chest.

'Despite how he's behaving, I still love him,' Lily said, looking crushed. 'I miss him dreadfully. My whole life has been about making him proud. Yes, he's stern and strict and I thought I wanted to get away from him completely, but without him to make proud I wonder who it's all for.'

How dreadful, Audrey thought to herself, to not stand beside your adoring daughter in her hour of need. She bit her lip, thinking that if she ever had a son or daughter she would put them first. Always. Family should find it in their hearts to forgive and love, no matter what.

Chapter Twenty-Eight

'I'll not have any fingers left soon,' Audrey said to Mary with a gentle laugh, as the little girl tightened her grip on Audrey's hand. 'There's nothing to be nervous of, Mary dear.'

The bakery shelves were empty at the end of another busy Saturday and while Maggie swept up the crumbs and tidied up the shop, Audrey was taking Mary to the Evacuee Centre, which had been set up for local evacuees to meet their mothers or families, whenever they were able to travel.

'It'll be lovely to see your mother, won't it?' said Audrey, suffering a pang of regret about how disastrous her meeting with her own mother had been. 'Perhaps you can tell her about helping me with the cakes. You're very good at making the currant buns. And eating them, I might add!'

Audrey chuckled and Mary looked up at her with enormous brown eyes. She gave a slight, nervous smile and Audrey squeezed her little hand in reassurance.

Inside the centre there were signs of Christmas already. A fake Christmas tree was waiting to be erected, half in and half out of a cardboard box, and there was a Christmas collection box for Bournemouth lads in services overseas. Audrey tried to hide her concerns, but why was Mary so nervous about today? Was it something to do with the reason she didn't talk? Audrey had put her silence down to being evacuated and thrown into a new life in Bournemouth, but now she questioned that. What if her mother was a cruel person, or had damaged Mary in some way?

'Can you see her?' Audrey asked.

Mary pointed to a woman sitting stiffly on a hard-backed chair, facing in the opposite direction to the door, staring out of the window. Dressed in a threadbare grey dress that looked two sizes too big, she held a cup of tea and sipped it slowly.

'Is that her?' Audrey asked and Mary nodded.

Mary's mother, Dot, was so quietly spoken Audrey had to strain to hear her. With skin as grey as her dress and pronounced purple circles around her eyes, she looked as if she hadn't slept in months, and it seemed to cost her a great effort to smile. She opened her arms slightly and, though she was hesitant, Mary moved in towards her to receive a hug. After a few moments, she moved away and perched on the edge of a chair, staring down at her shoes. Audrey looked from Mary to Dot in confusion. This wasn't the joyful reunion she had anticipated.

'Dot, is everything okay?' said Audrey. 'I'll leave you to it, if you like, and come back later? I was going to have a look in WH Smith & Sons.'

'No,' said Dot, grabbing Audrey's hand. 'Please, I'd like to speak to you first. There's something I must explain. Mary, can you play outside for a moment?'

Mary, relieved at having been released from the awkward reunion, flew into the garden and kicked around in the leaves that had fallen from the poplar trees.

'Has she spoken yet?' asked Dot.

Audrey shook her head. 'Not a word. Is there something I should know?'

'I hoped moving away would "cure" her,' said Dot. 'Help her forget about what happened. Help her forget…'

Dot held her hand over her cheeks, where the colour was rising.

'Our house was hit by a high-explosive bomb and incendiary bombs,' said Dot. 'The roof caught fire and collapsed. We were all in the house, me, Mary and her brother, Eddie.'

'Brother?' Audrey said. 'I didn't realise she had a brother.'

Dot shook her head, briefly closing her eyes. 'There was no siren warning,' she said. 'One moment we were asleep, the next the house was on fire. Part of the wall collapsed in the children's bedroom and the bricks crashed onto Mary's bed, but Eddie was sleeping in with her. He often climbed into her bed to keep warm and cosy even though I kept telling him to stay in his own bed. He was buried by the bricks. Mary tried to dig him out. Her fingers were bleeding from scraping at them. She was screaming his name and he was screaming hers until—'

Dot's fists screwed up into tight balls and she took a sharp intake of breath. Audrey forced herself not to weep.

'They were that close, the two of them, that it broke Mary's heart. It's broken my heart. Eddie's coffin was only this big.' She gestured a small space with her arms. 'He had blonde curls, pink cheeks just like the baby on the Pears soap advert, and he'd hold his arms up like this for me or Mary to pick him up for a cuddle. He was a beautiful boy. Always giggling, loved cuddles. Of course, Mary thought it was her fault, because she'd said he could get into her bed.'

Dot paused to take a sip of her tea. Her hands were shaking so much she could barely put the cup back down in the saucer.

'After that the house was unsafe, so we went to stay with my sister and Mary kept calling Eddie's name out for nights afterwards and I just couldn't stand the screech of her voice,' she explained. 'It haunted me. One night when she was calling "Eddie, Eddie", I screamed at her to shut up. Like a wailing banshee I was, and I'm so ashamed, I said if she hadn't let him in her bed, if she'd followed my instructions—'

Dot stopped speaking for a moment and closed her eyes. It was clearly painful to go on.

'I saw all the love and trust drain out of her in that one moment,' she continued. 'It was like I killed something in her too – her voice. That night I lost her as well... both my kiddies, gone.'

Dot's voice dissolved into tears and Audrey's heart smashed into smithereens as she listened to her cry and watched Mary playing in the leaves.

'You haven't lost Mary,' said Audrey quietly. 'She's still here.'

'I don't know what to do,' said Dot, trembling now and quickly drying her eyes. 'How do you undo such a thing? And her father is overseas fighting and I've not had the heart to send a telegram telling him his boy is dead. His children are his reason for surviving. I dread to think what he'd do if he knew. Probably stand in the line of fire, God forgive me. He so wanted a son. Here I am, supposed to be strong, and I've never felt so lonely and so hopeless. What kind of mother am I?'

Mary turned around at that point and stared at Dot and Audrey talking, pure desolation written on her face.

'I think you should tell her it's not her fault,' said Audrey, giving Mary a wave. 'I'll come back in a while, but you two need to be together.'

Beckoning to Mary to come back inside, Audrey left the centre and stood outside in the fresh air, trying to make sense of what she'd just been told. Anger at the senseless loss of young life infected her, but as quickly as the anger came, a feeling of helplessness engulfed her. At times the war felt like an insurmountable force of evil that she was powerless to confront. It was wrecking lives, not just on the battlefront but here at home. Glancing back through the window, she saw Mary and Dot sitting awkwardly side by side, the pain in their hearts like a physical wall between them. She silently pleaded with Dot, or Mary, to reach out to the other one, to hold a hand, or smile, or embrace, but neither did, or seemed able. It broke Audrey's heart. From her own experience, she knew very well that what should be such a simple thing to do could be indescribably complicated. Showing a person how you felt wasn't always easy, even when you loved them with your entire heart.

Tears blurring her vision, Audrey stopped to wipe at her eyes with a hanky and looked blankly at the shopfronts on the opposite side of the road where posters advertised Christmas gifts, warning there were only half as many tins of chocolates and toffees available this year, or that if you wanted to buy a serviceman a gift, you should only buy him Bakelite. Audrey's mind drifted to the Christmas parcel she wanted to send to William, packed with cigs, cards, a shaving stick and a fruit cake. *Would he even receive it?* she thought despondently.

Sighing, her eyes settled on a serviceman who was waiting at a bus stop holding a bunch of anemones. Sitting on a nearby bench to gather her thoughts, she watched as a bus drew up at the stop and saw Elsie, helping passengers get on and off. She looked splendid in her green uniform and Audrey felt proud to be her sister-in-law-to-be and friend. 'Elsie!' she called, but she couldn't be heard above the roar of the bus engine. Hugging her coat closer around her, she watched the serviceman get on the bus and hand Elsie the flowers. Audrey's heart skipped a beat as she saw the surprised smile burst onto Elsie's face. Then her stomach sank to her shoes – was Elsie's heart being tempted away?

'Oh William,' Audrey whispered. 'Please come home.'

An hour later, feeling utterly subdued but putting on a bright, brave face, Audrey collected Mary and quietly asked Dot if she had spoken.

'Not a sound,' Dot said.

'Perhaps you could write to her,' suggested Audrey, as they waved goodbye. Seeing Dot's distress at having to separate again from her silent daughter, she kept the farewell as brief as possible, giving Mary's hand a tight squeeze as she ushered them outside.

'You and your mum just need time,' Audrey said, as they walked together hand in hand. 'Shall we go home for some toast and tea in front of the fire?'

Mary nodded, and even though she still hadn't said a word, Audrey sensed that there was nothing the girl would rather do more.

'Anemones?' said Lily, when Elsie came home late that night after her shift and put the flowers in a vase on the windowsill of their bedroom. 'Who are they from?'

'A pilot gave me them,' Elsie said, her cheeks red as cherries. 'I've told him I'm engaged. I couldn't very well throw them in the bin. He doesn't mean any harm. Some of the servicemen and women who take the bus open their hearts to me – they're missing home, I expect.'

Elsie sniffed the flowers before sitting on her bed and yawning, circling her ankles to stop them aching and massaging the back of her neck. Standing up all day on the bus made bits of her ache she didn't even know she had.

Lily was on her bed, threading old buttons from a jar onto strands of wool, making necklaces for Christmas presents. Open on the blanket next to her was a copy of *Woman & Home* magazine, which suggested the necklace idea as a cheap and cheerful festive gift, along with rag dolls made from dishcloths.

'Some men are very persuasive,' said Lily. 'Be careful, won't you? I know that's rich coming from me, but I have first-hand experience of being gullible. One minute you're accepting flowers, the next you're having a baby.'

Elsie and Lily both laughed gently.

'Why are you up so late?' asked Elsie. 'Can't you sleep?'

'No, I got a letter from my father today,' Lily said, stopping threading buttons for a moment. 'Audrey visited recently and he's written to say that Henry Bateman has moved on and that my old job at the Ministry of Information would be willing to have me back. He's given me a choice. He says he won't support me if I choose to keep the child, but that if I don't, he'll welcome me home and help me with the job.'

'Oh Lily,' Elsie said, frowning. 'What kind of choice is that? It's emotional blackmail.' She shook her head with concern, while Lily's eyes brimmed with tears.

'He says he would like to put the whole thing behind us and get back to normal,' said Lily, taking a deep breath.

'Normal?' replied Elsie. 'There's no such thing as normal in wartime, is there? What gets me is how can your father, or anyone for that matter, be upholding such values when life and death have taken on a whole different meaning? I think the rulebook needs tearing up and rewriting and I reckon it will be once the war's over. Think of all those girls who are working now, earning a wage and enjoying it – they're not going to go back to staying at home, are they? So what will you do?'

'I don't know,' said Lily. 'I love my father. I don't believe he means to be cruel. He thinks he's doing the right thing.'

Elsie's heart ached for Lily. Her father would never behave like that, thought Elsie. Oh how she yearned to see her papa, to hear the sound of his voice and throw her arms around his neck. Just like normal. She craved normal. An ordinary day, where the sun rises and sets with nothing much going on in between.

'I need to talk to Audrey,' said Lily, yawning and bundling the button necklaces into a small tin and putting them under her bed. 'I'm going to talk to her tomorrow, but right now, I need to sleep. Goodnight Elsie.'

'Goodnight Lily,' replied Elsie.

She lay blinking in the darkness, unable to get to sleep, inhaling the sweet scent of the flowers that filled the room, reminding her of Jimmy Browne. Feeling guilty for thinking of him, she conjured the image of William's face, desperately trying to capture the sound of his voice in her memory and the sensation of his touch on her skin.

Eventually she drifted off, but woke hours later at 3.30 a.m., covered in a film of sweat, convinced that William was sitting at the bottom of the bed, shaking her legs. She sat bolt upright, her eyes searching the dark, and registered that it was in fact Lily shaking her legs.

'The siren,' Lily said. 'Sounds like someone's getting it! We need to get up!'

Breaking through the fog of sleep, Elsie heard the terrible sound of enemy planes and fire nearby. Stumbling through the dark, the girls made their way down the stairs and to the shelter with Mary and Audrey, while Bournemouth suffered hits by parachute landmines and incendiaries that set the town ablaze, causing unprecedented death and destruction.

Chapter Twenty-Nine

'Have you heard?' said Pat, the morning after the bombing raid. 'Alma Road Elementary School was hit last night. Hundreds of homes in the area were damaged, and the fire service are still battling with the blaze. There were casualties, some fatal I'm sorry to say, but there are no numbers yet.' She gestured with her hands to show the magnitude of the wreckage. 'The bomber came in the dead of the night,' she continued. 'When everyone was sleeping, the no-good— well, you know what I'm getting at.'

A shiver ran through Audrey as she listened and the muscles in her stomach tightened into a knot. It was a bitterly cold Saturday morning in November, a busy day in the shop, and some women waiting in the queue openly wept at the news. In her hands she held a box of last year's Christmas cake decorations she had found in the storeroom and, feeling desolate, she looked at the figures of Father Christmas and red robins on frosted logs, as if they were postcards from a different life.

In the last few weeks, there had been numerous bombs dropped on Bournemouth and many worrisome hours spent in shelters. Thankfully most bombs had fallen on open spaces, but this time a residential area had borne the brunt of the raid.

'That's absolutely awful,' said Audrey, holding her hand to her brow and rubbing at an invisible stain. 'How can they hit a school? Poor littl'uns will be so upset. I expect they've been decorating it ready for Christmas too. I know Mary's school have been making paper chains. I suppose we must be grateful it didn't happen in the daytime! Heaven forbid! How can we help?'

The women in the shop huddled together, listening to the stories of people being rescued from the wreckage. Everyone looked pale and worn out. Even Pat, in her role as messenger, was listless.

'I think they'll need help serving refreshments to the AFS and ARP and to the people who have lost their homes,' she said. 'As you say, just before Christmas too, what a terrible thing to happen.'

'Blast this war!' said Elizabeth, who was in the shop. 'And it's so cold. Imagine being without a home in this weather. Anyone who needs somewhere to stay can come to my house.'

'I'll help out, Pat,' said Elsie. 'I'm not working on the buses today.'

Audrey leaned against the counter, shaking her head in dismay. 'Coventry has had it bad too,' she said. 'Did you see the picture of their cathedral in the paper? Blown to smithereens. Hundreds dead.'

'It's a wonder we all keep going,' said Pat. 'The country's taking such a battering.'

'We might just be at the start of it,' said Elizabeth, bleakly. 'Last war went on for four years! We were all half-starved to death. To be honest, I think it'll be a miracle if we win this time around.'

'Oh don't say that,' said Pat. 'You can't give up like that. Where will that attitude get us?'

Audrey's eyes travelled across the faces of the women in the shop, all of them usually so set with determination, grit and resilience. Today their faces revealed their deepest fears and darkest thoughts and Audrey wished she had something to tell them, a wand to wave that would renew their positive spirit. Christmas was coming, but would anyone be able to celebrate? Beyond the shop window the sky was slate grey and as people walked past, their umbrellas blew inside out in the wind. Feeling thoroughly depressed, she longed for the war to be over, but what good did longing do? You just had to get on with life, doing what you could and making the most of the little jewels of happiness that shone out of the darkness. Casting her mind back to one of Churchill's speeches, she remembered his words: *Come then, let us go forward together with our united strength.* Audrey looked at her customers and thought they could all do with reminding themselves of that speech.

'I sometimes think we'll have to give in,' said Elizabeth. 'If they invade, we'll just have to let it happen.'

'Absolute rot!' said Pat. 'That kind of opinion will be the death of us, Elizabeth!'

'We have to keep going and feeling strong,' said Audrey, firmly. 'We have to keep going for each other and for the future. That's what we do, isn't it? We don't give up. We *can't* give up. Let me make some rolls for the firemen and the people whose homes have been destroyed. Lily, grab some bread and give me a hand, will you? Ladies, Maggie and Elsie will serve you, I won't be long.'

In the kitchen, Audrey and Lily worked side by side, packing bread rolls into crates as a donation to the families in the respite centre or for the AFS personnel who had been working throughout the night. When Audrey had finished and put the kitchen knife down on the breakfast table, Lily moved over to the window and stared out at the dark sea, which was only discernible from the grey sky by the white froth thrown up by waves, like spittle. A silence fell between them and Audrey stopped what she was doing, aware that Lily was staring at her.

'Audrey, I need to talk to you,' Lily said, her voice sombre.

'Of course,' said Audrey, her heartbeat quickening.

Aware of the minutes ticking by while she should be in the shop helping Maggie and relieving Elsie, Audrey moved closer to Lily, both women looking out to sea from the kitchen window. Lily took a deep breath.

'You've been so kind to me,' Lily said, continuing to look at the sea. 'Thank you.'

Audrey squeezed Lily's arm affectionately. 'You're my family,' Audrey said. 'I care about you.'

With quivering lips Lily managed a small smile.

'I have been thinking about the baby,' said Lily. 'My father wrote to me and said if I keep the baby he will consider it to be a rejection of him and everything he stands for, just as you told me after your visit to London.'

'But what about you?' Audrey said. 'What do you think?'

Lily took a deep breath and looked down at the floor. Her voice trembled as she spoke. 'I miss him and I'm not ready to be a mother. I don't think I have it in me to be one yet,' she said. 'I know how cold this makes me sound, but I made a dreadful mistake and I wholeheartedly regret it. I don't want this baby to start its life as a "mistake". I want to know this baby will be loved and looked after, especially in these uncertain times, and I…'

Lily paused and looked at her hands. Audrey felt light-headed. Holding her breath, she waited for Lily to finish speaking, keeping her eyes fixed on the ebb and flow of the waves.

'I would like for you to adopt the baby,' said Lily, barely able to form the words, glossy tears streaming down her cheeks. 'If that's what you still want to do and are able, I think it would be best for everyone. Best for the baby.'

A myriad of emotions hit Audrey all at once. She broke out in goosebumps, a brilliant smile burst onto her face and her eyes pricked with tears. This was her chance to become a mother, to cherish and love Lily's baby as her own. There was no doubt in her own mind that she would be honoured to care for the baby, but a Charlie-shaped question mark pinged into her head. Though she had talked to him about it in theory, it wasn't until now that she'd had a clear indication from Lily that this was what she really wanted. Creasing her forehead, concerns suddenly began to fog her mind. Had Lily searched her soul before making this decision? As if reading her mind, Lily nodded her head.

'I've thought about it until I can think no more,' said Lily. 'It feels right. I can still know the child, but as an aunt. My father doesn't have to have anything to do with him or her, he's made it quite clear that's what he wants, and Henry Bateman, well, why I ever got tangled up with him I'll never know. He wasn't the person I thought he was. Audrey, you're the kindest person I know, you would be a better mother than I will ever be.'

Lily was trying her hardest not to cry.

'Come here,' said Audrey, throwing her arms around her. 'Dry your eyes.' Hugging Lily, Audrey's heart soared at the thought of being a mother, but also at the prospect of being able to help Lily. With William away and Daphne estranged, every instinct in her was telling her to hold on to Lily and the baby and never let go. 'Thank you,' she said, her head and heart spinning.

Audrey couldn't wait until Charlie had woken from his nap. She had to speak to him urgently. Creeping into the bedroom where he was sleeping, she quietly closed the door behind her, her heart hammering.

'What is it?' Charlie said, sitting immediately upright. 'Is it the siren? Is it the ovens?'

'No, love,' said Audrey, sitting down on the bed next to him and grabbing hold of his hand. 'It's Lily.'

Charlie rubbed his eyes, which were red from lack of sleep, and Audrey felt guilty for waking him up. He worked so hard.

'Is she well?' he said, pushing back the eiderdown. 'That fella's not back is 'e?'

Audrey made a decision to be matter-of-fact with Charlie. She would tell it just like it was and hope that he supported her. The Charlie she married would, but what about the distracted, irritable man Charlie had been since war was declared? She wasn't so sure.

'Lily told me she would like us to adopt her baby,' Audrey said softly. 'I want nothing more.'

Charlie let his head drop down back onto the pillow with a thud, but said nothing.

'Charlie?' Audrey said, a feeling of dread sinking into her stomach.

He looked her in the eye. 'Who would look after it?' he asked. 'You're needed in the shop. Someone's got to help me look after this business, else we're done for. Our accounts aren't looking too rosy you know, love.'

Though her stomach was flipping, Audrey smiled reassuringly. 'Let me work that out,' she said. 'I can manage. There's plenty of us to help out with caring for a baby.'

'You can't just put it on the shelf like a loaf and carry on working,' said Charlie. 'Who would do the counter goods?'

'Me,' Audrey said. 'I know I can manage this. I know it.'

Closing her eyes for a moment, Audrey instructed herself not to get upset.

'Charlie love, this is difficult to say, but I don't think I'm able to have a baby,' Audrey confessed. 'We've been trying religiously for five years and I've not caught. But it's more than that, Charlie. Lily's baby was an accident of wartime, a random coming together of two people with uncertain futures. Lily came to me. This is my chance to do something important. I can't stop the war, Charlie, I can't get William back from wherever he is, or bring back Jacques or the Stringer boys, but I can love this child. It's what I need to do. I have to do this. Do you understand how that feels, when you're driven to do something, almost regardless of everything else?'

Quiet for what seemed like an eternity, Charlie finally spoke. 'Yes, love,' he said gently, squeezing his wife's hand. 'I do.'

Chapter Thirty

Audrey poured black treacle into the enormous bowl of deliciously fragrant fruity, spicy mixture and held up the wooden spoon.

'Who's first?' she asked, glancing up at Charlie, his Uncle John, Elsie, Lily, Mary, Pat, Elsie's mother Violet and the twins, who were all gathered around the kitchen table, which was crowded with dried fruit, mixed spice, butter, grated carrots, brown sugar, flour, peel and treacle. It was Stir-up Sunday and the day that Audrey made her Christmas cakes and puddings to her grandmother's recipe. As tradition ordered, everyone in the family would stir the family Christmas pudding mixture for luck. And never did they need luck on their side more than now.

Though the kettle was boiling on the hob and the kitchen warm and snug, one glance out of the window at the forbidding grey sky sent chills running up Audrey's spine when she thought of the future. It had been a year since she'd seen William and months since they'd had word from him. The RAF were bombing Berlin, Hamburg and Bremen in retaliation for the bombing of London and Coventry, and there were hundreds dead in Birmingham and Southampton. In Audrey's eyes it seemed like everyone everywhere was killing everyone else, ironically justified by being in the pursuit of peace. And now in the run-up to Christmas, families were desperate to be reunited with their loved ones, even if rationing meant festivities would be modest. Lord Woolton had said it was patriotic to be content with one Christmas pudding this year, and wait for shipments of dried fruit to arrive from Australia in January, so it hardly felt like a time to be celebrating. But, looking at the faces of those she loved in the kitchen – and knowing that each one carried their own private heartache – Audrey was determined to lift their spirits with some traditional festive cheer, however slight.

'Ladies first,' said Charlie, accepting the spoon and stirring the mixture. 'And gentlemen just before.'

Laughter rippled through the room and Audrey whacked Charlie on the arm, waiting until he'd stirred and then passing the spoon to Elsie.

'You know what I'm wishing for,' said Elsie. 'For William to come home.'

'We all wish for that, darlin',' said John, accepting the spoon after Elsie. He closed his eyes and stirred the mixture, his strong baker's arms making light work of the dense mixture. 'Bottle of brandy, or whisky,' he muttered in jest, opening his eyes a crack. 'Tobacco… and a box of chocolates wouldn't go amiss.'

'John!' laughed Audrey, elbowing him. 'What are you like? Lily?'

Lily, eight months pregnant now, blushed a little, but accepted the spoon and stirred the mixture. Audrey touched her arm.

'You'll be 'oping that there baby is not born while there's a raid on!' said John. I 'eard a young woman gave birth to twins in her Anderson shelter last week! She gave the twins the middle name "Anderson", believe it or not!'

'I was born in the privy,' said Charlie, his eyes twinkling. 'Arrived in a hurry, didn't I, Mother? That's why I've got this flat bit at the back of my head. Had all the sense knocked out of me before I'd even started.'

'Thought there was something funny about ye!' said John with a laugh.

'The less said about your birth the better,' said Pat, flustered. 'But yes, you were. And don't you forget it!'

The spoon was passed around the guests until everyone had had a stir and then, after dropping in a threepenny bit, Audrey made several small puddings out of the mixture and covered the basins with a piece of cloth, securing it with string and placing them in a vat of boiling water to steam. She had had a dozen orders for Christmas cakes and puddings, but with fewer ingredients available from the wholesalers – and almost no nuts at all – she had to be creative, adding grated carrots to add sweetness and moisture. There would be no marzipan or icing for the cakes this year, though she was going to experiment with mock marzipan made from flour, sugar, margarine and almond essence.

'What did you wish for, Mary love?' asked Audrey, as she poured tea for everyone from the teapot and put out a plate of sandwiches. Audrey glanced over at Mary, witnessing a wave of sadness pass over her face. Though she knew Mary wouldn't answer, Audrey always made sure to ask her questions to include her in conversation.

'I wished for my brother to come back from the dead like that Shearing boy,' Mary said in the tiniest squeak of a voice. Everyone fell silent as the enormity of what had just happened sank in. It had been months since Mary had arrived at the bakery and this was the first time she'd spoken. Audrey threw a stern look at the adults, not wanting anyone to make a scene, and carried on calmly pouring the tea.

'You're a brave girl, Mary,' said Audrey, giving the girl a cup and smiling at her, before turning away to tend the puddings, which were bobbing on the water, filling the kitchen with the bittersweet scent of Christmas.

Later, when the puddings were ready and the cakes baked, Audrey stored the ordered cakes in a tea chest in the cellar, ready for feeding with a drizzle of brandy. She let Mary poke holes into the cakes with a cocktail stick ready to absorb the alcohol, and wondered how best to ask her about her brother.

'Mary,' Audrey spoke quietly and slowly, 'sometimes it's difficult to say goodbye to someone we love. You loved your brother very much, didn't you? Just like I love my brother, William. The thing is, Mary, though Eddie has passed on, he's still with you in some ways, safely tucked into your heart. Even though you won't see him again, you'll carry him with you everywhere in your head and heart, for the rest of your life. He's part of you.'

Mary managed the slightest nod of her head before she threw herself at Audrey, flinging her skinny arms around Audrey's waist, weeping into her pinny.

Chapter Thirty-One

Pulling her old woollen coat around her body to protect against the harsh wintry wind, Elsie traipsed through Bournemouth town centre after her shift on the buses. Snow had been forecast and all day passengers had been wondering if this winter would be as bad as last, when temperatures had reached a record low. As she walked, Elsie mourned the loss of the pretty festive lights that normally lit up the town's shop windows and Christmas trees. The blackout had put paid to that, and combined with fog, it was almost impossible to see which way her boots were heading, but eventually she arrived at the Goat and Tricycle public house, which even though it was shrouded in the regulation darkness could be heard from the street.

Feeling for his handwritten note in her pocket, Elsie opened the door a crack and spotted Jimmy Browne sitting alone at a table in the corner near the piano, where someone had half-heartedly draped a string of tinsel across the top. Closing the door again, her heart thundered in her chest. She wasn't used to going into public houses alone. Though it was more acceptable these days, especially now that women were doing jobs that men traditionally did, some publicans still frowned on it. Why her money was any different to a man's, she didn't know.

Come on, Elsie, she buoyed herself up. *Get on with it.*

After the count of ten, she burst through the door into a cloud of tobacco smoke. Twenty or more men craned their necks, including the publican, who wore a Father Christmas hat, to peer at her as she quickly walked towards Jimmy, who was nursing a beer, his hat on the table in front of him. He greeted her with an enormous grin, standing to pull out a seat for her to sit on. Reaching into her pocket for his note, she cast it down onto the table.

'What's the meaning of this?' she said, glowering at him. Staring at the note, she watched him scan his own words, which said he had an urgent message for her. He'd left the note on the bus tucked into her bag and, for a crazy moment, she thought perhaps he had news about William. 'It's nearly wash time for my sisters,' she said crossly. 'They'll be waiting for me and wondering where I am. I said I'd be there tonight.'

Jimmy turned his face upwards from the note and smiled at her, with a dash of amusement in his eyes. It was then that her vague hope that this was a message about William dissolved and she felt ridiculous for coming.

'I didn't think you'd come unless it was an emergency,' Jimmy said. 'This will only take a minute. Can I get you a drink?'

Though Elsie felt she should leave immediately, she was physically exhausted after twelve hours on her feet. She put her elbows on the table and rested her chin in her hands. In truth she was gasping for a drink, but she shook her head in refusal. The quicker she got this over with, the better. She had been silly to come at all.

He gave her a long and meaningful look through the furl of smoke from his cigarette, before stubbing it out in the ashtray. Not for the first time, forbidden feelings stirred within her and she chastised herself. This war had thrown her whole life up into the air and right now she felt she had little control over where all the pieces were going to land.

'I know you have a fiancé,' he said. 'You've told me that you won't go on a date with me and that's fair enough.'

Elsie nodded and folded her arms resolutely. Ever since they'd had that chance meeting on the bus, Jimmy had been trying to convince her to spend time with him; fish and chips, a dance, the pictures, even just a turn around the Square.

'What's your fiancé's name again?' he asked.

'William,' Elsie answered, biting her lip. 'I haven't seen him now in a year. I haven't heard from him in almost six months. His last letter was very short. We were supposed to be—' Memories of the wedding day that never was rushed into her head, bringing with it the same colossal disappointment she had felt on the day. Her voice trailed off and she took a sharp intake of breath.

Jimmy stared at her for a moment, smiling in understanding, and took a sip from his drink.

'He's a lucky man to have you waiting for him to come home,' he said, before fixing her with a stare. 'Elsie, I'm going to be posted overseas before Christmas. I wondered if you'd grant me a Christmas wish? My regiment is helping to put on a Christmas concert party for the evacuee children. Some of us are playing instruments or singing a ditty or acting. I wondered if you'd come with me?'

Elsie looked at Jimmy quizzically. It seemed like a lot of bother to put a note in her bag urging her to meet him, just to ask her this, when he already knew she'd say no.

'So you're asking me on another date?' she said, raising her eyebrows. 'I've already said why I can't.'

He shook his head. 'It's not a date. I know you are off limits,' he said. 'I just like you, that's all. You're proud and unafraid and –' he looked up at her with a cheeky smile, before saying: 'beautiful.'

Elsie felt herself blush at the compliment. She glanced around the pub and was pleased to find that everyone was ignoring them.

'What were you doing before the war?' she asked.

'My father owns an ironmonger's shop in Sleaford,' he said. 'It's a small town in Lincolnshire, where the world moves slowly. He sold all sorts. Pianos in the basement, antiques in the corner, then all the hardware. Boxes of nails, hinges and doorknobs and it had this particular smell of wood shavings and varnish and rust that I have always loved. I was supposed to take over the business, but war was declared and here I am. Heaven knows where I'll be in a few weeks' time,' he finished quietly. 'I'd like to take a memory of

Bournemouth with me, one that feels connected to normal life, and so I want you to accompany me to this party.'

'Why me?' Elsie said. 'There are plenty of single girls in Bournemouth desperate for a handsome pilot to take them out. I know plenty. I could introduce you?'

'You're different,' he said, giving her an intense stare.

Elsie's anger subsided. She knew of many girls who went out with servicemen who were stationed in the town while their own sweethearts were away, quite innocently, but if she did, would it be disloyal to William? Or was it a simple case of helping keep up Jimmy's morale? Elsie made a snap decision. If she laid out clear boundaries, Jimmy would have to respect them. She wasn't doing anything wrong.

'I'll come,' she said. 'But strictly as friends. Can I bring Mary? She's an evacuee staying at my digs.'

'Friends,' he said with a grin, catching her eye and holding it for just a second too long. 'And yes, of course, Mary is welcome. Can I get you a drink now that's sorted?'

Elsie shook her head. 'Thank you but no,' she said. 'I need to get home.'

It was tempting to stay in the warm pub with Jimmy, but she stood and buttoned up her woollen coat, ready to face the biting wind outside. Feeling his gaze linger upon her as she slipped out of the door, she disappeared into the night.

Bournemouth was becoming a master at disguise. From the street-view, the hall looked empty and closed. The blackout blinds concealed the activity inside and only the music, a rowdy rendition of 'We're Going to Hang out the Washing on the Siegfried Line', gave a clue to the party within. It had been a week since Jimmy asked Elsie to the Christmas shindig and, walking towards the entrance clutching Mary's hand, she felt increasingly nervous about the prospect of the evening ahead. Only an hour ago she had begged Lily to accompany her.

'Aren't you forgetting that I'm the size of a house?' Lily had said, pointing to her bump.

At least Mary was there, pretty as a picture in a dress Audrey had made from an old pyjama top. Her presence made Elsie feel more justified in coming along. Now, tucking her hair behind her ears, Elsie plucked up her courage and pushed open the door into what looked like the inside of a spectacular musical jewellery box. Despite rationing the organisers had pulled out all the stops for the evacuees.

'Isn't it lovely, Mary?' Elsie said, watching Mary's eyes glitter as she stared at the paper chains and decorations strung across the hall where couples were dancing on the shiny parquet floor. On the stage two young women dressed in pale satin dresses played accordions, accompanying a male singer dressed in a suit and bow tie, who was belting out a tune. At the opposite end of the room was a real Christmas tree, the tip of which touched the ceiling. It was decorated with stars and bells, and was surrounded by a selection of beautifully wrapped presents for the evacuees.

'Why don't you see what's over there?' she asked Mary, pointing at the group of evacuee children who were standing around a table, hands together, rushing through grace, while staring intently at the fairy cakes and finger sandwiches.

'They give ENSA a run for their money, wouldn't you say?' Jimmy said, suddenly by her side. 'There's a whistler and a trumpet player on next, then I think we're having a game of musical chairs and statues. They're serving cocktails too. Here, I got this for you. It's an "Air Force" – two-thirds gin, one-third lemon juice and a dash of maraschino.'

Elsie felt herself relax. How wonderful it was to forget her troubles and enjoy an evening out. She'd taken such privileges for granted before the war, and now appreciated a dance and a cocktail so much more.

'Yes please,' Elsie said, accepting the drink and laughing. 'It's loud in here, isn't it? We wouldn't be able to hear the siren if it went off!'

'I've had a word with Hitler,' Jimmy said, with a wink. 'He's going to give us all a night off to enjoy ourselves.'

Sipping her delicious cocktail, which was going straight to her head, and watching Mary tuck into the cakes, Elsie recognised Rita, a former colleague from Beales Department Store, who was obviously gossiping about her to her friend. Elsie waved back.

'Care to dance?' Jimmy said.

'No,' said Elsie. 'No, I'll watch instead. I've two left feet.'

'I don't believe that,' said Jimmy, his own left foot tapping to the beat. 'Come on and let your hair down. Please?'

There was something about Jimmy, maybe something as superficial as his dashing looks, that made Elsie give in to his demands.

'Oh go on then,' she said, breaking into a smile.

Taking Jimmy's hand, she straightened her back and waited for the next song to start. When the music began, Elsie immediately stood on Jimmy's toes and he shrieked in pain and hopped about on one foot. She let go of his hand and both of her hands shot to her mouth to cover her giggles.

'I told you so,' she laughed. 'I can't dance!'

'You're making it up,' he said, grabbing her hand so she couldn't leave the dance floor. Mary had come over to watch them dance, so Elsie pulled her onto the floor too, and the three of them gave up trying to dance properly, joined hands and spun around in a circle until the walls of the hall were a blur of paper chains and stars. Elsie felt ten years old, released from her worries and responsibilities. They threw back their heads, laughing hard, but then Mary's hand suddenly slipped out of Elsie's and the little girl careered backwards, landing awkwardly on her ankle. For a moment Jimmy kept hold of Elsie's hand, before letting go.

'Ouch!' Mary cried, crouching on the floor to grab her ankle, her big brown eyes filling with tears. 'It hurts!'

Elsie sat down next to Mary, rubbing the little girl's back to reassure her. Even though she had started saying a few things, Mary's voice was still a new sound for Elsie – and hearing her so distressed was sobering.

Jimmy rested his hand on Elsie's shoulder before inspecting the damage.

'Looks like you've sprained it, Mary,' he said. 'I'll find a bandage from the first aid box, how about that?'

Elsie smiled gratefully. 'Come on Mary,' she said. 'Let's get you over to a chair and take your shoe off, so we can look at it properly.'

Helping Mary hobble over to a chair, Elsie sat beside her, removing Mary's sock and lifting her ankle gently to rest it, slightly raised, on her lap. Scanning the room to look for Jimmy, she saw Rita approaching and lifted a hand to wave at her again.

Sitting in the chair beside Elsie, Rita sympathised with Mary before whispering in Elsie's ear. 'I thought you were engaged to William Allen,' she said. 'Have you broken it off with him?'

Elsie drew away from Rita and frowned. 'No! Of course not,' she said. 'Why would you say that?'

Rita hardly took a breath before replying. 'Because you're here with Jimmy the handsome pilot and he's all over you like a rash,' she said. 'That's what everyone's saying. You know how people will talk.'

Elsie felt her blood boil. She wanted to stand up and walk away, but Mary's swollen ankle was keeping her seated.

'Jimmy is a friend and nothing more,' she said. 'William has been away for a year and I miss him more than I can say. Why don't you keep your blasted nose out of it.'

'Don't curse at me, Elsie Russo,' Rita said.

'Then don't gossip about me, Rita Norman,' Elsie replied.

'I'm only saying what I'm seeing,' snapped Rita. 'Does William's sister know what you're up to?'

'I'm not up to anything,' said Elsie, moving Mary's ankle gently onto the chair, so she could stand. 'Shut up, why don't you?'

Rita stood up to face Elsie and moved even closer towards her. Elsie could feel the warmth of Rita's alcohol-fumed breath on her face.

'Why are you all tarted up then, when your sweetheart is fighting?' she said. 'I reckon William would be better off without you and I won't shy from telling him as much when he's home!'

Everything Elsie had felt over the last year – the disappointment, fury, longing, the helplessness – seemed to bubble and boil inside her like molten sugar. Raising her hand, she lashed out at Rita, landing a stinging slap on her cheek. There was a sharp intake of breath from the small crowd that had gathered around them.

'You can wipe that smug look off your face for a start,' said Elsie.

'Bitch!' said Rita, holding a hand to her stinging cheek, before drawing back her own hand and slapping Elsie on the face in return.

Elsie, red with fury and humiliation, shoved Rita in the chest and as she stumbled backwards, Rita grabbed hold of Elsie's hair and yanked it.

Hurling insults at each other, the pair tumbled to the floor. The music came to an abrupt halt and all eyes were suddenly on the scrapping women. All they needed was clapping and a chanti of 'fight, fight' and it would be a proper brawl.

'Ladies! Enough!' boomed a voice above them. Elsie lay on her back on the floor, staring up at a horrified Jimmy, who stood open-mouthed before offering his hand to Elsie. He pulled her up, his expression incredulous. Then he helped up Rita, whose lipstick had smudged halfway up her cheek, giving her the look of a demonic clown. 'I'm not sure what sort of establishments you normally frequent,' he said, 'but this is a peaceful one. Please everyone go back to enjoying your evening. There's nothing to see here!'

The music quickly started up. Rita glared at Elsie, who glared right back before turning to Mary, who was sticking her tongue out at Rita in revenge.

'Let's get this ankle bandaged up,' she said to Mary, pushing the pins back into her hair and smoothing down her dress. 'Then we'll have to go home.'

'What happened, Elsie?' Jimmy asked. 'Gosh, you've got some fire in your belly, haven't you? No wonder I like you!'

Elsie glared at him. 'This is your fault,' she told him. 'I told you I shouldn't have come. Why did you ask me?'

Jimmy's eyes fell to the floor, his smile disappeared and Elsie felt instantly guilty.

'I better take Mary home,' she said, more softly.

'Let me walk you,' he said. 'How will you manage if Mary can't walk?'

'I don't need help,' she said, grabbing Mary's hand and leading her outside. But Mary was hopping on one foot, clearly in pain, and couldn't even put the other foot down.

'Please,' said Jimmy. 'Let me help you home. I can easily carry Mary.'

Elsie sighed and gave a quick nod of her head.

Outside, the night was freezing and Elsie struggled not to slide on the icy pavement in her evening shoes. Their breath was visible in dragon's-breath puffs as they walked, and though Elsie didn't admit it, she was grateful that Jimmy was there. He carried Mary in his arms and, snug against his warm coat, she fell asleep.

When they reached the corner of Fisherman's Road and the bakery was in view, Elsie stopped walking. Lights were shining from the kitchen and bedroom windows above the bakery, where the blackout blinds hadn't been pulled. *The ARP warden will fine Charlie*, Elsie thought, wondering how Audrey could have forgotten. *Something must have happened*, she thought, a tremor of fear tickling her spine.

Outside the bakery Elsie turned to Jimmy and held out her arms so that she could take Mary. He passed her over, a warm, sleepy bundle, and kissed Elsie's cheek, so gently and quickly she wondered if he'd kissed her at all. At that moment, the door swung open, the figure of Audrey framed by light.

'Elsie, thank God,' she said. 'Lily's gone into labour. I need water, towels and a bloody big brandy.'

About to follow Audrey indoors, Elsie glanced back at Jimmy, who had moved a few steps away, his collar turned up to protect against the flurry of snow that had started to fall.

'Happy Christmas, Elsie Russo,' he said, giving her a beautiful grin and raising his hand to her in a salute. 'I'll remember you. Thanks for the memory.'

Elsie opened her mouth to reply, but he had already turned on his heel and a second later had disappeared into the black night. *Thanks for the memory.*

'ELSIE!' Audrey said, when a blood-curdling scream erupted from Lily. 'For goodness sake, come inside and help me.'

Chapter Thirty-Two

This is it, Lily thought. *The baby is coming.* Waiting for another contraction to pass, breathing through the pain, she felt almost delirious with fear. In her mind, the baby about to emerge from her body would look exactly like Henry Bateman, even down to the suit and polished shoes, a thought that filled her with dread. The man she had at first so admired had turned into a gutless philanderer – she wanted to strike him from her life, yet here she was tied to him forever. However hard she tried, she found it impossible to separate the baby from the thought of him. They were inextricably linked.

The weeks and months since she'd arrived at the bakery carrying this secret had passed so quickly and now here she was, the baby restless and coming earlier than expected, with Lily feeling utterly unprepared for the birth. Obsessive thoughts about how her own mother had died in childbirth crowded her mind. Would the same fate befall her?

Lily cast her mind back to being four years old. One day she was happily sitting on her mother's lap in a rocking chair listening to her mother sing to the baby inside her. The next day, her mother and the baby were dead. While Lily was packed off to an aunt's house, her father locked himself away in his study, pouring his feelings into a vault he would never again open, not even when Lily begged him to. Her father's stoicism suppressed all emotion, regarding it as vulgar and weak. And wasn't he acting the same way now?

'John, you get back to the ovens,' she heard Audrey saying outside the bedroom door. 'Deliveries don't stop for anything, bombs or babies. Elsie, who was that young man you were with? Never mind. You can help me. I sent Charlie for the doctor, but he's gone to see the Christmas pantomime! I suppose even the doctor needs a night off.'

As another contraction surged through her in a tidal wave of pain, the enormity of her situation struck her with such force, she let out a phenomenal scream. She was about to become a mother of a child she hadn't wanted. What kind of woman did that make her? When thousands of people were dying in the war – including dearest Jacques who she would never forget – how could she give up on this new life before it had even begun? Shouldn't she be braver? Wasn't she putting her head in the sand, just as her father did? Refusing to consider another path in life? Other girls in her situation really did have no option, but with Audrey's support, could she make it work to look after the child herself?

'You've left the blackout blind up,' Elsie was saying, in the room now, pulling down the blind.

'Oh gracious me!' said Audrey. 'I forgot all about it. We'll be fined!'

Lily was incredulous that Audrey and Elsie were talking about the blackout curtains of all things when her body was being ripped apart with pain. Feeling strangely detached from their conversation, as if she was watching herself from the corner of the room, Lily's eyes moved over the little bedroom that had become her home these last six months. It was so familiar now: the floral wallpaper, the framed 'Home Sweet Home' embroidery on the wall, the dark stained floorboards and windowsill crowded with her books, the white cage with Bertie inside and Jacques' sketch propped up on the bedside table. Her life in London felt more than 100 miles away. It felt as if it was on the other side of the earth. She knew she wasn't equipped to live a completely new life as a mother of a child. Look at her. She was hopeless, wasn't she? *It's the war*, she heard Audrey's voice in her head, *it makes people act in a way they wouldn't normally.* She thought: *Could I? Could I be a mother?* But she had promised Audrey she could adopt the baby. Questions without answers streamed through her head. It was the pain and the exhaustion making her confused.

As if reading her tumultuous thoughts, Audrey squeezed Lily's hand and said: 'You know what they say; if you aren't in over your head, how do you know how tall you are?'

After another three hours of agonising pain, in the early hours came the final contraction that delivered the baby into the world. With one last push, the baby shot into the room at the same time as Old Reg's wife, Milly, a retired maternity nurse, arrived at the bakery to help.

'Just in time,' Milly said. 'Well done, Lily, you've a beautiful baby girl.'

Audrey and Elsie had tears running down their cheeks as the baby let out her first cry, her little arms already punching at the air. Lily made an exhausted whimper, hardly daring to look at the child, unsure that she should. But when Milly wrapped her in a white baby blanket and gave her to Lily to hold, a kind of euphoria took over and she was instantly entranced.

The baby looked nothing like Henry Bateman. With a shock of copper hair and porcelain white skin, she resembled only Lily and seemed to hold the answer to all of life's questions in her face. Speechless, but holding the baby in her arms, Lily stared into her tiny features, enraptured by her tiny fingers and toes. Numb with shock, she looked up at Audrey and Elsie, who were gazing at her with pure love and friendship in their eyes. Lily felt that at this moment she was driven not by fear, but instinct. Moving closer to her daughter's face, she kissed her silken skin in amazement.

After minutes had passed, she faced Audrey, who she knew so wanted to be a mother and who she had already asked to take care of this child, but now she had held this baby girl in her arms, now that she realised that the baby was not a carbon copy of Henry Bateman, was not an embodiment of a mistake, but a brand new chapter, a brand new life, a tiny version of herself, she thought: *how can I part with her?* It was like a switch in her brain had been flicked.

'I didn't know it would be like this,' she whispered to Audrey. 'I don't know if I can… Oh Audrey, I'm so confused. I'm sorry.'

Lily burst into tears and Audrey sat down beside her and the baby, brushing back the strands of hair that were stuck to Lily's damp forehead.

'I know,' Audrey said in a barely audible whisper, a silent tear running down her cheek, a warm, wobbly smile on her lips. 'I understand.'

'When my father sees her, he won't be able to turn us away,' Lily said. 'She looks just like me and just like my mother.'

Audrey took a deep breath and straightened up. 'Let me make you a cup of tea,' she said. 'You must be gasping!'

'What will you call her?' asked Elsie, as Audrey opened the door to fetch the tea.

'Joy,' Lily said. 'Her name is Joy.'

In the hallway outside Lily's bedroom, the smile slipped from Audrey's face. Leaning against the wall, she took a deep, raspy breath, fighting the selfish disappointment that twisted in her gut. She'd known the instant the baby was born that Lily would not part with her.

It wasn't going to be easy for Lily, but Audrey would do everything she could to support her, and the baby of course; but the emotional turmoil of the last few months, not knowing what Lily would do and whether Audrey herself would have the chance to become a mother, had taken its toll. She felt suddenly exhausted and wanted to be with Charlie, to have him hold her in his arms and comfort her. She had to accept that perhaps she would never be a mother. Perhaps it wasn't her role in life.

'I can't say I'm not relieved,' said Charlie, matter-of-fact, when she broke the news. 'But how the bloody hell is she going to manage on her own?'

Audrey was doing her best to remain positive. 'We can help her,' she said. 'I can help her.'

'I know you wanted the baby, love, but I'm not in a position to be a father,' said Charlie. 'Not now.'

'Why?' said Audrey. 'You'd make a wonderful father.'

Charlie looked at the floor. 'Because I've decided I'm going to sign up after Christmas,' he said. 'I've made up my mind and nothing you can say will change it.'

Audrey felt a flash of anger ignite in her belly.

'Winston Churchill said it himself,' she insisted. '"Workmen are soldiers with different weapons but the same courage." You're doing your bit for this country, for our community, for our family, right here in this bakery. Why do you have to kill yourself to prove your worth? You're no less of a man just because you're not holding a gun.'

Charlie's mouth was set in a determined line. He shook his head. 'I've made my decision and though my occupation is reserved I'm going to try again to persuade the authorities to let me go,' he said. 'I've spoken to John and he's willing to take over here, temporarily, as head baker. Albert can do more too. He's sixteen soon. We might need to take on an apprentice but I'm thinking on that.'

Audrey didn't say another word.

'It's the right thing to do,' Charlie continued. 'I'm doing the right thing.'

Though fresh tears were stinging her eyes and her throat was thick with the urge to cry, she nodded curtly at Charlie before turning away from him and walking outside. A freezing wind whipped her hair and stung her cheeks. Violently shivering in the cold, but needing to be alone, she stood with her chin raised, blinking into the darkness, searching the sky for stars. But there were none.

Chapter Thirty-Three

The telegram came at 6 p.m. on Christmas Eve. Audrey was in the kitchen chopping up rashers of fat bacon to add to onion, mint, sage, parsley, mushrooms and breadcrumbs to make the Christmas stuffing. At the table, Mary adorned bunches of pine cones and holly with ribbons and paper stars, making decorations for the Christmas table and mantelpiece. Above the fireplace was a string pegged with one of Charlie's old woollen socks, ready, Audrey told a wide-eyed Mary, for Father Christmas to leave his gifts.

'Can you get that please, Charlie?' Audrey said, when the telegram boy from the Exchange knocked. 'My hands are full of mixture in here.'

Since Joy had been born ten days earlier and in the run-up to Christmas, Audrey had been rushed off her feet – and glad of it too. The less time she had to think, the less time she had to ponder Charlie's decision to try again to join up. There was no end to hard work in a bakery and perhaps it would have been difficult to juggle the shop with the needs of a new baby.

Though the other shops on the street would be closed on Christmas Day, Barton's would still deliver the traditional mince pies and bread on Christmas morning, as well as cooking the neighbours' roasts in the bakery ovens while they were still hot.

'Those are pretty, Mary,' Audrey said encouragingly, half-listening to the exchange between Charlie and the telegram boy. Waiting while Charlie read the telegram downstairs, Audrey's heart raced. *Could it be William?*

Charlie seemed to be taking forever to come up the stairs. Losing patience, Audrey wiped her hands on the tea towel and called down, 'What was it, love?'

There was no reply. Instead, Charlie cleared his throat and then walked slowly up the stairs to the kitchen. The suspense was killing Audrey and she felt weak-kneed, imagining Charlie was going to give her the most awful news. He opened the kitchen door, his face even paler than usual. She raised her eyebrows anxiously and ran over to him.

'Is it William?' she said quietly, reading Charlie's sombre expression. 'Charlie, please, tell me?'

'No, love,' he said, shaking his head. 'It's not about William. It's... nothing.'

Audrey's shoulders dropped an inch as relief washed over her. 'It must be something,' she said, with a quizzical smile. 'Why are you not telling me?'

Charlie shook his head. 'It's about the coal delivery,' he mumbled, eyes scanning the decorations Mary was working on. He leaned against the table and patted her head. 'Mary, you've done a grand job of these. Hasn't she, Audrey?'

Mary looked up at Charlie with huge brown eyes, a smile creeping across her face.

Audrey frowned, as Charlie was clearly hiding something, but decided he would no doubt tell her later if there was a problem. Besides, she had so much to organise before tomorrow, she had to get on and concentrate.

'Try one of these,' said Audrey, surreptitiously passing him one of the cinnamon twist sweets that she'd made for Mary's stocking. 'They're for a certain someone.'

Charlie pushed it into his mouth and winked. 'Perfect,' he said. 'Right, I better get on.' Before he left the room, he turned to Audrey, put his arms around her and kissed her forehead. 'Thank you,' he said, gesturing at the table. 'For all this. I'm sorry that things didn't work out, y' know, with Joy an' that.'

Charlie's eyes were shining, the way they did on the rare occasion he had a few beers.

'You daft beggar,' she said, smiling an uncertain smile, a confused crease erupting on her brow.

Lily was in a bubble of love. Despite the fact that this was the second Christmas of the war and that the raids continued with a vengeance, with Joy in her arms Lily felt strangely secure, as if somehow protected from the ordeals of war. Walking into the cosy, warm kitchen to find Audrey cooking and Mary crafting only served to strengthen that bubble feeling. Carrying Joy in her arms, who was dressed in a white gown, pink baby slippers and a matinee jacket knitted by Pat, a wispy red cowlick sticking up in the air, it was almost possible to forget the burning cities, destroyed homes and devastated lives. *Almost.*

'It smells delicious in here,' she said, taking a seat by the fire. 'Can I do anything to help?'

Whenever she saw Joy, Audrey's face broke into an enormous smile. Though Lily felt guilty and awkward for her sudden change of heart, she was sure that Audrey understood and that there was no ill feeling between them.

'No Lily,' Audrey said. 'It's not yet been two weeks since you had Joy. Please rest. You'll never get these precious early days back and you'll be rushed off your feet before you know it. Mary, do you want to leave your pine cones and sit with Lily and the baby by the fire?'

Mary nodded and smiled. Though she had been pale and puny when she arrived at the bakery, she now had roses in her cheeks and a little more meat on her bones.

'You can hold her if you like?' said Lily. 'I know she likes you.'

'Yes please,' Mary said in a faint voice. Now saying a few words, Mary was still yet to use her lungs at full capacity.

'You sit here,' said Lily, getting up and indicating for Mary to sit in the chair. 'And put your arms like this, that's it, protect her head because they've no strength in their neck when they're this tiny. Well done, Mary. Look, you're a natural.'

Lily gently laid Joy in Mary's arms and watched as Mary stared at the baby's tiny features. Glancing at Audrey, she worried for a moment that it might trigger sadness about her brother, but Audrey smiled reassuringly.

'I'm going to write to my father,' said Lily, taking a seat at the kitchen table, leaning her elbows on the surface and resting her chin in her hands. 'I know after everything he said to you and in his letter that he might not want to hear from me, but having Joy has made me think about what's important. I need him to meet her and once he has, I know he will fall in love with her. There's nothing I would like more than for him to accept her into his life.'

'I know,' said Audrey sympathetically. 'But he's a stubborn man, with a rulebook a mile long.'

'He can't always have his way,' Lily stated. 'That's what my mother would have said. She was a redhead too. It's true what they say, you know: "the redder the hair, the hotter the temper".'

'Oh Lily,' Audrey laughed. 'You're one of a kind.'

'Not any more,' said Lily, gently lifting Joy from Mary's lap and smiling. 'There are two of us now.'

On the other side of town Elsie shivered in the freezing fog. The biting wind that ruffled the surface of the sea as it swept over the Channel turned the lips of the men guarding the beaches blue, and kept most people in their homes roasting chestnuts, trying to be festive, despite missing their loved ones in the Forces. Blowing hot breath on her frozen fingertips, Elsie was doing the final shift on the buses, delivering workers and revellers home to their beds. As the bus crawled through Bournemouth centre, she was struck by how unfestive the town looked in comparison to previous years. There were posters advertising the Christmas pantomime, and there were festive window displays in some of the shops, but they were not lit up and obscured by bombproof tape.

She thought about William and where he might be this Christmas Eve, her anxiety slightly assuaged by the fact that many others she knew hadn't heard from their loved ones in weeks or months. But how she longed for another letter, even if it was just as terse as last time – at least she would know he was still alive. *Be grateful for small mercies.*

Her thoughts of William were briefly interrupted by a memory of Jimmy. She wondered if he was still in Bournemouth or whether he had already been posted overseas. *Thanks for the memory.* A smile appeared on her lips as she remembered his kind words that meant so much in wartime. The smile was followed by a feeling of regret. Jimmy was a good man and she had been unfair to him, blaming him for Rita's cruel tongue. Releasing a sigh that could blow away clouds, she rolled her neck to straighten out the cricks.

'What's Father Christmas bringing you, love?' Barry, the driver, asked when they pulled into the bus depot.

'A new house would be nice as ours was bombed out,' she joked. 'My dad and fiancé home would be even better. How about you?'

'Tea and sugar rations are up for Christmas week, so I'll be having two cups tomorrow instead of the usual one. That and listen to the King on the wireless. That'll be enough of a celebration for me.'

'You can do better than that,' said Elsie, pulling out the sandwich Audrey had made her earlier. 'Look here, it's not much of a gift, but you can have my sandwiches. They're festive ones: cream cheese spread over with redcurrant jelly. I've no appetite today.'

'Don't mind if I do,' said Barry, taking one and stuffing it in his mouth. 'Right then, mind how you go, Elsie love, and Happy Christmas, if there is such a thing in wartime.'

'Happy Christmas,' she said.

Elsie cycled back to Southbourne through the dark, foggy streets, her eyes streaming in the icy cold. There were none of the usual festive, homely scenes in the windows of the family houses she passed. The blackout blinds were down and fearful of a Christmas raid; many people had hung their decorations in their shelters. Elsie arrived at the bakery to find Audrey and Lily sitting in front of the fire in the kitchen, Lily with tiny Joy in her arms, Audrey sewing a pair of felt slippers for Mary's stocking.

'You must be frozen, Elsie,' said Audrey, standing up and welcoming her with a warm hug. 'There's hot rum punch on the stove. You look like you need one. Put this shawl round your shoulders too.'

The three women settled by the fire and sat in silence listening to the crackle and spit of the flames.

'I've made some sweets for the twins,' Audrey said, handing Elsie a paper bag of cinnamon drops she'd made with sugar, cinnamon and water and wrapped in twists of paper. 'Are they still coming for their dinner tomorrow?'

'Yes, thank you,' said Elsie, feeling deeply grateful that Audrey had welcomed her family into bakery life, as if they were her own. 'I'll go to Pat's in the morning to see my sisters and mother. It'll be difficult without Papa there of course.'

Audrey rested her hand on Elsie's shoulder, giving it a gentle sympathetic squeeze.

'I can't stop thinking about William,' Elsie went on to say, choking back tears. She had become well-practised at emotionally detaching herself from the painful desire to see William, but now it was Christmas Eve, Elsie's heart threatened to break if she didn't hear from him soon.

'I hope he gets the parcel we sent,' said Audrey. 'That fruit cake should give him a taste of home.'

Home. As the hot rum and fireside seat warmed up Elsie, her mind drifted to Christmases past. Christmases at home with her family, with her papa wearing crazy hats and singing carols in a silly voice, making his girls laugh until their bellies ached. But with their house still in ruins, her father a prisoner of war, her fiancé disappeared, her mother and sisters staying with Pat, this Christmas would be very different indeed. The war had displaced her family, like so many others across the world. *Home*, as she had always known and loved it, may have changed this year, but Audrey had welcomed Elsie with open arms. And for that, she thought as her eyes started to close in the warmth of Audrey's kitchen, she was truly grateful.

Chapter Thirty-Four

Overnight, heavy snow fell. Pure white snow coated the branches of trees, gathered in the corners of windows and lay perfectly undisturbed on the beaches like huge white rugs, sparkling in the bright morning sunshine. Though the church bells didn't ring out – as they were only to sound in the event of an invasion – and William's absence was felt, Audrey did her best to create a festive atmosphere for Mary.

Scooping up a little fresh snow into a teacup, mixing it with the cream from the top of the milk bottle and a teaspoon of sugar, she handed Mary a spoon. 'Merry Christmas, Mary dear,' she said. 'This is snow ice-cream. My dad used to make it for me when I was little. Do you want to try?'

'Thank you,' said Mary, her eyes widening in delight, dipping in her spoon. 'It's delicious.'

After Charlie returned from delivering the mince pies and Christmas Day bread, with cheeks red from the icy cold, they gave Mary a small gift of a new dress for her dolly and a picture book, and swapped small token gifts amongst themselves. Wartime was not the time for splashing out on expensive gifts; the government had actively encouraged people to instead give war bonds.

Late morning, Audrey polished the cutlery until her face was reflected in the blades of the knives and the curve of the spoons. Laying the Christmas table, she felt William's absence more strongly than ever, and decided to set a place for him. He wasn't present in person, but he was present in hearts and minds. Lighting a candle and placing it in the centre of the table, with Mary's pine cone decorations, she smiled at the people taking their seats at the table. Elsie, Violet, the twins, Mary, Pat, Charlie, Fran, Pearl, Vivian and

John crammed around the table together, elbows touching, they all seemed determined to spread goodwill and cheer.

'It's not much of a spread,' Audrey said, bringing in the Christmas dinner she'd cooked to uproarious applause. 'But it'll keep the wolves from the door.'

'You've done us proud,' said John, tucking his napkin into his collar. 'What is it exactly?'

'Mock turkey,' said Audrey. 'We decided we couldn't spare the chickens, for the eggs they lay. Next year we've got to tighten our belts even more, haven't we Charlie?'

'Indeed we have,' said Charlie.

'So mock turkey is…?' asked Lily.

'Rabbit,' said Audrey, raising an eyebrow. 'Rabbit stuffed with stuffing in the shape of a…'

'Turkey?' said Elsie, with a smile.

John fell about laughing.

'You're quick,' said Audrey, affectionately tapping Elsie's head with a serving spoon. 'So on the menu today, ladies and gentleman, is clear soup, mock turkey with Brussels sprouts and chestnuts, potatoes and carrots, with my wartime plum pudding for afterwards served with a dollop of rum sauce. Please everyone, tuck in. Let's eat while we can. I don't fancy carting this lot into the shelter.'

At 3 p.m., Audrey turned on the wireless for the King's speech. Hush descended on the room as King George VI's voice crackled into life.

'…In days of peace the feast of Christmas is a time when we all gather together in our homes, young and old, to enjoy the happy festivity and goodwill which the Christmas message brings…'

Everyone listened to the sombre speech, and Audrey took Joy from Lily to give her arms a rest, each of them in their own private world of worrying about the future.

After ten minutes, the speech ended with a rousing statement: 'The future will be hard, but our feet are planted on the path of victory, and with the help of God, we shall make our way to justice and to peace.'

Charlie pushed back his chair and raised his glass. He rarely touched a drop, but today his cheeks were flushed from the beer. 'I'm not sure what God's got to do with it because if God were involved I'd prefer to think that the thousands of men and women who have lost their lives would still be here with us,' he said, slightly choked. 'But what I say is; let's raise a toast to justice and peace.'

Chairs scraped against the floorboards as the group stood.

'Justice and peace,' said everyone. 'Justice and peace.'

Clearing away the plates after they had listened to *Christmas Under Fire* on the wireless, a radio tour of the Empire in the front line, followed by Handel's *Messiah*, Charlie and Audrey stood in the kitchen together. Charlie quietly closed the door and pulled up a chair so Audrey could sit down. Exhausted after all the preparation and cooking, she was pleased to take the weight off her feet, but concerned about what Charlie was about to say. From the expression on his face, it wasn't good.

'I waited until now to tell you,' he said, keeping his voice low.

'What is it?' Audrey asked.

'You know the telegram that came yesterday?' he said.

'Yes,' she said, sitting up straighter in the chair. 'What did it say?'

Charlie rubbed his jaw with his hand. Suddenly looking older than his years, he shook his head and breathed a heavy sigh. 'It was about Mary's mother,' he said. 'She's dead. She took her own life.'

'Oh gracious me, why?' said Audrey, her hand on her mouth. 'The poor child. Why didn't you say anything?'

'Because it's Christmas,' Charlie said. 'Because I wanted her to enjoy today and for you not to be worrying about it, but we'll have to break it to her.'

'I don't know if she'll be able to withstand that news, Charlie,' said Audrey. 'She's only just started to talk again after what happened to her brother.'

'I know,' said Charlie. 'But we'll have to find a way. I don't know what will happen to her now.'

'Nothing,' said Audrey. 'She has a home here with us. We're the only certainty she has, poor child. Gracious me.'

Charlie wasn't one for emotional scenes, but he held Audrey's hands and squeezed them tightly, pulling his wife into his chest for a hug.

She leaned her forehead against his chest for a long moment before pulling away, giving him a tender smile and getting on with the washing up, eager to put her trembling hands to work.

It was almost 11 p.m. when there was a knock at the door. After many games, Pat, Violet and the twins had returned to Pat's house, Fran had taken Pearl and Vivian home to bed, Charlie and John were in the bakehouse preparing the dough for tomorrow's bread ('no rest for the wicked,' said John) and Lily, Elsie, Mary and Audrey remained in the kitchen, with full bellies and flushed cheeks, sitting in the lingering warmth of the fire, relieved that Christmas Day hadn't been interrupted by a raid. Though terrible uncertainty hung over the weeks, months and years ahead – especially if Charlie had meant what he said about joining up, and after the news he'd told her about Mary's mother – Audrey felt that she had done everything in her power that day to bring some festive cheer to the people she loved.

Rocking Joy to sleep in her arms, while Lily played another game of cards with Mary, who had been allowed to stay up late, Audrey went downstairs to open the door, expecting to see Old Reg or one of the neighbours.

'Hello?' she said, when she opened the door to find nobody there but the black night and a bright moon spilling a shimmering spotlight onto the snow and sea.

Chapter Thirty-Five

'Hello Audrey,' came a voice from the shadows a few feet away. *William's voice.*

Audrey gasped. Clutching the sleeping baby in her arms, she stepped outside into the darkness, towards the shadows, squinting to see if that really was William, or if her mind was somehow playing tricks.

'William?' she said, her voice tremulous and her heartbeat quickening. 'William, is that you?'

'It's me,' he said, shuffling out of the dark shadows towards her, his voice catching in his throat as he tried to stifle tears.

'Who is it?' said Elsie, suddenly in the doorway behind her, holding open the door, the glow from the house casting a dim light over William.

For the first time, Audrey saw William properly and, running her eyes over him, she sucked in her breath, biting her lip so hard it bled. William had lost his right foot, he had a large white bandage over his right eye and the right side of his face was covered in flaming red burn scars. Blinking in astonishment, light-headed with shock, Audrey grabbed his left hand and held it tight. 'Darling William,' she said.

'I didn't know if you'd want me back like this.' He shrugged, his familiar smile lighting up his disfigured face.

'Oh William,' Elsie said, rushing from the doorway and throwing her arms around him, kissing his face all over, weeping with shock and relief. 'Oh, I can't tell you how glad I am!'

By now, Lily, Charlie and John had come to see what the commotion was – Mary hiding behind Lily – and quickly ushered William inside, hugging him, weeping tears of relief and welcoming him home, into the warm.

Though she was overwhelmed with relief that he was back, Audrey felt a ball of anger form in her gut as she watched her handsome, strong, musical, cheerful younger brother go into the bakery, a shadow of his former self. William had clearly endured unimaginable physical pain and mental torment, all alone. Audrey could not bear to think of the loneliness.

'Sis,' William called, 'are you coming in? I'm hoping for some Christmas cake. I've waited a year.'

'Coming,' she said, her voice cracking as the icy wind chapped her wet cheeks.

A hush descended upon the kitchen as William took a seat by the fire and Audrey immediately thrust a glass of rum into his hand. Everyone huddled around him, lost for words. Audrey was desperately trying not to stare at his injuries, but she couldn't help herself. Steadying herself on the back of the chair, she shook her head in dismay. What words of comfort could she offer him?

'Will your foot grow back, sir?' asked Mary, breaking the silence.

'Mary!' scolded Audrey. 'Don't ask silly questions.'

'It's okay, Sis,' said William, with a gentle laugh. 'No it won't. I shall have to learn to live without it.'

'What happened, William?' Charlie asked bravely, his eyes full of concern. Audrey felt thankful to him for asking what they all needed to know.

William set down his glass and held Elsie's hand. She was sitting beside him, gazing at him with tears in her eyes.

'I was driving a truck when it happened,' he said. 'I was due to come home on short leave, for our wedding, Elsie, but the truck suffered a direct hit. The other men I was travelling with were killed outright. I tried to save them, but it was hopeless. I was taken to a field hospital and there I remained until I was brought back to England to recuperate.'

'Why didn't you tell us?' asked Elsie.

'Because I feared you wouldn't want me, but that you'd feel obliged to marry me,' he said. 'My face, under these bandages, isn't at all pretty. I thought, in time, you might be better off finding love elsewhere.'

'William, I love you,' said Elsie emphatically. 'You're my one and only, no matter what.'

She tried to hug him and kiss him, but knocked into the bandaged side of his face. He cried out in pain and she quickly retreated, startled.

'I'm sorry,' she said. 'I'm so sorry.'

'No… no, it's…' William's shoulders sagged as he battled with his emotions.

Audrey's heart broke a thousand times over.

'It's going to take time to heal,' said Audrey, resting her hand gently on his shoulder. 'But you're home now and we all want to help you recover. You've been on a journey none of us can begin to understand, but I hope in time we will.'

William's eyes shone with tears and though Audrey felt her throat thickening with the urge to cry, she raised a brave smile. William smiled in return. There were lines to be drawn in the face of suffering and this was one of them. She would not now cry tears of sorrow or anger about what was lost. Whatever life threw at their family, Audrey was determined not to be defeated by sadness and regret. Instead she would live in hope. Hope was the future. Hope was all she had.

A letter from Amy

I want to say a huge thank you for choosing to read *Heartaches and Christmas Cakes*. If you enjoyed it, and want to keep up to date with all my latest releases, just sign up at the following link. Your email address will never be shared and you can unsubscribe at any time.

www.bookouture.com/amy-miller

I have loved writing this book and was inspired to do so after thinking and reading about life on the Home Front during the Second World War. So much has been documented about the men who fought in battle, but as a mother of two children trying to imagine how it must have felt for the women left at home, I am fascinated and amazed by how women coped in wartime. Not only did many women who previously hadn't worked enter male-dominated professions, they also coped with displaced families, heartache, poverty and the challenges of rationing. The number of accounts I've read where people remember their mothers creating a meal 'from nothing' is striking.

Stories of women's resilience have inspired me to create my characters and base them in the comforting setting of a bakery, which was, at the time, at the heart of the community. Bread was not rationed until after the war, and so it was incredibly important in keeping hunger at bay.

Another source of inspiration has been a desire to record memories that are now sadly dying out with those people who lived through the war years. Their stories are so full of colour, I cannot thank enough all those people who have recorded their memories, either online or in books. They are a great source of information and inspiration.

I'm also deeply affected by the kindness evident in a time when the unimaginable brutality of war was being played out in the battlefield. An anecdote of a Dunkirk survivor who arrived on British shores to the welcome sight of local women running onto the railway tracks to give the exhausted soldiers tea and sandwiches truly moves me. These days, when something terrible happens in the news and my children ask me, with fear in their innocent eyes, how such a thing can happen, I have adopted the advice widely given on social media, to tell them to 'look for the helpers'. It seems, even in the most appalling situations, hope can be found.

In terms of the historical accuracy of this book, I have tried to base events around those that happened in Bournemouth and the wider world during 1940, but I have definitely used artistic licence to carry the story forward, for which I hope you can forgive me! Though the location of the bakery exists in reality, in a beautiful part of Bournemouth, I have changed street names.

I hope you loved *Heartaches and Christmas Cakes*, and if you did I would be very grateful if you could write a review. I'd love to hear what you think, and it makes such a difference helping new readers to discover one of my books for the first time.

I love hearing from my readers – you can get in touch on my Facebook page, through Twitter, Goodreads or my website.

Thanks,
Amy Miller

AmyMillerBooks
@AmyBratley1

Acknowledgements

Writing this book has been a steep and fascinating learning curve. Not only have I learned a great deal about the war years, especially on the Home Front, it has also been a joy to discover more about the history of the area I live in. I do not claim to have any expertise in baking and so I am incredibly grateful for the conversations I had with John Swift, of Swifts Bakery, and team members at Leakers Bakery, Cowdry's Bakery, Burbidge's Bakery, as well as various relatives of wartime bakers, including Anita and Betty. I also am indebted to the residents at Bournemouth's War Memorial Homes, who gave their time to share memories over coffee and doughnuts.

I am very grateful for the information from historian Dr Elizabeth Collingham, who wrote *The Taste of War: World War II and the Battle for Food*, and for the generous advice from historian Dr Annie Gray. I've read many books to inform this story and the book I found most helpful was *Bournemouth and the Second World War, 1939–1945*, by M.A Edgington, a brilliantly researched and detailed documentation of exactly what happened in Bournemouth during the war years. Also tremendously helpful was the information in the Heritage section of Bournemouth Library, where I enjoyed many hours studying the archived *Bournemouth Echo* from 1940, using the microfilm reader. Other books I must mention are *Christmas on the Home Front*, Mike Brown; *A Baker's Tale*, Jane Evans; *Bread: A Slice of History*, Marchant, Reuben & Alcock; *The Wartime House*, Mike Brown and Carol Harris; *Eating For Victory*, Jill Norman; *Wartime Women*, Dorothy Sheridan; *My Wartime Experience*, Charles W Swift; *The View From The Corner Shop*, Kathleen Hey, *Our Daily Bread – A History of Barron's Bakery*, Roz Crowley and *Spuds, Spam and Eating for Victory*, Katherine Knight.

Finally, I found huge inspiration in looking at photographs from the era, found on the Imperial War Museum's website and many others, as well as wartime poster-advertising campaigns, and in the incredible personal stories told on the BBC People's War website, an invaluable archive of Second World War memories, written by the public and gathered by the BBC.

I do hope I have remembered everything and everyone. Heartfelt thanks to them all and, last but not least, my long-suffering family.